Thief of Reason

Thief of Reason

a novel

Judy J. Johnson

IGUANA

Copyright © 2021 Judy J. Johnson
Published by Iguana Books
720 Bathurst Street, Suite 303
Toronto, ON M5S 2R4

This is a novel of pure fiction. All characters' names and identities, and most names of places and locations, are fictionalized.

Publisher: Meghan Behse
Editor: Amanda Feeney
Front cover design: Meghan Behse

ISBN 978-1-77180-471-4 (paperback)
ISBN 978-1-77180-472-1 (epub)

This is an original print edition of *Thief of Reason.*

For my son, Marc Shandro, and my three Grandies:

Morgan Shandro
Aaron Shandro
Nicola Shandro

"Understanding the 'other' will pose the 21st century's greatest social challenge."

— Charles Taylor (1931–)

Chapter 1

I want to love him, but I can't, Rick thought as he watched his father, 55-year-old Dick Wright, generously fill seven crystal wine glasses then bow his head in prayer.

"In the name of Jesus Christ our Saviour, we give thanks for our blessings, especially family—my wife, Dorothy, my loyal brother, Harry, and his lovely wife, Rose, my charming daughter, Joy, and her partner, Al, and my...only son, Ricky. Amen." Dick lifted his chin and looked at his wife of thirty years, raised his glass and said, "And a toast to you, my long-suffering wife. Thank you for bringing us together to enjoy another of your special Boxing Day feasts."

"To Dorothy," everyone proclaimed, hoisting their glasses and sipping traditional Beaujolais.

"Thank you," Dorothy said, leaning across the maple dining room table and repositioning the platter of crown roast beside the large bowl of fluffy mashed potatoes, a gravy boat, and colourful vegetable serving dishes.

Rick pondered his father's rare streak of largesse. *Could it be? A tender-hearted moment?* "Nice touch, Dad," Rick offered, hoping his compliment would extend his father's magnanimity.

Joy reached up and patted Dick's shoulder. "Thanks, Dad. That was lovely," then half winked at Rick and said, "Please pass the beets and sautéed mushrooms."

Sporting a full white beard that suited his short, stocky stature and basketball belly, Harry gave a throaty "Ho, ho, ho," and raised his glass. "Here's to my lovely sister-in-law, Dorothy, who keeps the family ritual going and works magic with aging."

"Hope I have Mom's magic genetic mapping," Rick joked, then tapped his temples. "Got a few grey hairs that make me look like an old man at twenty-eight. Then again, I am pushing thirty…no career, no wife, no children."

Rick's uncle winked and grinned at his nephew. "Get a move on, Ricky! You're on the cusp of death and taxes." Having had no children of his own, he had a special place in his heart for Rick, who, in turn, cherished his uncle's unconditional acceptance and easy banter.

"Bloody taxes!" Dick proclaimed. "I'm sick of paying taxes and sending all those royalties to eastern Canada. Bloody Liberals don't give a rat's ass about our oil and gas industry." As usual, Dick's eyes were concentrated on his son, who was hoping against disaster that his father wouldn't start another harrowing, threadbare political argument.

Joy dared to intervene. "I don't like taxes either, Dad, but without them, we'd lose universal access to public health care. Albertans would have to buy private insurance and those premiums would cost more than we currently pay in taxes."

Rick pointed to Al and shouted across the table, "Hey, Al! You, me, hiking boots. Kananaskis. This summer, man. You game?"

"All in," Al said through a mouthful of glazed carrots. "Five days off, end of June. Let's tackle Mt. Kidd."

Rick liked Al's friendly, easygoing disposition. Just the kind of guy this family needs, he'd concluded shortly after his sister, Joy, had introduced him to the family three years ago.

Dick refilled his empty wine glass and topped up the others, most of which were a couple swallows short of full, then watched his brother lace his mound of food with a generous sprinkling of salt.

"Harry, salt's bad for yer heart! We talked about that in the hospital, remember?" Dick shook his finger at the salt shaker. "Don't kid yerself; that's the leading cause of heart disease."

"How *are* you doing, Uncle Harry?" Joy said, with strained cheerfulness. "Haven't seen you since your bypass. Are you on the three Rs: rigid rehab routine?"

"Yep. Regular exercise and no second helpings," Harry said, smiling and looking directly at Dick. "I've already taken off five pounds of blubber."

"Stick with it," Dick said. "I figure you've got at least thirty to go. Here's the thing about exercise. Good for the heart, but—"

Joy covered her face with her hands and peeked between her fingers at Harry, who scowled at Dick and said, "Please, not another tirade. I've cut back on everything that's bad for my heart and I'm working out on the torture equipment my darling wife bought me. Body bag included."

Laughter lightened the air as Rose looked pensively at her husband and said, "Really, now. After your pretend version of morning exercises, you reward yourself with another coffee, loaded with cream and laced with sugar. I hate nagging, honey, but heart attacks are deadly serious and I'd like to keep you a while longer." Vigorously massaging her hands and looking directly at her nephew, Rose said, "Ricky, have you been to our magnificent Central Library?"

"Masterpiece of architecture, isn't it!" Rick said. "World class. I could spend a whole week hanging out there…reading, snacking, doing homework, or gazing at the panoramic view of Calgary's bustling downtown." Rick looked over at his mom. "Beats the community branch you took me and Joy to as kids, eh Mom?"

"Sure does," Dorothy said, "but I'm grateful we haven't lost our little neighbourhood one."

"I remember how books were scattered all over your living room when the kids were young," Rose said. "How they loved having stories read to them."

Dick said, "Look, Rose, books are obsolete. Libraries are a waste of taxpayers' money. Digital's the only way to go."

Rick gulped a mouthful of wine, looked over at his uncle and shrugged. "Looks like you're fixin' to say something, Uncle Harry."

Harry tossed Rick a knowing glance. "How are classes shaping up for next semester?"

"Got the three courses I want…need to ace them all to get into grad school."

"My money's on you, Dr. Wright," Harry said. "Then what?"

"Who knows? Short stories for magazines? An English prof?" He flippantly added, "The Man Booker Prize for literary fiction?"

In a deep, gravelly voice, Dick complained, "After wasting years bumming around Europe, you're now a professional student. Full marks for dilly dallying."

"Jeez, Dad! Why the snide comment?" Rick pinched his bottom lip and chastised himself for breaking his morning pledge. Hours ago, he'd paced the worn circles on his carpet and worried that his father, who'd been relatively civil during Joy's Christmas Eve dinner and Dorothy's turkey feast on Christmas Day, was surely overdue for pontification. *If Dad dangles the bait, I won't bite*, he'd promised himself and Joy, who'd interrupted his pacing with a phone call. *Not during happy hour. Not during dinner. Not during Christmas pudding and Irish coffee. Today, Dad wins.*

According to that plan, Rick was hovering on the edge of a losing battle.

In the awkward silence that followed, everyone focused on their dinner as if they sensed Dick was about to offer another hefty helping of something more pungent than political acrimony, salt, and library books. Dick didn't disappoint. He poked his fork at Harry. "Hey, little brother, why weren't you and Rose at Christmas Eve mass this year?"

"Thought I told you we wouldn't be there," Harry said, reaching for one of Dorothy's homemade dinner rolls.

Clutching his wine glass, Dick said, "Don't tell me you've become the family's infidel. A proud heretic."

The only sound was the scrape of cutlery on dinner plates until Dick pushed his chest out and said, "Speak up, Harry! Say something for God's sake."

Harry gently nudged Rose and arched his eyebrows as if to encourage an answer.

Rose looked like she'd bitten into a chunk of mouldy potato. She gulped, glanced at Dick, and said, "This year, Christmas Eve was like none other—peaceful as the falling snowflakes." She took a sip of wine. "Harry and I decided to honour our religious differences. Packed cheese and nuts along with cinnamon rolls and a thermos of hot chocolate and went snowshoeing in the Kananaskis."

Harry chuckled. "And a flask of hot rum."

With a long, rumbling belch, Dick made it clear he'd heard enough, but Rose hadn't finished.

"You might recall, Dick, that although I'm agnostic I *am* spiritual. The Church of Kananaskis, in all its breathtaking splendour, is my place of worship."

Dick spoke to Rose, but his eyes were still on Rick. "C'mon, Rose, Kananaskis could never compete with the beauty of our church's Christmas Eve mass. A good Catholic shows up. Gives thanks to our merciful Saviour."

Rose drummed her fingers on the arms of her chair. "There's a deep spiritual truth in the land of our majestic Rockies, especially in summer. Nature's bountiful wildflowers, the aquamarine lakes and fascinating wildlife that roam the mountain valleys—they connect me to my God." Rose raised her glass to Dick in what looked like an abortive toast, then took a quick slug of wine, opened her arms, looked up, and said, "Thank you, Kananaskis Country, for letting me be part of all that you are."

"Hee-haw and yahoo!" Rick cheered, throwing his head back like a cowboy in the Calgary Stampede Parade. "Bravo, Aunt Rose! Love it—a prayer to the Church of Kananaskis!"

Dick's resounding table thump rattled the silverware. Broccoli florets bounced in their bowl as Dorothy's red wine splashed onto the white linen tablecloth and slowly bled into its delicate weave. Looking at his son and making boxer jabs through a spray of spittle, Dick said, "Ricky! When it comes to religion you're as ignorant as a toad, so I'll thank you to keep your mouth shut on every blessed word about it."

"Stop trying to prove you're saintlier…" Rick's voice cracked, "and wiser than everyone else."

Joy threw her napkin on her plate. "Ricky, you promised!"

Dick's face reddened. "Goddammit, Ricky! After all I've sacrificed for you, this is the thanks I get? Give me some respect or get the hell outta here." Dick dropped his fork on his plate and vigorously rubbed his forehead.

Rick's eyes moistened as he stared at his food, hardly touched, and wondered whatever possessed him to wade into another religious argument, especially at Christmas. In the most controlled voice he could muster, he said, "I simply want us to make room for all points of view. If things get too heated, we'll summon the good manners of our upbringing and agree to disagree."

Dick's voice trembled. "Might that be all from the genius in the family?"

Silence blared.

Rick studied his father's frown line. *Deep enough to plant carrots in. Or a fist.* He forced an odd version of a smile at Harry and Rose. "My apologies," he said. "Even though it's Boxing Day, I shouldn't put the gloves on."

Harry shook his head from side to side. "No need to apologize."

Dick's eyes looked about to detonate. "Not so, Harry! An apology's in order."

Dorothy passed the broccoli to Harry and, in her sweetest tone of voice, said, "Second helpings are mandatory at Christmas."

That's Mom, Rick thought. *Maintaining order in the face of madness.*

Al, who usually refrained from commenting during disagreements in the Wright household, looked at Joy and said, "Family feuds like this have paramedics like me loading someone on a gurney."

As if to calm his racing heart, Rick pressed one hand against his chest and turned toward his father who glared at him. Rick glared back. "I've been stretched too hard for too long. I appreciate my free rent and working part-time for you and Uncle Harry, but jeez, Dad, I'm tired of feeling like an outsider looking in…like I don't belong in my own family. Tired of not being able to state my views without coming under your almighty wrath. Why does it have to be this way? Especially now, in front of everyone. At Christmas, for Chrissakes."

Dick flung his hand toward Rick and yelled, "Enough!" He refilled his wine glass and siphoned off the top third.

Sensing that his father wouldn't let up, Rick inhaled deeply, pushed his dinner plate forward and his chair back, then stood tall, as if subconsciously reminding people that he towered over everyone in the family, especially his father who was a good six inches shorter. He tugged at his shirt as if to make a formal address then froze when he caught the injured expression on his mother's face.

Dorothy pleaded, "Ricky, please relax and finish your dinner. Like you said, it's Christmas."

"I'm truly sorry, Mom, but there's no way out but down to my room. Thank you for making this delicious meal."

Dick punched his right fist into his left palm. "Listen to your mother! Sit down and eat!"

Rose propped her elbows on the table and rubbed her eyes as if trying to erase the tumultuous scene, and Harry looked like he'd just passed a small kidney stone. Al stared in disbelief at Joy, now feasting in sensuous oblivion and intermittently clucking her tongue as if she were calling the chickens home to roost.

Nodding ruefully to each family member except his father, Rick left the table and descended the stairs to his basement suite where he stepped inside and stood motionless at the entrance, lit only by a street light that shone through a sizeable basement window. The kitchen, dining, living room, and study nook blended together in a large, angular room that once looked welcoming and homey, but now looked cold and dingy. Rick grabbed his novel, which late last night he'd struggled to put down. He read the same paragraph three times. Thinking booze would mellow his mood, he tossed the novel aside, twisted the cap off a beer, and dimmed the lights. *How many fathers in this city ruined today's family dinner? What stitched their obnoxious behaviour into the fabric of their being? Genes? Parenting? Childhood trauma? Drugs?*

Rick traced the same old carpet circles he'd trampled on earlier and continued his quest for answers: *How many sons ruined today's family dinner? Why am I so bent on proving Dad wrong? So fuckin' obstinate? Can't get out of my own way. Should go upstairs and apologize.* He mulled that idea over, then said aloud, "Can't. Won't." Putting his hands together in a sloppy prayer to the God he didn't believe in, he begged, "It's been a long time, but please God, if there's any chance you're out there, help me and Dad find a way to heal our hurt."

Twice, the upstairs front door firmly closed. *Nine o'clock and everyone's gone,* Rick thought. *Even Joy and Al left earlier than usual. Dad will go to bed soon, and I'll go up and help Mom with the dishes.* He flopped back down on the sofa and journeyed into his favourite painting that hung above his desk—a lone, scraggly tree stood at the side of a long, barren highway that narrowed and vanished into snow-capped mountains poking holes in a melancholy sky.

Suddenly, heavy thuds grew louder until the basement door burst open and slammed into the wall behind—doorknob lost in the drywall. Dick's face, sweaty and coloured by rage, burned like an asteroid plunging through the stratosphere. "*YOU* make my blood boil! Correcting me in front of everyone! Cursing Jesus Christ our Saviour!"

Rick stepped closer to his father and braced himself for unfinished invective.

Dick's hands sliced through chunks of air as he emphasized each word. "In this house, I call the shots!"

Something inside Rick snapped and before he could stop himself, he shrieked, "Shove it up sideways!" then turned and started walking away.

Dick grabbed the heavy broom that Rick used to sweep the walks and slammed it into his son's back.

Rick screamed as he spun around and caught the edge of the kitchen table. "What the fuck!" He lunged at his father, who raised his arms to shield himself and yelled, "Don't you touch—" but before he could finish his sentence, Rick pinned his dad's shoulders against the wall and pushed his face within inches of his fiery eyes and hot breath.

Like a llama flaunting dominance over a lower-ranked male, Dick spat in his son's face.

Enraged, Rick wrestled his father to the floor, rammed his right knee into his chest, and held his shoulders to the carpet. With rhythmic, unrestrained punches, he dragged out every word, "Give *me* some respect, goddammit!" He pounded Dick's face until his nose and mouth oozed blood. Until his dazed eyes closed, his arms dropped to the floor, and his legs stopped flailing about.

Physically and emotionally drained, Rick stared down at his father, now reduced to a speechless, motionless old man. "Why do you *hate* me, Dad? *Why*?" His voice quivered. "I can't take it anymore." His heart throbbed, his hands shook, and his mind went blank. Scarcely stopping to think, he jumped up, grabbed his winter jacket and key ring, then flew up the stairs and out the back door.

Rick jumped in his car and started the twenty-minute drive to his only safe refuge—his uncle and aunt's. Frightening images of his father's bloodied, sagging face and vacant stare blurred his vision as he traversed a safer side route. To keep his foot from trembling on the gas pedal and get a grip on more than the steering wheel, he stopped beside a playground, buried his face in his hands, and tried to stop the dizzying flashbacks. With the brute force of that heavy broom, guilt hurled him into a terrifying scene—a whole new world walled off by heavy prison doors, clanging key chains, and strange sounds. A world where he huddled in a corner, trying to shake relentless shame and unresolved anger. A world that, until tonight, was inconceivable. Rick's stomach began convulsing so violently that he flung the car door open and coloured the snow with a stream of emotional, projectile vomit. He wiped his face with a fistful of snow. *Stop it!* he ordered. *Dad assaulted me. I needed to defend myself. Keep calm. One step at a time. Turn the key. Check rear-view and side mirrors. Drive. Don't speed.*

Rick rang the doorbell and waited patiently. He rang it again and was about to leave when Harry appeared in his new Santa Claus pyjamas and winced at the sight of his nephew. "Come in, come in! Holy moly! Did everything go haywire after we left?"

Rick stumbled over his words. "Dad attacked me first...can't stand the sight of me. Christ, we could've killed each other!"

"Have you been drinking?" Harry asked and, without waiting for an answer, added, "Could've phoned me."

"Nothing serious—didn't finish my wine at dinner and had one beer since."

Rose rushed into the living room. "Ricky, my God! Are you okay?"

Rick felt as sober as the look on his aunt's face. "Dad drilled me with the heavy broom I use to sweep the walks. I hit him back. Pulled no punches. It's all a blur." Rick frantically patted his jacket pockets. "Where's my phone? I should call Mom, ask about Dad."

Rose said, "Your mom phoned after she got your father upstairs and into bed. Wants me to let her know how you are if you come here...doesn't want to talk to you, at least not tonight. She's very upset, with both of you. I'll call her in a bit and tell her you're spending the night with us." Rose stepped closer to Rick. "Where did your dad hit you?"

Rick slipped his jacket off and raised his shirt to expose the damage.

"It's a real doozy," Rose said, as she ran her hand over the red, swollen lump, "but the skin isn't broken."

Harry stepped back from his own examination of the damage and put his hand on his nephew's shoulder. "Your father's so angry...so set in his ways. After every family dinner I swear it's the last. Then I start feeling guilty. Your mom gets the Nobel Peace Prize for keeping their marriage together."

Rick closed his eyes and nodded hesitantly as Harry beckoned to follow him into the kitchen. "How about a cup of tea?"

"Thanks, Uncle. Need something to calm my nerves."

"I'll check out the guest room," Rose said, "and you can call your mom in the morning."

Rick sat down at the kitchen table and looked at his uncle, who leaned against the counter as he waited for the water to boil and smiled at something known only to himself. Talking more to the kettle than his nephew, Harry said, "Bet you haven't heard about the time your dad—" Harry looked at Rick, shook his head and chuckled. "You should've seen it. Grade eleven. Dick had the hots for Marylou Fancy Pants…that's what all the guys called her. A feisty, wild one, if you know what I mean. Didn't give a damn about social values or decency."

"Yep," Rick said, grinning. "The type of girl guys want but don't respect."

Harry smiled and nodded. "Miss Fancy Pants' locker was beside your dad's and one day, or so the story goes, they got into a shouting match and be damned if Dick didn't go gaga over her. Said he'd bring lunch and a couple beers if she'd meet him over the noon hour next day and go down to the river."

"Seriously?" Rick asked.

"Uh huh. Marylou agreed, and to prep for the big date, Dick spent an hour in the bathroom, slicking his hair back with greasy goop and doing God knows what all else. Under some phony pretense, he borrowed our father's leather jacket, stashed three beers in his school bag alongside his usual peanut butter and jam sandwiches—a couple extras for Marylou—and chocolate chip cookies."

Harry peeled a mandarin, put half of it in his mouth and gave the rest to Rick.

"Then what?" Rick asked.

"Next day at noon, I stood a safe distance from their lockers and watched Marylou Fancy Pants scream her lungs out in a strange, seductive way…didn't let up until your dad opened a can of beer, dumped most of it over her head, and guzzled the rest. Marylou just stood there looking stunned, then ran to the washroom."

"Did you do anything?"

"Nope," Harry said, shaking his head from side to side. "By then, Dick's classmates had gathered, and it soon became clear—at least to all the girls—that no one argued with Dick Wright and won, not even Marylou Fancy Pants."

Rick raked his hair and racked his brains, amused but not knowing what to say.

Harry poured tea and sat down at the table. "Your dad! After that crazy sideshow, the girls shunned him, and believe you me he was quite a hunk in his younger years."

Rose walked into the kitchen and adjusted the sash on her fluffy red bathrobe. "Guest room's ready for you," she said, then walked over to the fridge and rifled through it. "You didn't have much supper."

"Please, I don't want to put you out. You were already in bed when I rang the doorbell."

"No problem, I wasn't asleep."

Rick looked at Harry and said, "Years ago, I asked Dad what it was like growing up in a small town and he said that it's never easy when everyone knows your business. Since then, I've only heard bits and pieces about his past—grandma died from cirrhosis, and grandpa was killed in a car accident. Joy and I never got any of the details, but I always sensed those tragedies left Dad with deep wounds—wounds that haven't healed."

Harry stacked the orange peelings. "Do you remember the Boxing Day dinner a couple years back when we were all having coffee and Baileys and I started describing our alcoholic mother? Your dad said, 'Stop right there! We owe it to Mom to honour her for who she was. Period.' So you see, your dad had a soft spot for our poor mother, as if he understood that alcoholism was a disease, not a weakness."

"That's touching. I always knew he didn't like to talk about his past, and all Mom ever said was how horrifying it must've been for both of you to lose your parents at such a young age. I kept hoping that someday Dad would let it all out, but it looks like Marylou Fancy Pants will ask him to marry her before that happens."

Harry chuckled. "What a miracle that would be! But yeah, too much of Dick is all tangled up in childhood rage."

"Childhood rage?"

"Mm-hmm. Our family was as unstable as a rotten barn ladder, so poor Dick had to practically raise me." Topping up their tea, Harry continued, "When I was about nine, I remember Dad—your Grandpa Wright—telling Dick and me, 'Life's cool when all your mother does is sit and nod her head.' Dick asked him what he meant by that and Dad muttered something about Mom's drinking, but we both knew by his tone of voice not to say anything more about it."

"Was Grandpa Wright a bit like Dad?"

Harry scratched his thick, tinselled beard as Rose, listening in from the kitchen counter, glanced back at him and said, "From what you've told me, your father was a stern, God-fearing man at the best of times."

Harry looked agitated. He walked over and put his hand on Rose's shoulder. "Dad was as gruff as a grizzly but could turn on the charm like tap water. He liked women, beer, and curling, in that order." Harry dropped his chin. "Poor Mom. Had no career or close family ties, just us and her absentee husband."

"Except for the curling and philandering, Dad's got Grandpa's love of beer," Rick said, looking forlorn.

"You got that right. As for philandering, I'm sure all the realtors and curlers gossiped about the town's infamous womanizer. But he did sell lots of real estate. Won so many prizes in company sales that we ran out of space on the mantle for his trophies."

Rick swallowed hard. "Still and all, Grandpa must've been a real embarrassment to Grandma."

"Yep. She hardly ever poked her nose out the door. No wonder alcohol became her best friend…and worst enemy."

"Alcohol's becoming Dad's best friend too. Maybe it's in his genes."

"Possibly, but I doubt he'll ever be the alcoholic Mom was." Harry sauntered back to the table and tapped his foot on the kitchen tile. "Every day before your Dad and I got home from school, Mom was well into her liquid salads—vodka and orange or tomato juice, with celery stir sticks. By supper time, she was pretty well wasted, and Dad, good ol' Dad, was either wheeling and dealing or rutting with the ladies. That's when Dick became the parent. He'd make mounds of popcorn smothered in melted butter, or we'd fix ourselves the same old sandwiches we'd had for lunch. To this day, the smell of peanut butter makes me gag."

Rick shook his head. "That's so sad. Did Grandma and Grandpa fight a lot?"

"They rarely spoke. Dad must've known it was only a matter of time before booze would take her."

"At least my parents talk," Rick said. "Well, Dad does most of it. I hate it when Mom doesn't stand up to him."

"That's what I love about you, honey," Harry said, winking at Rose. "Won't take guff from anyone."

"Including Dad," Rick said, grinning. "You didn't let him get away with anything tonight. Loved everything you said."

"Really? I told Harry on the way home that I should've known Dick would take his frustration out on you. Wish I'd kept my mouth shut."

"Glad you didn't. He needed to hear from you," Rick said. "If family doesn't challenge him, who will? Most people wouldn't bother."

Rose studied Rick's facial expression then placed a tray of cheese, whole-wheat crackers, ham slices, and dark fruitcake on the table. She squeezed her nephew's shoulder as she passed slowly behind him and said, "I'm off to bed. Get a good sleep and we'll talk over breakfast."

Rick yawned into his cupped fist. "Thanks, Aunt Rose. I'm so grateful for your help." He glanced at Harry and added, "Both of you."

Harry nodded and asked Rick, "Where was I?"

"Grandpa, the realtor…among other things."

"Right," Harry reached for a slice of fruitcake and talked more about how it's taken years to appreciate that, overall, Dick tried to be the good parent who watched out for his younger brother.

"Did your father spend any time with you and Dad?" Rick asked. "Take you to hockey games, go camping, fishing, play catch…stuff like that?"

"Nope. But one thing he did do…then we better hit the hay. Sundays were special. Your grandpa would cook Dick and me a big breakfast, then we'd dress in our proper church-going duds…and be sure to comb our hair. Dad got hot under the collar if our hair wasn't clean, parted straight, and nicely combed for all those church-going ladies. At supper time, he'd treat us to a full meal at the Family Diner where we'd order the regular special—roast beef with gravy, mashed potatoes, some vegetable or other that I didn't touch, and dessert, usually pie." Harry paused. His eyes had a faraway look. "Dick and I ate lots, said little; Dad drank lots, ate little. And lectured us." He glanced at the wall clock and groaned faintly. "Now that we've had our tea and a bite—a few years ago I would've brought out the scotch—maybe we should pack it in."

Rick smiled. "Yeah, I'm losing steam too. Thanks for the bedtime story. Never knew the half of it."

Harry raised his eyebrows and said, "Family histories. Because of ours, Ricky, I've always cut your dad a lot of slack."

In the pitch-black guestroom, Rick tossed and turned until the sheets, soaked in perspiration, were as knotted as his stomach. The discomfort he felt from his wound was drowned by crashing waves of guilt and grotesque images of his father's bloody face, his glassy stare and immobile body. When sleep came, it didn't last long.

At 8:05 in Calgary's dawning light of winter, Rick awoke to the sound of a garbage truck in the back alley. Dazed, he slowly got his bearings and gasped aloud, "Oh no…NO! Dad!" Hearing voices downstairs, he pulled on his wrinkled clothes and lumbered into the kitchen.

Harry looked up from his newspaper. "Good morning, Ricky. How did you sleep?"

"Hope you were comfortable," Rose piped up, then poured Rick a cup of steaming coffee.

"The bed was comfortable, thanks, but I only caught a few hours," Rick said as Harry passed him a large plate of pancakes. "Is it okay if I call Mom?"

"Yes, yes, of course, you can do that now if you like." Harry reached for the cordless and plunked it in front of his nephew.

"I'm almost as worried about Mom as I am about Dad." Rick frowned and slowly shook his head. "Wonder why she didn't want to talk to me last night?"

Harry stood up, gave Rick's shoulder a squeeze, and beckoned Rose to leave the room with him.

Rick pushed pieces of pancake around on his plate as he waited for his mom to answer.

"Good morning, is that you Rose?" Dorothy said.

"No, it's me, Mom. Can't tell you how sorry I am for last night."

In an unsteady voice, Dorothy said, "Come home now. Joy's here and we need to talk to you."

Rick's voice was strong. "Look. Dad attacked me first. When I wasn't looking, he slammed that heavy broom into my back. Dammit, Mom, I *had* to defend myself."

The phone connection crackled. "Hear me! Come home now," Dorothy said, sounding impatient.

Rick wolfed down a few bites of pancake and dragged himself into the living room. "Mom hung up on me. Ordered me to come home immediately." He went to the door and reached for his jacket. "Time to settle this family matter, then do some soul searching on gentle ski slopes." Rick walked over and gave his Aunt Rose a hug.

"We'll always be here for you if you need us," Rose said.

Harry followed his nephew to the door, lifted his arms, and wrapped him in a bear hug. "I admire you for standing up to your old man. That took guts."

Rick's deep blue eyes glistened as he lowered his head, stepped out the door, and tossed Harry a loving wave.

Traffic had narrowed to a single lane on Calgary's busiest rush hour street. As Rick crawled along, accelerating then decelerating, his thoughts drifted from his favourite ski slopes to his parents' kitchen table where he pictured his mom and Joy waiting to pounce. *What if Dad's there? Nah, too early. Even on his good days.*

Rick gently knocked and opened the kitchen door, walked in, and boldly said, "Before either of you say anything, keep in mind that I could've called the cops." His voice grew louder and more urgent. "Could've charged Dad with assault."

"Mother of God, I'm glad you didn't do that," Dorothy moaned.

"How is Dad?"

"Had a fitful night, but I just checked in on him and he's sound asleep. What on Earth got into you two? I heard the racket…the shouting. Should've come downstairs, but…" Dorothy's voice trailed off.

Rick's voice softened. "Please tell me, Mom. How *is* Dad?"

"Cut and badly bruised. The gash on his forehead took forever to stop bleeding. Needs stitches, but he refused to let me drive him to the hospital."

"I'm…I'm still in shock. And I'm sorry," Rick said. "So sorry."

"And I'm so disappointed…in both of you," said Dorothy. "Dad was belligerent at the table, but you…*you* practically sent him to an early grave."

"Why, Ricky? Why?" Joy said, in a tone that complemented her mother's scorn.

"Go ahead, give me hell. But remember this, Joy, in case Mom didn't tell you. Dad assaulted me first."

Dorothy repeatedly sniffled; her eyes were tearful. Shielding her face, she left for the bathroom, a common escape route when Dick railed about some unpardonable mistake, like not putting the lid on the pickle jar tight enough, or flinging the towel over the shower rod instead of hanging it "properly."

Dorothy's absence gave Joy permission to have at it. "Even though Dad hit you first, why in God's name did you beat him within an inch of his life?" She sat back and took a deep breath before continuing. "You showed amazing restraint during Christmas dinner when he went on about his wacky conspiracy theories, and I thought you'd decided to let him have his stupid ideas and ignore—"

"Look! I tried to ignore him last night too, but there's a limit to my endurance."

"Just one more night, that was all, Ricky—for Aunt Rose and Uncle Harry. For Mom. For Christmas! You made things worse than they already were. Listen, all kinds of fathers in this world act like Dad, but their sons don't retaliate like rabid animals."

"*You* listen!" Rick snarled. "All kinds of sons confront their fathers' stupidity, but their *fathers* don't attack them like rabid animals. Dad was the worst he's ever been…to Uncle Harry too."

"Cut the melodrama! Dad was just being Dad," Joy said. "Mom's right, he was belligerent, but when will you get over your endless grudge?"

"*My* melodrama? Did you see how Dad glared at me? How he looked for any excuse to hammer me with another spiteful insult? I'm always in his crosshairs, in case you haven't noticed."

"I *have* noticed. But the minute Dad disagrees with you, you become an arrogant, pompous ass who sounds like one of those ancient philosophers you love to quote. All that's missing as you stride back and forth is a white toga draped over your shoulder."

"Fuckin' enough! Try imagining that *you're* that little kid Dad rejected. Vividly imagine it instead of doing what you always do—defend him."

Joy gave what sounded like a painful squeak. "And you can try imagining what our lives would've been like without this nice home and heaping wad of financial security we'll inherit. Doesn't that prove Dad loves us?"

"Loves *you*! Your little love alliance is sickening. And don't tell me to stop feeling sorry for myself. After twenty years of calculated cruelties, I finally exploded. *Understandably* exploded." He stared at Joy, who now sat expressionless and speechless. "I'm trying to hold it together, Sis. Trying to see what role I play in this fucked up family."

Dorothy had returned from the bathroom and as she busied herself at the kitchen counter, Rick asked, "What happened after you went downstairs, Mom?"

"Couldn't believe what I saw." Dorothy leaned heavily on a dish cloth she pushed back and forth across the counter top. "Dad was lying on the floor, his face covered in blood. For a split second, I actually thought you'd killed him, but as soon as he heard my shocking reaction he mumbled, 'Get me outta here.' I helped him up the stairs and into bed, cleaned the blood off his face and wondered where you'd gone."

"Did he say anything about me?"

"Said something about you having to move out. Good idea if you can't control your anger."

"Mom! It's not like you to take sides. You haven't said anything about Dad having to control *his* anger. I'm controlling my own right now…toward you."

"Now just a minute here, Ricky. You're bigger and stronger than Dad. Why didn't you take that broom out of his hand and calm him down? Or escape upstairs?"

"You're kidding, right? Wild animals don't let humans calm them down. I told you, he attacked when I wasn't looking." Rick pushed his chair back and announced, "I'm going skiing…need to find true north."

Joy's brooding…they've abandoned me, Rick concluded as he descended the stairs to his suite. *Feels like I'm sneaking down some grotty stairway in the Roach Hotel…my very own House of Horrors.* Frazzled and unfocused, he changed his clothes three times until he got the right layering, then threw together two cheese sandwiches that he put in his backpack along with a water bottle and shortbread cookies.

Fresh fallen snow sparkled in the brilliant sunshine as Rick bore down on every push—one stride of pity; one, disgust. One stride of guilt;

one, anger. As always, nature had the upper hand and it wasn't long before she smoothed the edges of Rick's jagged emotions. Two hours in, he chanced upon a small opening where he flopped down on the soft snow and devoured his lunch, then rested his head on his backpack and thought of his fun-loving friend Gabe. Compassionate, witty, easygoing Gabe was spending Christmas with family in Vancouver. *He'd know just what to say at a time like this. Never felt so bereft. So alone.*

Snow had seeped into Rick's clothing and the slow melt made his return trip bone-chillingly cold. Gliding into the final clearing before his descent to the trailhead, he stopped and stabbed his ski poles in the snow. Streaks of orange-tinted sunlight had burst through a veil of cloud, and although Rick had seen many awesome sunsets over the years, this one had special impact.

Ah, twilight, he mused. *A tranquil gift for tortured souls.*

Chapter 2

Bang, bang, rattle, rattle.

"No need to fix this flimsy lock," Dick shouted as he opened the door and brazenly barged into Rick's kitchen. "Your free ride's over!"

Rick's mouth went dry. He motioned his father to take a seat at the table. "Let's talk, Dad."

Dick braced his stance and pointed to each black and blue swelling on his face. "This oughta be reason enough to make my case. We can't live under the same roof."

Sensing an impending eviction notice, Rick sat down at the table. "I promise you it won't happen again. Word of honour!" He resisted lifting his shirt to put his own wound on display.

"Right! It won't happen again cuz you'll be outta here by mid-January. Let that sink in."

"Are you giving me the pink slip too? Surely you've seen how I pull my weight at work."

Sounding less like a drill sergeant, Dick said, "I'm not kicking you outta my life. Besides, Harry wouldn't agree to letting you go."

"I'll gladly pay more rent, and I'll—"

"Your mother says I should let you stay if you see a shrink and get a grip on your anger. Not just a one-time shot either; every week for three months at least. Fat chance you'll do that."

Rick desperately tried a compromise. "I'll go if you do…family counselling could benefit us both."

"The truth of the matter is, shrinks are for adults who can't get beyond their diapers," Dick said contemptuously.

Rick winced. "But Dad, why can't we work things out together?"

"Cuz I'm standing in enemy territory, that's why."

"This is killing me," Rick said, voice trembling, eyes watering.

"Pay the moving company and I'll reimburse you." Dick blew a heavy sigh, lowered his head, and walked out, gently closing the door behind him.

Rick folded his arms on the table and docked his face in the crook of his elbow. Sadness and regret soaked his shirt sleeve. *What to make of it? No remorse. No apology.*

One ring, two rings, three. Rick trimmed his nails with his teeth.

"Good morning, Doctors Chang and Grey. May I help you?"

Rick faked confidence. "Oh, I'm surprised you're open during the holidays. I'd like to book an appointment with one of your therapists. It's, um…fairly urgent."

"Can you come on short notice? Dr. Marion Grey just had a cancellation and can see you at three o'clock today."

"I…well…I—"

The receptionist waited.

"Yes. I can be there at three. See you then."

Done. A sanity probe. Exercise in humiliation, Rick told himself, then unexpectedly, from some cranial fold came the vision of a large poster he'd seen on the side wall of a bookstore. A rag doll was stuck in the ringer of an old washing machine over which the caption read: "The truth will set you free, but first it will make you miserable." *Go with truth and freedom at the expense of misery?* he asked himself. *Too late to ruminate. How much should I tell this woman? Can't bullshit a therapist. Clean-shaven face, crisp white shirt, newest old jeans…good first impression.*

Rick frantically tidied papers on his desk and picked up the clothes strewn about his bedroom, then absent-mindedly found himself spraying cleaner into the toilet bowl.

Toilet? Rick wondered. *Why now?*

"Please fill out this information form before I take you to Dr. Grey's office," said the receptionist, passing Rick a questionnaire.

When he read the form's last statement: *Do you have a criminal record?* Rick considered that, in the interest of accuracy, the *Yes* or *No* forced choices should have included a third option: *Almost.*

The receptionist knocked on Dr. Grey's office door and poked her head in. "Meet Rick Wright, Dr. Grey. Your three o'clock appointment."

Dr. Grey rose from her desk and smoothed her short black skirt. "Nice to meet you, Rick. Please come in." She motioned him to take a seat, then sat in her usual position behind a low coffee table in front of the client's chair.

The image of professionalism, Rick thought. *Younger than Mom; a lot older than me. Forties or fifties…yeah, fifty something. Could lose a few pounds. Silver-streaked auburn hair. Sophisticated.* He tried to casually settle into the billowy, leather chair.

"Feel free to call me Marion, if you prefer."

"Thanks. Nice gesture, but I'm comfortable with Dr. Grey."

Dr. Grey smiled. "Please tell me a bit about yourself."

Rick tore a chunk of skin from his bottom lip. "Dad threatened to kick me out of the family home—my nice basement suite—unless I get therapy." He leaned forward to pressure his bouncing leg. "Thumper's doing his disturbing dance…without music," Rick said, pounding his right thigh with his fist. "Maybe coming here makes me more anxious than I want to admit."

"Your first visit to a therapist?" asked Dr. Grey.

"Yes. Can't quite believe I'm sitting here. My ex was in long-term therapy until the day her therapist asked, 'What's the big lie you're telling yourself?' That did it. Never went back. Should've. The big lie was clear to everyone but her."

Dr. Grey gently probed. "Can I assume you weren't blinded by passion or the idea—so common among lovers—that you could change her?"

"Yeah, I guess you could say that."

"What about you and your dad? Sounds like the two of you aren't getting along."

Avoiding Dr. Grey's invitation, Rick digressed. "My ex and I got on reasonably well until she glommed onto the QAnon conspiracy—thinks the banks are funding a secret New World Order the rest of us are too dumb to figure out. But she's special…one of the select few who are unafraid of the truth. Unafraid to challenge all traditional media…thinks it peddles nothing but fake news. To her, personal testimonials and Googled articles dressed up to look like a million scientific bucks are more valid than peer-reviewed studies that test hundreds, even thousands, of subjects. She once said that until I'd read as much as she had, I didn't know what I was talking about. Where do you go with such arrogance? Dad's a lot like her—won't change his mind and won't change the subject. Feels entitled to hold court, but I can't have my say because I'm not worth listening to. Sorry, I'm ragging the puck."

Rick couldn't tell whether Dr. Grey's rhythmic nod was one of sympathy, politeness, frustration, or something else.

"The Internet rewards extremists and people prone to paranoia, especially those who feel a profound loss of control in their lives," Dr. Grey said. "Then again, Copernicus was considered a conspiracy theorist in his day, yet his propositions were eventually proven true. But I agree, the example you gave, and many others, are ludicrous."

Rick started to talk about his father's anti-Semitism and a revisionist theory of the holocaust, but Dr. Grey interrupted. "I'd like to hear more about you, particularly your apprehension about the usefulness of therapy. What most concerns you? How can I be helpful?"

Rick answered her question with one of his own. "What are the ground rules?"

Dr. Grey straightened her back as if suddenly aware of sagging posture. "One rule I'm legally bound to honour is confidentiality. Also, I won't waste your time and money with friendly chitchat about the weather or last night's hockey game. In turn, I hope you'll be open and honest about personal issues, even embarrassing ones, so that, together, we can discuss changes that could make your life more meaningful. More enjoyable. I'm not going to tell you why, when, or how to change, but I will ask you to consider what you might give up if you do change."

"I get to do the heavy lifting," Rick sighed, then noticed a drooping peace lily in the corner of the room. *Needs watering. Or an antidepressant.*

"I'll appeal to your healthy side," Dr. Grey said, "but I'll also confront that which may prevent inner peace and fulfillment. I should state upfront that without effort from both of us, therapy won't magically give you what you're hoping for."

Rick swallowed hard. "Inner peace is missing. I've lost my way…need a reboot."

Dr. Grey said, "To quote Maya Angelou, 'If you don't know where you've come from, you don't know where you're going.' With all clients, I like to begin working on small changes to remove their stumbling blocks."

"Sure, but getting back to your earlier question about what I'd like to have happen in here, I'll be upfront. I didn't come to talk about me. I came for professional advice about my father because unless I figure out how to get along with him, I'll lose my free rent and part-time job with his company—two sweet deals."

"Working for your dad and living at home are important because…?" Dr. Grey steadied her gaze.

"I need at least one advanced degree in English—four more years of university—if I'm to have any chance at becoming a professional writer."

"Professional writing, an exciting career. I gather something serious happened between you and your father that could put that in jeopardy."

"Yes, and if things don't improve, one of us could get hurt, most likely him. Frankly, that scares the shit outta me. Pardon my slanguage,

I'm trying to clean it up. Vulgar language indicates a juvenile mind…a sex-obsessed, male mind. Cripes, I'm blathering again. Less is more. I think you asked a question."

"There's no need to censor yourself with me. In therapy, more is sometimes more. You're being open, and it's quite natural during a client's first visit to give a wealth of information, even if a bit disjointed. I'll rein you in if necessary. Is what happened between you and your father the problem that most concerns you?"

Unlike his jumpy leg, Rick's mind ground to a halt. He stared at the carpet's abstract design. *A fuckin' Rorschach rug…looks like soldiers swinging bayonets while marching through a sea of blood. Wrong answer.*

Rick crossed and uncrossed his legs, then did the same with his arms.

Silence dragged on until Dr. Grey broke it. "Working silences are the necessary pauses that help clients consider issues and questions that arise." She cleared her throat. "Take your time."

Very considerate, Rick thought. *Sensitive. But I should keep the conversation moving.* He unbuttoned his shirt cuffs and rolled up his sleeves. "It's just that…well, I don't quite know how to put this, so I'll be blunt. Dad is seriously damaged. He pontificates about politics, religion, people he idolizes—political leaders, presidents, Forbes billionaires…you get the picture. Probably adores Hitler too, but I'm afraid to go there. And he acts like he knows everything about everything—as if that were humanly possible. How's this for Dad's favourite, friendly little jab? 'Of course I'm right! What's the matter with you?'"

"Insulting, for sure," Dr. Grey said. "Given what you've just told me, I see why you want to talk about your father, but I wonder if focusing more on him is the best use of our time, especially since he isn't here to give his perspective on your concerns."

"But my main concern is *him*—takes all his frustrations out on me. Has dedicated his life to finding signs of stupidity in his feckless son. When I was about six, he told me that my name should be Ricky

Wrong." Rick finger-combed his hair. "Like I said, I need help handling him because he's my main problem."

"I'm noticing the cords in your neck. Will you close your eyes and make your jaw muscles as tight as possible?"

"Tight?" Rick closed his eyes and quickly reopened them. "Can't make them any tighter."

"Take a slow, deep breath, then exhale fully," Dr. Grey said, then watched Rick's mouth and jaw muscles soften.

"Did you notice any difference in your facial tension, your neck muscles?"

Rick took another easy breath and Dr. Grey gently coached him to fully exhale.

"Didn't realize how tense my muscles were until you told me to tighten them." Rick sat back in his chair.

"You loosened their grip through body awareness and deep breathing, a good start to managing your thoughts and emotions. We'll delve into that more deeply if you like," Dr. Grey said, then crossed her legs and traced airborne circles with her foot. "For the time being, I'll honour your request to talk about your father. What's his name?"

"Richard Wright, but he's always gone by Dick."

Nodding slowly, Dr. Grey said, "You'd like to better understand him in relation to you, so sure, let's start there and see where it takes us. Greater understanding opens the door to hope."

"Hmm." Rick squinted, then stared at his feet. "I don't…." he fell silent. "Whatever it is with me and Dad, we're caught in something awful. *I'm* caught in something awful."

"Was there anything in particular that led you to book this session?"

Rick lowered his head and struggled to accurately describe the Boxing Day dinner and the vicious beatings that followed. He ended by saying, "It's the kind of savagery we think couldn't happen in our family…stuff we see on TV and movie screens." He tapped his prominent nose with his index finger. "I've tried not to turn that gruesome event into something other than it was, but I've put up with years of Dad's abuse so it's hard to be objective about him."

"Quite insightful, Rick. No one can be totally objective about the ongoing dynamics in fractured relationships."

Back and forth, back and forth, Rick ran his hands under his eyes. "Here's what terrifies me. As I knocked the bejesus out of Dad, I didn't realize what I was doing. Quite simply, I lost my mind."

"What was that like for you?"

"Chilling. I was…still am confused about the whole mess. The Incident, capital *T*, capital *I*."

"Prolonged abuse grew and grew until you couldn't take it anymore?" Dr. Grey said, part statement, part question.

"Yeah, blind rage."

"My first concern is that you and your father might still be in danger. Before we go any further, I should tell you that I'm officially bound to break client confidentiality if I think you're at risk for harming yourself or others."

Rick scratched at a small stain on his shirt sleeve and agonized that he'd said too much too soon. He looked squarely at Dr. Grey. "No worries; rest assured I have no such plan. We obviously don't do conflict well, but that's the only time Dad ever attacked me and I retaliated. With your help, I'll get through this."

"What needs to happen for you to get through it?"

Rick watched his thumbs twiddle in his lap. In a tearful voice, he said, "My mind needs to let go of the images…they weigh me down. Can't stop, *cannot* stop the hideous sight of Dad's bloody nose and mouth. The purple pouches under his eyes…hollow eyes. The ropey veins on his temples."

Dr. Grey moistened her lips and waited until Rick said, "For years I've imagined Dad tearfully apologizing for the pain he's caused. Instead—and this is why I'm sitting here—I now have to replace that fantasy with the stark reality that a ferocious father caused his equally ferocious son to hammer him into submission. Scary stuff." Rick pounded his foot on the floor. "Thumper's at it again."

"What are you feeling now, Rick?"

"Rocks in my gut. Big, fat boulders."

"Stay with your feelings."

Rick held his face in his hands for a few moments, then looked up, teary eyed and silent.

"This is difficult for you," Dr. Grey said.

"Mm-hmm."

"Are you working hard at holding something back?"

"Part of me wants complete control of my emotions; another part wants to let go. Part of me wants to love Dad; another part, not far from the surface, wants to hate him."

"Poised between control and letting go; between love and hate. Let's work at integrating those thoughts and feelings. They're at war with each other."

"How so?"

"It's as if your brain's cognitive parts aren't listening to the emotional parts. You can't love unless thoughts and feelings of love are within you, which makes me wonder if, long before The Incident, your anger may have crushed your capacity for love and compassion."

Rick rubbed the bridge of his nose and contemplated Dr. Grey's comment until she asked, "Can you tell me about the part that wants to love your dad?"

Thumper finally rested while Rick said, "He works hard to provide for his family, but twenty-some years of constant criticism and put-downs are bloody awful no matter how hard I try to remember his finer qualities."

"No matter how hard? We'll work on that effort later, but your father...he's been a steady provider for the family?"

"Yes. Dad and his younger brother, my Uncle Harry, are joint owners of Wright Brothers. They're not corporate titans, but they've done amazingly well at building new homes and small condo complexes. Dad manages a couple dozen tradesmen, including me, his unskilled imbecile. I work in the warehouse—receiving, stocking, and shipping materials. Best part is operating the forklift at building sites. Keeps me and Dad at a safe distance."

"That's the logical, analytical you speaking."

"Maybe so, but despite trying to make sense of Dad's endless verbal abuse, I can't find any good, logical answers."

Dr. Grey raised one brow. "It's easy to feel…?"

"Pissed off with him. Angry. Too angry. That's what I need to control because he always draws me into his narrow, cynical world."

"Is that what led up to The Incident on Boxing Day?"

Rick rubbed his hand across his cheek as he scanned the room, then demonstrated his skill at deflection. "I should also tell you that after travelling around Europe for a few years, picking up odd jobs here and there, I went back to school. Took Abnormal Psychology in my second year of university…wanted to satisfy my curiosity about crazy behaviour. I'm taking Personality Theory next semester…speaking of which, can I ask for your opinion of Dad?"

Something indecipherable crossed Dr. Grey's face. "I don't have enough information to form a valid opinion, but I'm slowly developing a portrait…in black and white. Let's get back—"

"Picture perfect! Dad's ideas are either totally black or pure white. People are totally honest, or complete liars and cheats, brilliant or stupid, right or wrong. And his beliefs about politics and religion, the economy, the military, marriage, sex, how to bring up kids, the environment—you name it, there's never room for that lighter shade of black or darker shade of white, if you know what I mean…Dr. Grey."

Dr. Grey looked perplexed, then unrestrained laughter filled the room. Heartened to see her burst of amusement, Rick felt the tension drain from every muscle in his body. "For Dad, the only grey zone is *on* his head, not in it."

"I can see you've given black, white, and grey serious thought," Dr. Grey said, laughter subsiding. "Grey is the difficult area alright; black and white are the easy, slender threads of reason. I prefer a more colourful approach to understanding and solving problems, one that makes room for a variety of interpretations and solutions. But yes, grey is that difficult area…makes me wonder how you approach complex problems."

Rick chewed on his thumb knuckle. "This might sound odd, but I'm okay with not having answers to the big questions everyone struggles with…except people like Dad, whose extreme thoughts diverge so far from the rest of us we tread gently when he's around. But he does have a good sense of humour, even if it is at my expense."

"Humour can hint at what we'd like to say without saying it. Often keeps tension at a minimum."

"Like when a TV commentator reported a 3% rise in university tuition. I told Dad that if our government wants citizens to receive a world-class education, it should lower fees, even cancel them. Dad raised his beer mug and said, 'Congratulations! An idea with more beer than foam.' After that patronizing compliment, he accused all students of being too lazy to work at menial jobs and pay for their own education. So you see, I'm not the only failure in Dad's small world…and mind."

Rick's thoughts were again on a long leash he tried to control but couldn't, perhaps because Dr. Grey looked relaxed, yet concerned. Contemplative.

"Sorry. Once again, I'm as unfocused as a feather in the wind."

"Not a problem. One more question about your father, then I'd like to get back to you. Are there other strengths you admire about him?"

"Admire is too strong a word for someone who's slow to think and quick to judge." Rick scratched his stubble. "He's loyal to his employees…and Mom, as far as I know. And he's a decent citizen— volunteers for the Alzheimer Society's annual fundraising casino. A good move since he might need their help some day. He drinks too much."

Dr. Grey slowly brushed her bangs across her forehead. "I find that when I better understand people, I'm less inclined to judge them.

Less inclined to give them power to emotionally upset me. Problem is, understanding's difficult; judgment's easy."

Rick nodded while recalling his strange, inexplicable feelings the night his Uncle Harry reminisced about his childhood with Dick. Until now, Rick hadn't fully understood how deep emotional awareness was the first step to transformative change.

"The day after The Incident," Rick said, "I knew there was no way out. Had to talk to a professional. But I now wonder if you're worried that a man capable of violence is sitting across from you."

Dr. Grey didn't flinch. "A thoughtful concern, but no, I'm not worried. You're aware that you have a problem to solve, and you've taken steps to do that…to move closer to where you'd like to be, and *who* you'd like to be. In my books, that's a real plus. What are some other strengths?"

How am I supposed to answer that, Rick mused. He knew that learning had always been easy in grade school and university, but he remained conflicted about a remnant of his childhood learning—one his mother had drilled into him. Bragging about accomplishments was sinful. Humility was a virtue.

"I'm not comfortable promoting myself," Rick said, squirming in his chair, "but since you've asked, I get top grades in my English, Psychology, and Political Science courses, probably because I read beyond the required text and make use of professors' office hours. Here's hoping that's enough to get me into postgraduate studies. That'll piss off Dad, knowing that I'm better educated than he is, especially when it comes to politics. Maybe then he'll soften his uncompromising views."

"And satisfy your desire for revenge?"

"Revenge? That's not why I'm going to university. I'm doing it for me. Do you think I'm doing it for revenge?"

"Not necessarily, but I get concerned when university students say, or imply, that a degree will finally prove themselves to their parents. They're adults; they don't need to prove themselves to anyone. Please their parents, yes; compete with them or prove their worth, no."

"Maybe I am trying to prove myself. Whatever me and Dad are doing to each other, it never ends."

"Sounds oppressive," Dr. Grey said. "Have you ever thought of moving out…putting your frustrations behind you?"

"Friends and my ex have insinuated I'm a wimp for staying…for hoping things will change. But I can't totally reject him. He is my father!"

"Rick, everyone has emotional reasons, some unknown to themselves, for tolerating what others wouldn't."

"Yeah. I keep thinking that if I were more accepting and understanding of Dad—a high-wire act with no safety net—his arguing and arrogance would fade away. But it hasn't. I dunno…maybe it's me."

"From your father's perspective, might his attempts to lure you into an argument be the first step to winning it?"

Rick shrugged his shoulders. "He does get a sickening grin on his face when I've been baited, hooked, and landed, so yeah, to Dad it's a game he needs to win. I like Mark Twain's warning to be careful when we argue with fools; onlookers might not see the difference."

Dr. Grey chuckled. "Frequent arguing rewards some people with desired attention. If so, behaviour that's consistently rewarded seldom changes. Have you tried ignoring your father, or switching the topic?"

"Yes, but he gets even more belligerent…makes it impossible to bite my tongue."

"When we remove the payoff for undesirable behaviour, it usually increases. A test, so to speak. But if you don't bite, your dad might stop offering the bait. Consistency's the key here; long-term consistency."

"Long-term consistency with the master baiter," Rick said, snickering.

Dr. Grey managed a weak smile.

"Here I am, wanting to figure out how to confront Dad's lizard logic without getting enraged, but you think I should simply walk away?"

Expressionless, Dr. Grey said, "It's your father's turf. His rules. Perhaps you fulfill two of his needs: first, you give him permission to draw you into a losing competition; second, you allow him to make you angry…initially at him, then yourself."

Rick pondered the idea. "Are you saying I *let* him control me? *Let* him make me angry?"

"Does he have a loaded gun to your head?"

"Well no, but he needs to understand that his arrogance and crazy beliefs make him look stupid…ridiculous. Racist and pig-headed. He embarrasses himself. Need I say more?"

"Is that when you step in to rescue him? Correct him? Or protect him?"

"I want to expose his ignorance. That's all."

In a semi-playful tone, Dr. Grey said, "I see. Have you appointed yourself the guardian of your father's intelligence? And reputation?"

Rick started to raise his arms in protest, but quickly dropped them in his lap, saying, "Wow! You've laid on a lot. Maybe I'm just embarrassed to be his son."

"Is it possible that aside from feeling ashamed, you feel somewhat responsible for changing his behaviour?"

"All I know is this: on Boxing Day the animal that was locked up inside me finally burst through the barricades and went wild."

"Let's work on taming that animal," Dr. Grey said.

Sounds like she's talking to a purring cat. "Will you perform the exorcism?" Rick asked, then felt himself physically dwindle. *Dumb comment*, came the voice in his head.

Dr. Grey looked at Rick as if trying to improve her focus. "I feel like you're mocking my profession. Exorcism? Really? What else? Frontal lobotomies?" She stared solicitously at Rick.

Rick geared down like an eighteen-wheeler on a turnpike. "Please give me a moment," he said, cracking the knuckles on one hand, then the other. "I'm sorry. The beast was in control—Mom's favourite metaphor."

"Thank you. Apology accepted." Dr. Grey said with a bemused smile. "How *are* things with you and your mother?"

"We're good, but I wish she were more assertive. I've encouraged her—pushed might be more accurate—to stand up to Dad. Tell him to stop drinking or she'll leave, then leave if he doesn't."

"Did your Mom hear you?"

"Sort of. She told me she's tried to persuade him to lay off the booze, get a hobby, take walks together, anything to get him out of that TV chair and away from the fridge. He'd get angry and call her an old hound dog. Guess she eventually decided it was impossible to change him."

"Sounds like your Mom would agree that the harder we try to fix people we care about—disguised as helping—the more we insult them."

Rick tilted his head to one side. "But isn't it natural to try to help family and friends? People we worry about? Doesn't that show we care?"

"You've raised an important question. As I see it, factual information is different from unsolicited advice for a self-change project. Too often we tell anxious friends or relatives to settle down, take a course in meditation, get more sleep. That's disrespectful; they've likely thought about our nagging suggestions a hundred times over. What's the unspoken message?"

"Shape up or ship out?" Rick said, raising his brows.

"Yes. Here's another well-intended but mistaken assumption: You need me to help you solve your problems. No, they don't. Listening and respecting them as a person is more helpful than giving advice."

"Are you saying I should never give anyone advice, Dad included?"

"Not unless they ask for it, then be brief. Tell them once. Give them space. If the problem's deeply personal or emotional, you could suggest that somewhere within, they know how to solve it."

"Doesn't sound like that would help much."

"But you've recognized the problem as *theirs*, not yours. You've given them agency. You could also say: You've found your way back before; I have no doubt you'll find it again. Just know that I'm here for you if you want to talk."

Rick stared at his nails as if seeing them for the first time.

Dr. Grey added, "My suggestions are only meant for adults who aren't psychotic, suicidal, or psychopathic. But let's get back to you. I'm afraid I've given a sonorous lecture."

"It doesn't seem like a lecture. I'm taking it all in," Rick said sincerely.

Dr. Grey knit her fingers together. "You and your father. As you talked about him, I heard both caring and bitterness in your voice. Two contradictory emotions."

Rick pressed his hands to his thighs. "I want to love Dad, but...but I can't. There's nothing to build on: no foundation, no mortar, no wood. Could you love your father if his daily mission was to put you down and trip you up?"

"I'm not trying to avoid your question; it's entirely reasonable. But I need to know if your dad ever physically or sexually abused you as a child?"

"No. Do things have to be that bad to justify not loving one's father? Haven't I given reason enough?"

"Yes. It makes sense to me why you feel the way you do, but perhaps if we work on a few ideas and strategies, your feelings will change...and your relationship. For the better."

"Hopefully. Up until now, I've ignored psychological problems."

Dr. Grey said, "Ignore them and they'll go?"

"Sounds stupid when you put it like that, but yeah, that's pretty much what I've done."

"Psychologists believe differently. Ignore them and they'll grow. Over time, it might be more damaging and take more energy to repress problems than confront them."

"So it seems, but when I try to deal with them...surprise! They get worse."

"Tough problems are like that. They show us what we're made of, and I think you're made of sturdy stuff. Shall we get back to The Incident?"

Rick tightened his grip on the armchair and finished summarizing The Incident: his overnight stay at Rose and Harry's, the kitchen chat, the phone confrontations with his mother and sister, and his escape to the ski trails. Tears welled up when he described his Aunt Rose. "Women like her make me wonder what kind of mothers they have. I'd go out of my way to help her."

"Ah, yes. We teach people how to treat us."

Rick's eyes glowed as if switched on by an inner light. "Dad's brilliant at teaching me how to treat him. Knows how to push my buttons."

"When you were a little kid, how did he teach you to treat him?"

Rick fiddled with the top button on his shirt. "He taught me to fear him…to not trust him. And obey him without question or I'd be scolded. Even punished."

Rick looked up at the ceiling and said, "In Grade nine, I took on Harman, the schoolyard bully…a year older and slightly taller than me, but weaker. I threw him to the ground and put my knee in his groin. By then, a small band of spectators—little pagans from Rome's Colosseum—egged us on, eagerly waiting to give us a thumbs-up or thumbs-down. When I gave Harman the honour of apologizing for calling me 'Rick the prick,' he obliged. Stopped bullying me too."

Dr. Grey said, "Hmm, that was one way of teaching him how to treat you."

"Yeah, but here's the weird part. One of the pagans squealed on us, and later that afternoon, when Dad got home from work, the principal phoned. I figured I was in serious trouble, but after Dad hung up, he gripped my shoulders and proudly declared, 'Attaboy, Ricky! Your testicles have descended. Don't let anyone push you around.'"

In a flat tone of voice, Dr. Grey said, "Your father applauded your aggression. How did your classmates respond the next day?"

"I can't remember. I only know that I continued to feel left out most of the time. And angry."

Dr. Grey discreetly checked the time and said, "Speaking of anger, let's discuss some safety measures when frustration builds between you and your father. Specifically, what will you do differently next time to handle a touchy situation?"

Rick answered with an air of confidence. "The next time he gets belligerent I'll say nothing and leave the scene before things get out of control. Really."

"Excellent. Sit back, close your eyes, and take a few deep breaths, then vividly imagine yourself doing that."

Rick uncrossed his legs, leaned back in his chair, and breathed deeply. Slowly, a subtle look of satisfaction crossed his face. "That might help," he said.

"I'd like to spend more time on coping strategies next session, but before we end today, I also want to ask about support systems beyond your uncle and aunt—friends and family you can count on in difficult times."

"Unfortunately, two of my good friends have finished university and taken jobs in eastern Canada, but I'm close to my sister, Joy, and even closer to my good friend Gabe, who's studying journalism. We met in a first-year university course and, ever since, there isn't much we don't talk about. Oh, and an older coworker in the warehouse knows how critical and narrow-minded Dad can be. We usually have lunch and coffee breaks together; he'd be there for me if I needed him."

"Would you phone one of them, without hesitation, if you felt seriously threatened…or threatening?"

"Yes, count on me to do that."

"Remember too that if you're in severe distress, don't hesitate to phone me." Dr. Grey handed Rick her professional card. "There's someone on call from the agency 24-7."

Rick pulled out his phone. "I'll enter that number now."

"You've given a lot of yourself today, Rick—all very helpful for me to hear."

"This session was nothing like I expected. What a relief to sound off to someone who didn't tune out."

Dr. Grey smiled warmly. "With all clients, I suggest a time limit of six sessions, after which you might want to take a break to work on things we've discovered or uncovered. But you can continue, terminate, and resume sessions anytime it feels right to do so."

"Fair enough. A little self-education is as important as anything I'm learning at the university." Rick reached for his jacket. "I'll book another appointment on my way out."

"It wasn't easy for you to come here today. I'm glad you did."

Dr. Grey shook Rick's hand as he smiled and said, "A reasonable start to...wherever."

Chapter 3

The din and pace of rush-hour traffic had diminished notably enough for Rick to lower the window and breathe in the crisp winter air. *Ignore Dad? That's all I'm supposed to do? And what was that bit about letting him control me?* Deep in thought, he ran a stop sign and almost hit a delivery truck. Barely had he calmed down from that near miss when he rounded the corner of his home street and saw, parked in the driveway, Vermillion—the shiny red truck his father named and described as, "Good vermillion miles."

Rick parked a short distance from the house, cut the engine, and leaned against the steering wheel. Watching the low-flying, ring-billed gulls swoop below the swirling storm clouds, he recalled another of his father's sayings: "Sometimes I just sits and thinks and sometimes I just sits."

Rick just sat. Edvard Munch sat with him. As fog slowly worked its way across the inside of the windshield, Rick used the pad of his index finger to etch a meagre imitation of Munch's "The Scream," then sat back and briefly revelled in his burst of creativity.

Get on with it, coward, he scolded himself, then held his head high and briskly walked his usual route along the house to the back entrance, crept downstairs, and gently closed the door to his suite—the door with the flimsy lock. Voices from the upstairs TV were loud enough for him to picture his dad, beer firmly in hand as he watched Fox news and rhythmically nodded like Howdy-Doody, the famous finger-puppet.

Rick went upstairs and strode into the living room. Faking confidence, he said, "Hey, Dad, I've taken you up on your offer. Just finished my first therapy session with Dr. Grey, a psychotherapist who had a cancellation this afternoon. How about putting me on probation for three months while I continue seeing her?"

"Really now!" Dick cleared his throat as if a small swarm of flies were trapped in it. "And how much will that set you back?"

"No worries, I've worked it out. A tuition refund for my History course will cover most of the sessions, and as long as I can keep working for you, I'll manage the rest...even if I go in debt."

"I'll see about giving you more work at the office. If therapy goes well...if you shape up, I'll consider meeting you halfway on the fees."

"Thanks. Glad I don't have to move out." Rick turned on his heels and sock skated across the varnished hardwood into the kitchen where his mother was scrubbing a frying pan.

"Did I hear you right?" Dorothy asked. "You've actually seen a therapist today?"

"Yep." Rick stood beside his mom and whispered, "Thanks for suggesting that to Dad. He looked stunned when I told him...said he might help me with the cost *if* I shape up. He wasn't the least bit thankful or impressed with my desperate attempt to work things out."

Dorothy gave Rick a wet, partial hug. "Well, *I* appreciate what you're doing."

Keeping his voice low, Rick said, "I told Dad that I thought family therapy was a good idea, but his reaction was so crude it's not worth repeating. Jeez, Mom, how have you put up with him all these years?"

Dorothy leaned toward Rick and said, in a low voice, "Now, now...don't be cheeky. I have my ways. Might tell you about it someday, but not tonight." She dried her hands on the dish towel. "You haven't eaten. No leftovers, except lemon pie. How about some scrambled eggs and toast?"

"Thanks," Rick whispered, "but I need to keep my distance from Dad. If he comes into the kitchen, I'm afraid I'll say something I'll regret."

Dorothy whispered, "Okay, but quickly, how'd your first therapy session go?"

"Let's just say I have lots to think about—going downstairs to do just that. I'll tell you about it when Dad's not around." Rick started toward the door, looked back, and smiled at his mom. "Actually, I'd love a piece of pie."

Dorothy asked as she cut him a big piece of pie, "How's your back?"

"The wicked welt's going down," Rick said, raising his sweatshirt.

His mother stepped closer and ran her fingers over the injury. "Quite the bruise, but it'll heal with time."

Rick went down to his suite, opened a beer and sighed after the first long swallow, the one he says soothes a parched throat; the one— and only one—he usually sips as he prepares his routine supper. Some days he goes all out: sautéed cubed chicken, broccoli, carrots, and frozen peas over steamed rice. Today, he settled for a fully loaded pizza from the freezer.

Slice of pizza in one hand, TV remote in the other, Rick watched a grizzly claw open its captured salmon. As it gnawed on its catch, Rick gnawed on Dr. Grey's meatier interventions, which he later recorded on his computer. Into the night, a flurry of uncensored thoughts filled a document he titled Therapy Session #1, the last sentence of which held a cliché that bore down on him: The apple doesn't fall far from the tree. With that, Rick crawled into bed where, losing his battle with insomnia, he remembered his mother saying, "I have my ways." *What if she's having an affair?* he wondered in all seriousness, then questioned his ability to think rationally. *A staunch Catholic like her? Nah. She'd spend the rest of her life in the confessional. Then again....*

Midnight munchies had Rick staring into his kitchen cupboard and reaching for a crumpled bag of chocolate chippers. Polishing off the cookies, he contemplated the term shrink, then grabbed his phone from the bedside table and chose one of Google's several definitions.

Shrink: Slang for shrinking a patient's narcissistic, inflated sense of self-importance. *Has the Doc shrunk me down to that diagnosis, or simply concluded that I'm a failed specimen of Homo sapiens?* On and on his thoughts unravelled until finally, into the cavernous darkness, sleep descended. Unmerciful, nightmarish sleep.

Rick dreamt he was in a broken-down cemetery anxiously wandering among rows of sunken graves and weathered boards, once markers for the long-since dead. In a damp, dirt hollow lay an old, weathered coffin with filmy hair-like fibers creeping along one wall. Streaks of moonlight flickered across the face of a grey slab crookedly poking up from the ground, its sun-bleached name still readable: RICKY.

Unaware that he'd been holding his breath, Rick bolted upright and gasped as a burst of consciousness assured him he was well above ground. Shaken but grateful to be alive, he flopped back down on his pillow and drifted into deep, restorative sleep.

Hours later, Rick snuggled under the covers to block the glare of sunlight flooding his room. *How strange*, he thought, *that we yearn for sleep despite knowing that unconscious forces may take us to unknown, scary places with strange faces—some, complete strangers; others, long-since dead. Or wished dead.*

Dick Wright was upstairs sounding off to his new 50-inch TV when Rick hauled himself out from under his duvet and turned up the volume on his favourite music channel. He sauntered over to the window and watched puffy snowflakes gently fall from a hazy, grey-blue sky—a scene that contrasted nature's soft winter beauty with the echo of his father's hardened, cynical view of the world.

After devouring a toasted bagel smothered in cream cheese, Rick showered and shaved, grabbed his winter jacket, laptop, and library book, then crept up the back stairs to the landing. Hearing loud voices, he turned and climbed the remaining five steps to the kitchen door, cautiously inched it open, and gingerly peeked in. From what little he could see, his mother was kneading and turning dough at the pastry counter; further down, his father's elbow protruded from the coffee nook.

"Cripes, Dorothy, when will you learn to open the right end of the milk carton!"

Rick eased the door close to its casing and listened to what he and Joy dubbed his mother's little girl voice—high pitched, with an apologetic tone that signalled anxious to please.

"I can't stop worrying about you and Ricky," Dorothy meekly protested.

Rick wanted to scream: *Lower your voice and say what you'd say if you weren't afraid.*

Dorothy continued, "Please have a man-to-man talk with him about Boxing Day. I'm begging you. *Please.*"

Curious to hear his father's reply, which was anything but hesitant, Rick listened in on Dick's unmistakable imitation of a Wild West cowboy. "Keep outta this! It's between Ricky and me so don't you be worrying yer pretty little head about me not handlin' things. How about another pot o' coffee."

Dorothy said nothing as Rick reframed his parents' relationship: *Mom's giving Dad another lesson in spousal abuse.* When he shifted his laptop and novel to his other arm, the thick, hard-cover book slid off the laptop and bounced down the stairs to the landing.

Dick opened the kitchen door and watched as Rick snatched the book off the floor, then slapped the palm of his hand to his forehead.

Life slowed right down for both.

"Was just heading out to the car," Rick said, hoping his dad hadn't clued into his eavesdropping.

"Come into the kitchen," Dick said, voice noticeably calm. "Yer mother has something to say."

"Good morning, Ricky. It's time to clear the air," Dorothy said, in a stronger voice, as if Rick's presence bolstered her confidence.

"Hi, Mom." Rick sauntered over to the large kitchen window and gazed out, hoping the beauty of snow-laden trees would steady his racing heart.

"I just asked Dad to talk to you about Boxing Day," Dorothy said. "Never again will I stand frozen in fear as I listen to the two of you go at it. So help me, I'll call the police and report a case of domestic violence at 846 Sunset—"

"The police!" Dick's voice echoed throughout the house as he forcefully pulled out a chair from the kitchen table. "Why in God's name would you do that? So things got a little tense. Listen, honey bunch, that's no reason to call the cops and have the whole neighbourhood think our family's gone psycho."

Dick shook his finger at his son. "You attacked me first, Ricky boy, in front of the entire family."

Bud, the neighbour's big Newfoundland hound and unrivaled guard dog, began barking until it reached a feverish pitch of howling.

Rick's eyes refused to meet his father's. "Once again, Bud's joining another hostile, win-lose battle in the Wright household."

Dorothy wiped the flour from her hands and slowly circled the kitchen table, raising and lowering her arms in desperation. "For heaven sakes, Dick, Ricky simply disagreed with the way you grilled Harry and Rose. There's a big difference between arguing with your son and physically assaulting him."

"Wrong!" Dick said, in a tone that suggested his tolerance was fast approaching zero. "He rudely attacked me, even if only in words. Verbal attacks bring on lawsuits."

"And physical attacks bring on jail sentences," Rick snapped.

Dick's face turned a deep scarlet. "You got some wild hair up yer arse or what! Let me know when you two are finished preaching." He glared at his son. "And kindly remember who's boss in this household."

Rick stared his father down. "Someday you might want to ask yourself why you're so domineering and disrespectful, so vulgar."

"For a man who spent years loafing around Europe and now expects free rent, *you* might want to ask yerself why yer an ungrateful freeloader. As for you Dorothy, quit yer bellyachin'. I have every right to demand Ricky follow my rules as long as he lives under my roof. His shrink needs to teach him the finer points of respect."

With a deep sigh of resignation, Dorothy slumped into the nearest kitchen chair and let her arms dangle over the sides. "I'm afraid, Dick. Afraid of your anger."

"Afraid! Since when were you afraid of me? I've never raised a hand to you…never will."

Dorothy closed her eyes and pressed her palms together. "Dear God, please help us get past this." Slowly lifting her head, she pressed on. "For years I've wanted to hear either of you say: I'm sorry, I shouldn't have said that. Or: Sorry, I was wrong. So simple to say. Everything's over and done with."

Dick harrumphed, grabbed his coffee mug, stomped into the living room, and turned up the volume on his favourite sports channel.

Rick hugged his mother. "Stay strong, Mom. I'll be at the Caffeine Castle if you want to get away for a while."

"I hope you heard what I said about simple apologies. Will you ever say you're sorry to Dad? Will you?"

"I heard you, Mom…even louder and clearer now. When the time's right, I'll apologize." As Rick opened the door to the stairway, he looked back and added, "Thanks for defending me."

Rick sipped his vanilla bean latte and listened to a growing crescendo of voices from a corner table where two older men argued about climate change. Their charged conversation reminded him of an encounter two weeks ago at Joe's Bar where he'd stopped for a beer and burger before braving the mall to finish his dreaded Christmas shopping.

Laptop open, he described the bar scene, hoping he could use it for his English assignment.

Perched on the edge of a worn leather stool at Joe's Bar, I ordered a pint, thinking it would help me effortlessly plan my shopping list. Billy-Bob, a regular client, nodded at me from the far end of the counter and smiled vacantly. "Slide on down and join me for a couple."

Not much daylight there, I thought, then foolishly, tempted a conversation I didn't want to have. "Did you just emerge from a near death experience?" I asked, chuckling.

With a swift return to the living, Billy-Bob plunked himself down on the barstool beside me. "Bloody assassins. NATO needs to carpet bomb the hell out of any country that harbours terrorists. Doesn't matter if—"

"What! Carpet bomb innocent civilians! Bombing them would only intensify their rage…strengthen their commitment to the group's messianic mission."

Billy-Bob said, "You don't get it, man! The problem lies with the jihadi cool. Frinstance, the Quran orders them to kill infidels wherever they find them. That, my friend, would be us."

As Billy-Bob railed about a dark future of immigrants who'd outnumber "us white folks," it crossed my mind that quite likely, he'd never met a bigot he didn't like.

I egged him on. "Lord Jesus man," I said, a little too loudly, "if we can't try to understand and respect each other, if we look for scapegoats instead of solutions, we're doomed."

Billy-Bob pushed up his shirt sleeves to show off his bulging triceps. "Listen, we need a strong leader who'll take on our enemies in this world."

"The kind of leader who thinks he's a very stable genius?" I asked. "The rest of us are gullible morons?" I pointed to Billy-Bob's forehead and slowly curled in my thumb. "I'm right, you're dead? *That* kind of leader?"

Billy-Bob narrowed his cold, steely eyes. "Stop trying to mess with my head."

I flamboyantly pushed my beer mug to the centre of the counter, slid off the stool, and reached out to shake his hand.

Billy-Bob recoiled in horror. "You're nuts, man!"

Rick sipped his latte and read what he'd written. *People like Billy-Bob are as welcome as wasps at a Sunday BBQ,* he thought, *and Dad's the most annoying wasp in the swarm.* Feeling exasperated that he and his father couldn't have a reasonable discussion about their differences of opinion, he opened a new file and typed *Wasps*, then went to the counter for a refill.

Back in his chair, Rick clasped his hands around one knee, and reread what he'd written. *Yes! Forget Christopher Hitchens' comment that everyone has a book in them and that's where most should stay. Not mine, Hitch! I'm jumping this horse full stride and riding it to the finish line.*

The afternoon flew by like autumn leaves in a windstorm and although Rick felt hungry, he didn't want to go home and risk a face-to-face encounter with his father. As the sky darkened, he thought about how, not long ago, his father would open the kitchen door and holler down, "Ricky, get up here. Hockey's on and the Flames are burnin'!" He missed how he and his dad would jump and howl when their team scored, or rail at the referee for a moot penalty call—the good old days when his mother would join them with big bowls of popcorn and help cheer their team to victory.

Rick munched on a ham croissant with a side order of Caesar salad, then sat back and reminisced about Liv, a woman he'd met recently. She'd been the guest speaker at a student rally that protested tuition increases, and Rick recalled how her soft beauty complemented a natural grace as she confidently encouraged students to negotiate with the Board of Directors. Dazzled, Rick eyed her slender fingers and, seeing no hardware, waited until she finished answering questions from the floor, then boldly slid in beside her and a student who looked about to leave.

Rick fumbled for the right words. "Hi Rick, I'm…oops, did I say Rick?"

Liv smiled. "No problem," she said, patting his arm. "I noticed you earlier."

She noticed me? Rick felt simultaneously relaxed and thrilled. "Your polished platform speech had students right here," he said, tapping his fingers on the palm of his left hand. They chatted briefly about their current status—she, a social studies teacher at a local high school; he, a fourth-year Creative Writing student at the U of C. Soon, the two of them found a corner table and talked more personally about binging on Netflix, their addiction to novels, and difficulty resisting the deluge of newsfeeds from the *Globe and Mail*, the *New York Times*, *The Guardian*, and others. The evening progressed alongside their mutual attraction such that at closing time, they agreed to meet for coffee or a drink after Liv returned from Christmas with her family in Edmonton.

That was then, Rick thought. *Now's the time.* He texted Liv: *How was Christmas in Edmonton?*

She replied within minutes: *Nice to hear from you. Ate and drank too much. How was your Christmas break?*

Rick noticed his pulse quicken as he tapped: *Slight family feud. Won't bore you with the details. Short notice, but would you like to meet for a drink and bite at Joe's Bar?*

Sure. Had lunch on their patio last summer.

Rick texted: *How about 6 o'clock?*

Okay, first one there snags a corner table, Liv replied.

Happy to oblige. See you there!

Rick was jubilant. *Easy peasy! In ninety minutes I'll be keeping company with the sophisticated Liv Janson.* To pass the time, he read the final chapters of his spy novel, but thoughts of his father disrupted his concentration. *So what if I run into Dad? I'll simply apologize.* He reached for his jacket, then flopped back down in his chair. *No, he should apologize first.* Rick pulled his phone from his pocket, put in the earphones, and opened a relaxing music file, but the word "coward" stubbornly tormented him.

Liv breezed into the bar and greeted Rick with an affectionate hug. She doffed her coat and glanced at the drinks menu while Rick tried not to gawk at her low-cut, pink sweater. Feeling somewhat self-conscious, he stammered, "Chilly one out there…the weather, I mean," then caught himself gazing hypnotically into Liv's blue-grey eyes with a striking dark ring around the iris. *Real gems*, he thought. *But why is she chewing on a piece of her hair?*

Smiling and leaning in closer, Liv said, "So, when do classes start, and what are you taking this semester?"

After Rick described his courses and challenging English assignment, he and Liv compared notes on previous courses they'd taken. Following an amicable silence, Liv rhythmically tapped the arms of her chair and said, "I don't want to pry, but I hope things work out between you and your father."

"I'll simply say this about that," Rick said, perfunctorily. "We had it out after our family's Boxing Day dinner. I still feel badly about it, but here's hoping I'll find a way to make things better between us."

Liv scrunched her nose like a rabbit. "Ah, the stress of Christmas. Takes its toll on family members, especially those with longstanding issues."

Sounds like a therapist, Rick inwardly balked. Not wanting Liv to think she was dating a mad man, he intentionally avoided describing The Incident, saying instead that his father has an ironclad grip on truth—"the expert who knows all there is to know about politics and religion. Dad gushes forth like a broken water main. Does anyone in your family have uncompromising ideas they flog to death?"

Liv thought a moment. "You might say my family's extraordinarily ordinary, but I have a colleague who wins the Oscar on that score. Ask her a simple question, especially about education standards or today's parenting styles, and she gives her usual speech from the pulpit. She also has that annoying habit of finishing every sentence with a rapid little nod and a high-pitched 'yes?' or 'right?' then checks to see if people are nodding in agreement. If they aren't, she sulks."

"How manipulative," Rick said, and deftly turned the conversation to the politics of today's polarized world. Not so deftly, he tossed in the word nihilism, then tore off another chunk of skin from his bottom lip and chided himself for being so pretentious. *I know as much about nihilism as I do about knitting*, he thought, then quickly passed Liv a menu.

Liv swayed closer to Rick. "I forget. Did you say you were born and raised in Calgary?"

"Yep. Me and my sister, Joy, grew up in the house I'm still living in…with my parents. Dad remodelled it until the original was buried beneath the new, including a fully furnished basement suite—the one I call home."

"So, we're both Alberta born and raised," Liv said. "My only relatives, other than parents and brother, Zeke, are an aunt and uncle who live in Cape Breton, Mom's birthplace. When Zeke and I were kids, we went with Mom and Dad to Inverness where we swam in the ocean and beach-combed for treasures…years long gone."

"Ah, Cape Breton," Rick sighed. "I've cycled most of the Cabot Trail. Gorgeous!"

"Yeah. Mom misses the sea." Liv took a slow sip of beer and demurely lowered her eyes. "At one time, she also missed Dad—trial separation a few years back. They've since hammered out a treaty, or so it seems. Occasionally they go for an after-supper walk and, recently, I saw them holding hands...the senior citizens' equivalent of sex?"

Rick grinned helplessly as Liv continued, "Does anyone ever know—*really* know—what goes on inside a marriage? What's centre stage in each other's hearts?"

"Probably not," Rick said, feeling obliged to challenge the male stereotype that relationship talk is scarier than Tyrannosaurus Rex. "I wonder how Mom truly feels about Dad. They seldom laugh together or playfully tease each other…maybe because Dad thinks too much fun and joy are signs of stupidity."

Liv put her elbows on the table and dropped her face in her hands. "What would it be like to live with someone you can't have fun with or tease a little now and then? From what I've seen of marriage, it begins with a loving, adventurous honeymoon and ends with a long, boring flight home…interrupted by rough turbulence."

Rick gave an easy laugh. "I know a couple whose entire marriage has been one turbulent plane trip—destination unknown."

After a moment, Liv said, "Destination, hell."

Rick winced. "That's Dad and Mom. She must've got tired of hugging a porcupine."

Liv looked like she didn't know whether to laugh or sigh. She did half of both.

"Mom's favourite word is sorry," Rick said, "which doesn't help their relationship. They're more like roommates than marriage partners. And their kisses are only suitable for a baby…you know, that extended little pucker that barely grazes the lips."

The waitress approached with their order of chicken wings and nachos with extra cheese. "Aha, snack time," Rick said, "needed something to end my marriage monologue." He smiled at the waitress and ordered a glass of red wine for Liv and another lager for himself.

As Liv daintily stripped flesh from the messy bone, Rick's imagination went wild. *She'd look classy slurping Japanese noodles with chopsticks.*

Liv leaned in. "Wait 'til you hear what I've done. The very thought is daunting."

Rick reached over and brushed a strand of hair from her forehead, then coughed into the funnel of his fist and waited.

"Shortly before Christmas, I agreed to let a colleague nominate me for the Liberal candidate of Mount Vista. I think that's your constituency too, no?"

Rick could barely restrain himself. "Whoo-hoo, I can vote for you! I knew you were a natural politician when you spoke at the student rally. Couldn't be more excited for you."

"Thanks, but at this point I'm only nominated for the candidacy; that election takes place in early January. A death wish or what?"

Rick laughed. "Keep your sense of humour, it'll serve you well on the front lines. When's the election likely to be called?"

"Our best guess is soon."

Rick talked through a mouthful of nachos. "What will you stress in your stump speeches?"

"*If* I win the candidacy, I'll commit to improving our education system, beginning with early child care. This province has a long way to go if we really value our children and their futures. Too many kids come to school hungry, thanks to the government's cancellation of school lunches. We also need to teach kids emotional skills beginning in kindergarten—they're as important as any other subject, according to recent studies. Enough. The beginning of my first press conference is officially over."

Continuing the conversation, Rick said, "I like your emphasis… addresses the ongoing problem with bullying and other student issues."

Liv did most of the talking as they discussed value differences between Liberals and Conservatives. When she asked Rick for his honest thoughts about the Liberal brand, he said, "I'm concerned about the hard swing to the right in this province and elsewhere. As I see it, too many politicians prevent respectful exchanges of ideas. Turns me off politics. Still, as adage notes, evil triumphs when good people do nothing." Rick sensed their knees gently touching under the table; above board, Liv's hand almost grazed his hairy forearm.

Soft background music and animated conversation filled the room as they then discussed their various travels across Canada, adventures in Europe, and unseen places on their bucket lists.

Confidence rising, Rick asked, "Hey Liv, how about celebrating New Year's Eve together? We could ski in the afternoon, have dinner somewhere and…well, do whatever you like."

Liv hand ironed her serviette as Rick worried that his question was laden with clumsy eagerness.

"Sorry, Rick. I told Noah, a former boyfriend, that I'd go to his New Year's house party."

Rick nodded as he dragged out a disingenuous, "I seeeee. Niiice," then wondered, *if Noah's a former boyfriend, why can't she invite me to go with her?* He licked the tip of his index finger and captured nacho crumbs from the plate. "It might be difficult to enthusiastically wish people Happy New Year, especially given the chaos in this world."

"Perhaps," was all Liv said, then sipped her wine.

"Excuse me," Rick said, "be right back." *Something isn't working here*, he told himself en route to the Men's Room. *Stay cool...it's not the end of everything. Yet.*

Returning to their table, Rick noticed the lights had dimmed just enough to give the room a romantic ambience. He paused and gazed at Liv before sitting down. Filled with unquenchable desire, he said, "You look positively glowing."

Liv smiled affectionately. "Charming compliment."

Rick was utterly in thrall.

"Excuse me; my turn," Liv said, and as she sashayed to the washroom, Rick ogled the snug black leggings that emphasized her curvature. *What a woman!* he thought. *But hold on. She just turned me down for New Year's Eve.* Feeling bereft, he parked his fanciful dreams alongside the serviette he'd squished into a tight ball of grease.

When Liv returned, Rick had convalesced enough to pleasantly comment, "It's getting late. Maybe we should close in on the C-train. If you like, I'll walk you over then sprint home...only a few blocks away."

Liv glanced out the window. "Yes, it's time. It's also dark and desolate out there so I'm glad you'll walk me to the platform."

At his insistence, Rick cleared the tab and during their short trek to the station, Liv took a deep breath and slowly exhaled. "Ah, the fresh, pure fragrance of winter air."

"Winter fragrance?" Rick sniffed as if trying to detect it. To him, the only fragrance was the lingering stench of Liv and Noah's New Year's Eve reunion.

"Look, a full moon lights our way," Liv said, gazing upwards with that same rabbit-nose expression Rick had noticed earlier.

Rick stared at her pearly teeth and imagined running his tongue across them, then quickly reminded himself that romantic imagination outperforms reality.

When the C-train rounded the corner, Liv hugged Rick and kissed him firmly on the cheek. As he turned and stepped down from the platform, she shouted, "Let's go skiing soon."

Rick looked back and waved energetically. "Great idea!"

Reinvigorated, he buoyantly jogged across a beaten path on a short-cut through the park. Beneath a cobalt sky, Liv's pink cheeks and blonde hair bounced alongside him until the evening he once thought was going sideways, suddenly became marvellously dreamy. Rick shouted as if he wanted the whole world to hear.

"I'm in love!"

Chapter 4

Holiday season over, Rick trudged into Wright Brothers' main office and braced himself for an unwelcome greeting.

"Good morning," Dick said, glancing at his watch and noisily tapping his pen on the counter. "Nice to see yer on time."

Rick looked at his father with pleading, sorrowful eyes. "Jeez, Dad. I'm always on time."

In a voice somewhat muted by a roaring engine out front, Dick said, "I take that back; yer seldom late for work." He twirled his fingers in the air as Rick pondered his apologetic tone. "Lately I've been thinkin'…" Dick gulped and covered his mouth with his hand and for a moment, Rick wondered if he felt nauseous from a hangover.

"I've been thinkin'," Dick repeated, "that somewhere along the way, we took a wrong turn."

Rick was pleasantly stunned until Dick, unable to sustain his oblique admission of regret, added, "Hope your therapist straightens that bend in the road."

Rick shifted his weight from one foot to the other as he watched a semi truck park out front. "Looks like we can't talk now; someone's here to see you." He yanked the fob from a wall hook, stepped into the biting north wind, and marched to his work station.

Straighten your own fuckin' bend in the road, he mumbled to himself. *Where's the doc when I need her? Time to think outside every box in the warehouse.*

At 5 o'clock, Rick went to Calgary's Central Library to work on his short story. He loved feeling surrounded by venerable knowledge as he sat in a partially secluded reading nook where natural light cascaded from large ceiling panels and massive bay windows offered a stunning view of Calgary's sprawling city below. Jean-Paul Sartre's timeless adage came to mind: "If you're lonely when you're alone, you're in bad company."

Within minutes, a digital visitor knocked on the door of Rick's phone. Excitedly, he opened Liv's text: *Would you like to join me New Year's Day for dinner and a pay-per-view movie? Six o'clock, 3327 Spruceline Boulevard, NW.*

Rick savoured the moment, then replied: *Thanks Liv—love to. Champagne's on me.*

As Rick entertained romantic possibilities, little did he know that his mother was realizing hers. Dorothy was blissfully spending her weekly afternoon tryst with a man she'd met two years ago. She'd become increasingly drawn to sixty-one-year-old Efner, a brawny cattle rancher who drove into the city once a week to volunteer at the same hospice where Dorothy offered her services.

A few months back, when Efner had arrived late, Dorothy poked fun at him. "It's the big man from the Big Country who's trying to keep his cattle this side of Sheep River." That day, during an extended coffee break, they exchanged ideas about a host of topics, frequently interspersed with playful humour. At the end of their shift, as they walked out together to the parking lot, Efner lassoed Dorothy's heart when he said, "I love the way you gently distract patients from their pain and suffering…their waiting."

It wasn't long before Dorothy and Efner satisfied their own heartfelt waiting with an entrée not listed on the drinks menu at a nearby hotel. Time was short and much too rushed, but before Efner slid out of bed in their private suite, he swooned, "My dear Dorothy, you make me feel so good, body and soul."

Having just recalled one of Dick's recent chastisements, Dorothy brushed a tear from her eyes. Efner passed her a tissue from the bedside table.

"Did I say something wrong?" he asked. "I hope you aren't feeling guilty."

"No, no. It's just that, well...honestly, I've never felt so alive. So respected."

Family, relatives, and Marg, Dorothy's only close friend, would've been shocked to hear of her clandestine affair. Mrs. Wright, the epitome of diplomacy, decency, and integrity, the personification of Catholic devotion, softly whispered in Efner's ear, "There'll be time enough for guilt, when the rapture's done."

A fiery red ball lazily disappeared from view as Rick drove the winding streets to Liv's condo late on the afternoon of New Year's Day. He parked his car, climbed the three flights of stairs to her unit, and welcomed her heartfelt embrace. Tweaking his nostrils, he said, "There's a fragrance in the air...redolent of my Grandma Davidson's charming little cottage in Winnipeg."

"Really? What's the particular smell?"

"A hint of...furniture polish?"

"Could be," Liv said, then hung Rick's coat and poured him a glass of white wine. Rick surveyed the living room's antique furniture and ornately framed prints, including Claude Monet's "The Garden at Giverny" that hung above a wooden cabinet from another era. He gently ran his fingers across its scarred, grainy surface.

"I love the warp of time in aged wood, especially oak," Liv said.

Rick imagined gently running his fingers across the brief warp of time on Liv's naked body. *Will she ever lead me to her bedroom?*

"There's something about antique collectibles that speaks to me," Liv said, passing Rick a tray of Thai shrimp lettuce wraps. The two chatted comfortably and munched on appetizers until Liv excused herself to tend to last minute dinner details. After she assured him there was nothing he could help her with, Rick perched on a bar stool at the end of the counter and listened to her cheerfully recite the unique ingredients in their dinner of curried carrot and ginger soup, stir-fried vegetables over Jasmine rice, and Thai coconut chicken. While waiting for the rice to steam, she and Rick exchanged stories about Christmas holidays past—family traditions and childhood memories, including Rick's embarrassing story about how he, at five years old, sneaked into the living room one early Christmas morning and tipped over the Christmas tree while reaching for a large present tucked behind a pile of smaller ones—the present he'd hoped was a train set.

"I can still see the look on Dad's face as he flung the tree into the back yard, decorations and all." Rick lowered his chin and shook his head.

"How sad," Liv said, reaching for her wine.

"Uh-huh, the year I ruined Christmas for everyone. Dad never forgave me…never lets me forget it either." Rick raised his glass. "But let's talk about happier times."

Rick helped Liv carry serving dishes to the dining room table set with flea market bargains: vintage goblets, dishes, cutlery, and slightly tarnished brass candleholders. After fumbling with an antique bottle opener, he filled the crystal wine glasses with a polite amount of red Bordeaux.

"May I say grace," Liv asked. Rick half nodded as she bowed her head and gave a lengthy prayer of thanks that ended with, "We're truly grateful for all that blesses us today."

Rick's attention had strayed to the soft background music and a voice he recognized as Leonard Cohen's, sighing through a wish for lasting love. Rick wished Liv wasn't religious. Instead of saying amen, he looked at her with a smile that barely lifted the corners of his mouth.

"Do I hear Leonard Cohen?" he asked.

"Yes. A deep loss to Canada's music culture," Liv said, handing Rick the curried chicken dish. "My parents have all his albums and I love it when Mom pulls out the piano bench and Dad, in his best Cohen-like voice, sings along."

"Cohen, Bublé, Sinatra…I like them all even though my sister, Joy, says no one listens to that stuff anymore. But she's younger." Rick grimaced. "In two years, I'll be bracing for the big three-o."

"Can't believe I passed that milestone four years ago." With a relaxed giggle, she asked, "Have you read any good books on dying?"

"Not yet, unless I count those dark novels we read for English Lit. Camus and suicide, anyone?"

Lively dinner conversation dwindled down with the candles. Liv reached for the snuffer. "I'll do a quick tidy up if you'll select a pay-per-view movie."

"Happy to do that," Rick said, and after helping Liv clear the table he looked through the choices, most of which he decided were too full of violence or dripping with sappy romance. Then he noticed *Spotlight*, a movie he'd recently seen.

"Hey, have you seen *Spotlight*?"

Liv poked her head around the kitchen corner. "Not sure I want to see a movie that trashes Catholics, especially since I am one. Did I tell you my family's Catholic?"

No wonder she said grace with such reverence, Rick thought, as he perched on the same stool at the end of the counter. "With a name like yours, I assumed your parents were Scandinavian."

"They are. Norwegian. So?"

"Aren't most Norwegians agnostics or atheists?"

"Yes, like my brother Ezekiel—Zeke for short—he's a None."

"A nun? Is he trans or does the Catholic Church have male nuns now?"

Liv laughed so hard she started coughing. Then she sneezed, and slowly spelled, "N-o-n-e-s. They're non-believers who don't identify with any religion, and they've been spreading throughout Europe and North America for quite a while."

"Seriously?" Rick said, excitedly. "I wonder how many believers became Nones after viewing *Spotlight* and hearing that the Catholic Church has protected its child molesters for God knows how long. Those creeps should be behind bars."

Liv said nothing as she put the leftovers in the fridge and finished loading the dishwasher.

Rick paced back and forth from the dining room to the living room, stopping only to notice a batik hanging on a side wall. He shuddered at its gruesome portrayal of dark red blood dripping from

Christ's hands and feet as he hung lifeless on the cross. Feeling distraught, he decided that Liv becoming a None was as remote as him becoming a priest.

"Remember how, at Joe's Bar, we talked about our parents?" Rick said, walking back to the kitchen counter. "We delved into their marriages, but I don't recall hearing much about your father."

"Dad? He's professor emeritus in the History Department at the University of Alberta, and Mom, a good Catholic, still teaches high school English at St. Thomas."

Perseverating on the topic he loves to hate, Rick felt compelled to ask, "Your Dad, is he also a good Catholic?"

"Apparently he wasn't keen on converting, but eventually got the Bishop's permission for a mixed marriage if he promised to raise Zeke and me Catholic. Dad's not devout like Mom, but Scripture says the unbelieving spouse is made holy through the believing spouse, who becomes a conduit of grace to the non-believer."

Rick looked like he'd just been doused with cold water. "In other words, your mother will save your father? How strange."

Liv motioned to the dishwasher and half joked, "Strange? Put your religious thoughts in with the dishes, they might need a good cleansing."

Rick shrugged his shoulders. Once again, he knew that religion—his annoying problem—would now become a problem with Liv.

"The Bible is the final authority on grace," Liv said, her voice sombre. You can be the final authority on the movie to watch."

"I'd like us both to decide but before we do, and just for the record, my family's also Catholic. When I was sixteen, I told my parents I wanted to take in a Unitarian Church service and compare beliefs and sermons. Truth be told, I was smitten with a super smart, pretty, and fun-loving classmate whose family is Unitarian. Figured that if I showed up at her church, she'd be impressed enough to get me to first base."

Liv smiled. "Bet you hit a home run."

"Nope. Never even got to bat, but here's the thing. When I told Dad why I was going to attend her church, he wagged his finger at me and said, 'You stay away from those people, they do the devil's work.' That's when I became an ex Catholic."

"You mean *lapsed* Catholic. You can't be an ex Catholic any more than you can be an ex human," Liv said.

Rick gave a sidelong glance. "So when people die we should call them lapsed humans?" He rapidly shook his head. "Never mind. I take it you aren't up for *Spotlight*."

"Well, maybe I should watch it, but will you agree to turn it off at the first sign of anything lewd?"

"Egg-zactly! That'd be obscene. Downright vulgar." Rick thought about how his dad would welcome Liv, the ideal woman who'd bring his apostate son back into the fold. The believer who'd be his conduit of grace.

Liv put a large tray of cups, a tea pot, and a candy dish of chocolates on the living room table, then selected *Spotlight* and flopped down on the sofa beside Rick, who sensed the coolness of her body against the heat of his own.

Halfway through the movie, Liv paused the movie, put her elbows on her knees, and dropped her face in her hands. "I need something to relax my nerves," she said. "How about a little Grand Marnier?"

"The champagne!" Rick shouted, opening his arms wide. "Break out the champagne!"

"Yes! Yes! Much better than Grand Marnier. Might need both for this occasion!" Liv sprinted to the fridge and reached for the champagne.

Rick uncorked the bottle, filled their glasses, and raised his own. "Happy New Year, Liv. May this one be your best ever."

Liv gave a warm, wide smile. "Same to you, Rick. Good luck with your courses…writing and grad school." After a slow kiss and a couple sips of champagne, Liv looked imploringly at Rick. "This movie isn't off to a good start, but I'll try to stick it out."

Rick squeezed Liv's arm and said nothing as she resumed the video. Michael Rezendes, starring as an investigative journalist at the *Boston Globe*, had researched hundreds of priests' sex crimes against young boys. Rick empathized with Rezendes' agonizing struggle to abandon his Catholic upbringing, but he also sensed Liv's growing discomfort. He casually placed his arm across the top of the love seat, almost, but not quite, grazing her shoulder.

Both sat solemnly until, during the film's rolling credits, Rick took a sip of champagne, looked at Liv, and said, "Hardly what you'd call entertaining."

Liv looked on the verge of tears. "Can't believe there were so many…" she paused, folded her arms tightly across her chest, and lowered her head.

Rick grew visibly agitated. "Rezendes' torment moved me deeply." Unable to restrain himself, he continued, "In what verse of the Bible does it state that clergymen can sexually molest hundreds of innocent boys without being criminally charged?"

"Nowhere. Don't be ridiculous," Liv snarled, then rested her head against the back of the love seat. "I understand how a lapsed Catholic might feel watching that movie, but you're moving into dangerous territory."

Rick reached for his glass and peered into it. "My friend Gabe said that I sound like an atheist on the rampage when I talk religion…might be right because words don't always come out the way I want them to." He sipped his drink and sighed. "But champagne always goes down the way I want it to."

Liv sat in glum concentration.

"How do you think most Catholics would react to this movie?" Rick asked.

"Catholics have known about the clergy's sexual abuse for years. We pray that God will show compassion, forgive, and cure the guilty."

How do I countenance that ready-made answer? I'd have better luck explaining garlic to a cat. Rick slowly shook his head from side to side. "Asking God to forgive abusers while moving them to different parishes as if nothing happened didn't stop their sex crimes…or solve their psychological problems. And while I'm at it, why does the Pope deny women birth control and abortions, especially in poor, over-populated countries?"

"He's obeying Scripture," Liv brusquely answered.

Rick proclaimed, "Obey Scripture and preserve the institution while sentencing millions of women and children to poverty and ignorance? Where's the almighty love and compassion in *that*? And why do intelligent women donate time and money to a church that practices such injustice? Such hypocrisy?"

Liv's body shook with indignation. She gulped her champagne. "You're over the top angry and judgmental, Rick Wright."

Rick softened his strident voice. "I'm simply facing facts and holding Catholics to account. Statistics say what Catholics don't want to hear. They're living in denial…and God saw that it was good."

Liv carelessly plunked her vintage glass on the coffee table. "That's an unfair swipe at all Catholics. Just as families don't abandon their children who transgress, the Church doesn't abandon its impure."

"But Liv, the Catholic Church isn't an ordinary family. It's a monolithic institution that should model decency and justice, not sexual abuse. And misogyny."

"But Rick, religion's a private matter. Gabe's right, you do sound like one of those holier-than-thou atheists."

"I *am* an atheist—literally without theism. I don't believe in the dogma of ancient religious texts because as far as I can tell, no theology can scientifically prove that words in the Bible, the Torah, or Quran came directly from God." Knowing he should stop his invective but unable to do so, Rick added, "*Origin of Species* is my holy book."

"Stop with the echo chamber!" Liv ordered, then pulled her knees up to her chest.

"I'm trying to be reasonable. May I say one more thing, then I'll stop?" Without waiting for an answer, Rick calmly asked, "Are Catholic men saintlier than Catholic women?"

"Of course not!"

"Then why can't women be Popes and Bishops?"

"The Church *is* modernizing. It now allows women to be lay priests, for your information."

"In my opinion," Rick said, as if at this stage, such a preface genuinely showed a more open-minded approach to the topic, "popes, priests, bishops—the whole tribe—chose religion as a profession. They're not any saintlier than physicians, bar tenders, teachers, truck drivers, housewives, or anyone else for that matter. Why don't we address all of *them* with Your Holiness? What's with that title? It's time Catholics came out of the tall weeds."

Liv pressed her middle finger to the bridge of her nose as if to dull a stabbing pain, then glowered at the man she'd earlier shown such affection. "Your belief that all religions are one big fairy tale that hoodwinks gullible followers is naive. Can't you see that strong beliefs have nothing to do with intelligence, which I'm sure you've decided I seriously lack. Pull out my fingernails one by one, why don't you."

To Rick's surprise, Liv allowed him to replenish her champagne. He left his full glass on the table and sat down on a chair across from her. "I certainly don't think you're unintelligent, but since reason didn't get you into religion, reason won't get you out of it."

Liv's dwindling reservoir of tolerance sprang a massive leak. "Religion transcends reason…far exceeds the limitations of our puny, human brains—yours and mine!"

Looks like she's trying not to cry, Rick thought. *I want to engulf her, but….* He walked to the living room window and stared out at a small plane flying overhead. On the surface, he looked composed. Below the water line, he was drowning in a fetid slough.

Liv sat upright and dug her hands into her hips. "I'd like an apology."

"Why in the name of God do you want an apology? I've given my honest views about religion, and there's no reason why we can't disagree without having a winner and loser—a loser who needs to apologize?"

Liv was no longer livid, she was spectacularly livid. "If you won't apologize, Rick, then kindly go fuck yourself. No one else will."

Rick drew a long, sharp breath. "Done that…many times!" Marching across the living room to the coat closet, he added, "I'll now go home and cut off my ear." A coat hanger clanged to the floor as he grabbed his jacket, turned to Liv, and said, "Thank you for a lovely meal and thought-provoking movie." He knew his words rang hollow.

From the sofa, Liv tossed a dismissive wave and mumbled inaudibly.

Rick forcefully closed the door behind him and thumped down the back stairs. *Did madam want me to fall on my knees and genuflect?* He stalled at the landing and leaned into the wall, breathless and sweating. *This time I've really done it,* his inner voice told him. *In the name of religion, I've sacrificed my relationship with Liv.*

In unit #303, Liv Janson had plunged her fingers into her hair and was sobbing uncontrollably.

Rick roughly calculated his blood alcohol level before driving to Joe's where he hoped to steady his conflicting thoughts and emotions. At the counter, he ordered a light beer and surveyed the room. To his utter surprise, there at a corner table sat his uncle and aunt, who sometimes came to Joe's to watch sporting events on the big screen.

"Fancy meeting you here! Happy New Year!" Rick said, walking toward them and raising his glass in a toast that sounded more like an apology than a heartfelt wish.

"Happy New Year to you," Harry and Rose said in unison. "We came to watch the last half of the Sugar Bowl on the big screen," Harry said. "Have a seat."

Good distraction, Rick thought, grabbing his mug and taking a seat at their table.

"What brings *you* here at this time of night?" Rose asked.

"Did a hatchet job on polite conversation with my…don't know what to call her now."

Harry said, "Hmm, a romantic row?"

"Um, yeah. Started a brand-new year by acting like an arrogant jerk."

"A man who admits mistakes," said Rose, who glanced at her husband with one eyebrow raised.

Avoiding any semblance of small talk, Rick said, "I won't bore you with the details, but happy to get any tips you two have on how to save a ruptured relationship."

To Rick's surprise, Harry stroked his grey beard and plunged in. "Seems the biggest problem with most relationships is open, honest…as in courageous, communication. Partners who talk to each other after the passion subsides—and it will—are more likely to celebrate their silver wedding anniversary."

Rose said, "Yes, but talk's cheap. Spouses can gab away from morning 'til night, but if they're disrespectful, they'll end up gabbing to lawyers, no matter how honest and courageous they are."

"It's taken Rose and me thirty-six years and some counselling to decide whether we'd rather be right, or have a relationship." Harry rested his hand on his wife's arm, grinned, and asked, "Agree?"

Rose, busily checking her fingernails, looked up and said, "We've certainly *tried* to stop turning arguments into competitions."

Rick said, "You never met my ex, but she badgered me about every little thing, like squeezing the toothpaste in the middle of the tube. Good Lord!"

Harry chuckled. "That damn nagging…love's little executioner. We gave up trying to change each other—"

Rose interrupted. "Not so fast, m'darlin'. You and I still have to work on that."

Harry flexed his fingers on both hands as if squeezing an imaginary stress ball. "I'll buy us another round…and cab fare home."

"I can drive," Rose said. "Two light beers on a full stomach over several hours—I'm well under the limit."

Harry beckoned the waiter as Rose leaned into Rick. "How did the meeting with your mom and Joy go after spending Boxing Day night with us?"

"It wasn't easy, but we've all had our say, except Dad, who was still in bed. Mom and Joy thought I overreacted, and they're right. The next morning, Dad said I needed to see a shrink if I want to continue living at home with free rent." As Rick began summarizing a couple key therapy points, Harry intervened. "Tell me, Rose, have I taught you how to treat me all these years?"

"Need to think on that," Rose said. "We've both been each other's teacher…and student?" She then talked about their holiday plans until the lights dimmed and Rick said, "It's closing in on closing time. I'll leave my car here and scoot home. The short walk will do me good."

After hailing the waiter, Harry insisted on clearing the tab.

"Thanks, Uncle Harry." The three of them stood up and put their arms around each other in a family hug. "So glad you were both here," Rick said. "And thanks for the helpful tips—bliss is just around the corner." He grinned, reached for his jacket, and firmly pushed his thumbs up.

Rick left his car in the parking lot and trudged along the familiar route home. Catching sight of the moon's crescent of ice in a dark blue ocean, he recalled how only a week ago, he'd soared home on Liv's parting words. Tonight, he horsewhipped himself. *What's wrong with me? What was I trying to prove?*

At home, Rick dimmed the lights, opened his laptop, stared into space, and searched for the right opening.

Dear Liv,

I'm struggling to find the words to apologize for my obnoxious, arrogant behaviour tonight. Anything I write will be inadequate to the task.

Religious conversations have always tested my tolerance. Remember the fight I mentioned between me and Dad at our family's Boxing Day dinner? Can't believe I treated you the same way Dad treated his younger brother that night—called him an apostate, an infidel, an embarrassment to the family, all because he and Aunt Rose, a wise, spiritual soul, didn't attend Christmas Eve mass. That's when I reminded Dad that in a democracy, everyone has the right and freedom to choose their beliefs. I insisted that he be tolerant of religious differences, yet tonight, I ruthlessly attacked you and your religion. I'm sorry. It's the institution of the Catholic Church that I take issue with; not the people who attend it.

Julian Barnes began his book, "Nothing To Be Frightened Of" with this touching first sentence: "I don't believe in God but I miss him." Even renowned scientists, particularly Einstein, Darwin, and Margulis, questioned their atheistic certainty and eventually became agnostic. Like them, I don't believe in a personal God, but I do respect common religious principles that have endured for centuries—kindness and honesty, among others.

I'd love to meet for coffee and start over again. If you'd rather not, please know that I wish you my very best, always.

With good memories, abundant affection, and sincere apologies, Rick

The next morning, Rick awoke early and thought about how, within two weeks, he had brawled with his father, immersed himself in therapy and writing, reconnected and fell in love with Liv, who later rejected him, and faced his bellicose father on the first day back at work. Reason enough, he decided, to linger in bed wishing he could again talk to his insightful uncle. Harry would tell him how to mend his ways. And broken heart.

Self-pity will get me nowhere, Rick decreed, then dressed and treated himself to a hearty breakfast. Partway through his plate of bacon and eggs, he heard an incoming text.

Hello Rick,

Thank you for your thoughtful message. Rather than inflict further damage, let's do the kindest thing possible—wish each other well and go our separate ways.

Sincerely,

Liv

Assuming Liv had strangled all hope for a romantic relationship, Rick ceremoniously dumped his breakfast into the compost and went back to bed. Under his fluffy duvet, he pulled the pillow tightly around his head and buried his thoughts in goose down.

"Liv," he repeatedly moaned. "Loss."

"Any questions?" Dr. Knowles' voice punctured the air as he marched to the front of Rick's first class in the winter semester.

A student flipped his red ball cap to one side and shouted from the back row, "About what?"

"Just checking to see if you're awake," said Dr. Knowles, glancing back at no one in particular.

Brash confidence, rumpled clothes, grey shaggy hair, and weather-beaten face—this guy must be close to retirement, Rick thought.

The professor opened the computer cabinet and said, "Psychology 401 will keep those billions of neurons dancing in your fertile brains. As we broaden our ideas about personality development, you'll think of relatives, friends, coworkers, and lovers...especially your exes, and by the end of this course, you might even gain a better understanding of those insufferable childhood bullies. But to *really* get your money's worth, dive into your own personality, if you so choose."

Feeling emboldened by his classmate's earlier comment, Rick said, "How about diving into our parents' personalities?"

Dr. Knowles said, "Interesting idea. From the time we're born, our parents' personalities certainly influence our own." He smiled good naturedly and added, "But I won't turn this class into group therapy." A slow giggle spread throughout the room.

"Understanding something as complex as personality is like lassoing the clouds," Dr. Knowles continued. "But that doesn't mean the entire effort's futile. To the contrary, I think you'll agree that we first need to better understand human nature if we're to survive as a species. But I want to stress that all psychological theories and the research they generate begin as narratives, and those that get published in peer-reviewed journals are, at best, probabilistic; none are deterministic. We'll get into that later, but for now it's safe to say that what you get from this course will match the effort you put into it."

Rick knew exactly what he wanted from the course—clues about his father's personality and strategies that could help the two of them live peacefully in the same house.

Dr. Knowles reviewed the online syllabus, then asked students to break into small groups and talk about personalities they'd like to understand—famous entertainers, sports figures, politicians, or anyone else who came to mind.

A student in Rick's group smiled alluringly at him. "I'd like to understand all the men in my life."

"I'd like to understand me," Rick said hesitantly. "And my father. I need to figure out how to live at home without Dad and I practically killing each other."

"Without Dad and me," came a voice from behind.

Frowning, Rick looked up at Dr. Knowles, who'd been circling the room, listening in on group discussions.

"That's what Dad does—corrects every little thing I say. Lectures me about what to think and what to believe."

Dr. Knowles said nothing.

Not my best reaction, Rick thought. "My apologies," he said, embarrassed. "I've overreacted."

Dr. Knowles half smiled. "In this class, I won't tell you what to think, but I will give you something to think about. The role of parents and educators, as I see it, is to teach young children emotional and social awareness—the foundation for critical thinking and human progress. Children would learn, for example, not to feel anxious or angry when they make mistakes—those valuable little learning opportunities."

Rick felt pressured to say something, but what? He tapped his teeth with his pen.

Hearing no further comments, Dr. Knowles returned to the front of the class and listened to group summaries. "You're off to a good start," he said. "For next week, please review Chapter One of your text—our first personality theorist, Sigmund Freud. Some students cringe at the thought of Freud, but he's still relevant today, so suck it up—a colloquialism Freud would've had much to say about."

Rick had a few things to say about Dr. Knowles' idea to begin the course with Freud. He'd learned in a previous class that Freud's psychosexual stages, Oedipus complex, penis envy, and dream analysis, were outdated. Feeling vaguely uncomfortable, he checked the university calendar and noted the last day to withdraw from a course without financial penalty.

Three more classes will help me decide what to do about Knowles; what to do about Dad will take a little longer.

Chapter 5

Rick sat beside his good friend Gabe who'd reserved a seat for him in their Creative Writing class. "You up for catching up in The Den after class?" Rick asked.

"You bet!" Gabe said. "Hope the intro doesn't run the full three hours."

Professor Evans, a plump, middle-aged woman, confidently sprinted to the front of the room. Her luminous brown eyes sparkled. "Welcome everyone! Today, I'll introduce the course and review the importance of literary conflict, crisis, and resolution. Those of you who aced your final exam for Creative Writing II can take a short nap. Neighbours will poke you if you snore."

Good sense of humour, Rick thought, then assured himself that this semester he'd revisit those literary concepts from a closer, personal perspective and apply them to the writing assignment—a short story, which the professor stressed was worth forty percent of the final grade.

"If writing a short story sounds intimidating, remember this," Dr. Evans said. "James Joyce was only twenty when he wrote *The Dead*, a novella with themes of love, heartache, and identity. You can do it too."

Some students smiled; others raised their eyebrows in disbelief. Or both.

"Why not start your assignment on a collegial note? Introduce yourself to the person beside you and brainstorm ideas about a possible theme and plot for your short story. You can work independently if you prefer, but it might be worthwhile to get to know at least one classmate."

Gabe turned to Rick. "Hmm…theme and plot. What about that camping trip when a bear rummaged around outside our tent? Remember how we trembled in our sleeping bags wondering where the fuck we put the bear spray?"

"Good suggestion, but I checked the syllabus over the holidays and decided to write about me and Dad, in disguise. I've already drafted a couple scenes."

"No shortage of conflict there! Got a title?"

Never short for a wry comment, Rick said, "How about 'Son of a Dick'?"

Never short for a wry comeback, Gabe stifled his laughter and said, "Too Kafkaesque. Wish I knew what to write about."

"Write something real. Something raw and personal."

Gabe flipped his pen between his fingers. "I could give Sally a pseudonym and write about how she turned me on a year ago, but her manipulations and crafty little hints soon told me she'd be high maintenance. Lately she's been hounding me to get married and have kids. Kids for fuck sake! That's all she talks about…all she wants." Gabe ran his fingers across the table and said, "I want a new pair of running shoes."

Rick laughed openly. "Could be your first sentence that hooks readers."

"Might think about it. By the way, how was Christmas—your dad and all?"

Rick slowly shook his head. "Dad and I need professional help. Had an explosive fight. Knock-down, drag-out brawl. Later. Tell you about it later."

"Sorry to hear that," Gabe said, looking momentarily hangdog. "Wasn't your first class with Doc Knowles this morning?"

"Yeah, not sure about him. Seems a bit too…don't know how to describe him, but he's starting the course with Freud, who I *do* know how to describe."

Gabe said, "I'm not big on Freud either, and from what I could tell, neither is Knowles. Thinks clinical psychologists should be trained in all major psych theories and apply the one best suited to the clients' problems. Eclecticism—that's the word. Anyway, I grew to like the guy even though he constantly moves his tongue and mouth like some kind of reptile. But he's never dull, and always available. You could visit him during office hours and talk about your dad. Get some ideas for your short story while you're at it."

"Hmm, might give him a closer look," Rick replied, unconvincingly.

Interrupting Rick and Gabe's side conversation, Dr. Evans said, "Sounds like some of you have zeroed in on exciting topics. My unfailing feminine intuition tells me this semester will be exceptionally good, and I've had years to test the precision of my instincts—accuracy, B+; optimism, straight A."

Controlled laughter filled the room.

"Before we end today, some final comments about your short stories. Be daring. Open your characters' hearts. Expose their inner lives and inject their intimate relationships with tension and conflict—the real sleep snatchers. If you haven't been rejected by someone you've fallen madly in love with, look forward to it."

Amidst nervous laughter, Dr. Evans said, "On that happy note, see you in seven."

Gabe tapped Rick's arm. "Den time."

"Yep! Let's drop a couple bills on the counter."

The students' Den was alive with the frisson of a new semester as Rick and Gabe did what they were good at—commiserating about women, courses, profs, politics, climate change, and their fathers. Rick described The Incident in vivid detail, and Gabe listened in a manner that deepened their honest, supportive friendship. As Rick snacked on yam fries, he thought about his friend's genuine gift of quiet listening, without harsh judgment or advice. *A special friendship*, he reminded himself. *Don't fuck it up.*

Rick tapped on Dr. Grey's door and poked his head in. "Happy New Year, Dr. Grey."

Dr. Grey looked up from her computer and with a welcoming smile said, "Hello, Rick. Happy New Year to you too. Come in and have a seat."

"In the coming year, may all your clients be more normal than the one you're looking at."

In a jocular voice, Dr. Grey asked, "When did you start your very own Pathetic Patients' club?"

Rick replied with silence, wondering if Dr. Grey was intentionally patronizing, confrontational, or teasing.

"My feeble attempt at humour," Dr. Grey said. "How are you?"

"Looking at everything from the wrong end of binoculars," Rick said, his right hand massaging his left, over and under in a ritualistic pattern. "Just getting out of bed empties my tank."

Dr. Grey slowly nodded. "Let's turn those binoculars around…better yet, replace them with a microscope."

"And zero in on this hell I've created?"

"But you're here…taking one step at a time. I haven't overlooked that strength. What's happened since I last saw you?"

"I lost it with Liv."

"I don't remember hearing about Liv in our first session."

"I met her at a students' rally. Simple twist of fate had me totally smitten." Rick's mood lifted as he detailed the thrill of meeting Liv—her sense of humour and balanced mix of courage with humility. When he described their emotional reactions and polarized views on the movie *Spotlight*, he became sullen. "Reason deserted me…had the impulse control of a two-year-old. I mercilessly attacked the Catholic Church and its followers knowing full well that Liv was a devout parishioner."

"You needed to air your views. How did Liv respond?"

"She valiantly defended her beliefs until I said that since reason didn't get her into religion, reason wouldn't get her out of it."

"Ouch!" Dr. Grey shuddered. "Then what?"

"Liv abruptly ended everything. Told me to go fuck myself. Didn't even see me to the door." Rick rested his elbows on his knees and pressed his forehead against clenched fists. "Total disaster."

"It's unfortunate things didn't go as you'd hoped, but I wonder if the evening was as much about her beliefs as it was about yours."

Rick sat upright. "Do you think *I* ruined the evening?"

"I'll answer your question in a moment, but first, to understand you correctly, how did you feel when Liv ended everything?"

Rick tried to get comfortable in his chair. "Devastated! Wouldn't any guy in my situation feel crappy?"

"Many would, and I still haven't forgotten your question, but do you agree that adults have the right to choose their own beliefs and make their own decisions in life, even if such decisions are harmful to themselves?"

"Of course," Rick tossed a curt nod. "The Human Rights Act was built on that principle. No government should prevent fair access to education and healthcare, or ban abortions, sex-change operations, divorce…" He suddenly noticed a gold chain around Dr. Grey's neck, the tip of which had slipped inside her blouse. *Fuck! What if it's a cross?* "I should've asked if you're religious," Rick said. "Catholic, in particular."

"That wouldn't matter. I'm here to understand your views—what they mean for you and how they impact your life. But to address your concern, no, I'm not Catholic. Humanism comes closest to my religion—a rational world view that's informed by science and motivated by compassion."

"I like that," Rick said, leaning closer to Dr. Grey. "But let me ask again if you think I was as much to blame for ruining the evening as Liv?"

"I'm not looking for blame. Can you suspend your certainty about the Catholic Church? Seems to me you're giving it a lot of power to determine your emotions."

Rick gave a protracted groan. "The *last* thing I'd do is give the Catholic Church power over me. Obedience be damned."

Dr. Grey said, "And Catholicism aside, you agreed that adults have the right to make their own choices…their own decisions." Rick felt Dr. Grey's penetrating eyes, as if she were waiting for confirmation.

"Makes sense to me." *Where's she going with this?*

"If you agree that adults have the right to choose their own beliefs, why would you insist that anyone, especially your father and Liv, agree with your views? Respect you? Not disappoint you?"

"Wait a minute! I don't expect anyone to obey or respect me, but people should obey employment contracts. And what about infants and children? Shouldn't they obey their parents if they want to survive past infancy?"

"Of course. I'm not talking about reasonable demands of employers and parents. Think of everyday beliefs and expectations adults have about themselves and others, especially family and friends. Is it reasonable to think people *should* respect us? Agree with us? Be considerate and sensitive to our needs? Be tidy, lose weight, know the proper way to peel avocados—"

"I get your point! Why are you harping about this?"

Dr. Grey's eyelids crinkled as if she were peering deep into Rick's psyche. "Perhaps I am harping, but words like 'must' and 'should' are weapons of relationship destruction. Dr. Albert Ellis, a renowned cognitive psychologist, said that if we should on ourselves and others, we'll have shouldy personalities."

Rick smirked. "I hope he didn't say we *should* stop shoulding on ourselves."

Dr. Grey smiled. "Except for rare and sudden life-threatening occurrences, events don't cause intense feelings and behaviours. What happened between you and Liv that upset you?"

"Liv told me to go fuck myself—her salty version of get lost, you prick."

"When Liv said that, how did you feel?"

"I thought she was rude."

"We're not always aware of emotions that hum in the background of everything we do…even boredom is a feeling state. Imagine the scene, and let yourself really feel how you felt." Dr. Grey comfortably waited. "You felt…?"

"Since I've fallen hard for Liv, I naturally felt like my heart had been ripped out. I was devastated. And pissed off."

"How did you deal with your feelings? What did you *do*?"

"The only thing I could do—grabbed my coat and left; slammed the door behind me and drove to my neighbourhood pub."

Dr. Grey asked, "What made you slam the door?"

"Liv's order to get the hell outta there. What are you getting at?"

"Something powerful…something within you happened between Liv's order, your emotions, and your leaving."

"Still not sure what you're getting at."

"What *belief* did you harbour about Liv's abrupt end to the evening?"

"I thought she shouldn't—yes, shouldn't—have ruined everything by taking my comments so personally. At the very least she was insensitive. Didn't respectfully hear me out."

"My next question might sound superficial," Dr. Grey said, "but stick with me here. Do you think it's logical to assume that at times, we're all insensitive and disrespectful of others? Quite unintentionally, in many cases?"

Rick grinned. "Yeah, but I think I know where you're going with this."

"Where?"

"If I agree that we can all be accidentally insensitive, then why did I think Liv *should've* been sensitive to my views of the Catholic Church?"

Dr. Grey smiled broadly, nodded agreement, and waited.

"Are most people that logical when they feel upset?" Rick asked.

"I don't know about people in general, but most of my clients are not. They overlook the intervening, inappropriate beliefs between what happens and their emotions and behaviours that follow. Your *belief* that Liv should've been sensitive to your views determined how you felt and behaved, not Liv's order to leave."

"So it's all about my stupid beliefs?"

With a warm but pensive facial expression, Dr. Grey said, "Inappropriate beliefs are all-powerful. I hear comments like, 'Don shot himself because his wife committed adultery.' More likely, Don killed himself because he firmly believed infidelity was *disastrous* and he *couldn't stand it*. Wives, most certainly his own, *must* always be faithful." Suicide was Don's reaction to his real problem—unrealistic beliefs about how others must think, feel, and act."

Rick said, "Maybe Don simply believed that living without her was impossible."

"Perhaps. But if I'd had the chance, I'd have asked him: Where is it written that you can't live without her? Where's the evidence? You managed to survive all those years before you met her."

Rick thought a moment and said, "Yeah, very logical, but at that point would Don give a damn what you or anyone else said?"

"At that point, the art of therapy would be sorely tested, for sure, but I don't want to turn this into a lesson on suicide intervention. Let's dig deeper into your thoughts. You said the evening with Liv was a total disaster."

"Mm-hmm," Rick replied. *Here's where she turns Freudian.*

"What if you believed that Liv's failure to respect your beliefs and her abrupt end to the evening were *unfortunate, unpleasant,* or *disappointing*? Not a total disaster. Might you have felt and behaved differently if you told yourself that?"

"Are you saying I wouldn't be upset if I thought Liv's order to leave was merely disappointing? Unpleasant?"

"You might have been less upset. It would've been *nice* if Liv hadn't abruptly ended the evening. *Desirable* if…, *preferable* if…, but was it a total disaster?"

Rick sat silently, thinking.

Dr. Grey sat quietly, motionless.

"I can't imagine calmly telling myself that it would've been preferable if Liv hadn't told me to go fuck myself."

"Strong feelings don't just happen," said Dr. Grey, "except in response to sudden, life-threatening events. In our relationships, what happens on the outside is less important than what happens inside…what we tell ourselves."

Her face is saying something, but what? "You make it sound like knowing this stuff is as crucial for understanding ourselves as $E=mc^2$ is for understanding physics."

Dr. Grey appeared to stifle a laugh. "I don't want to beat this idea to a pulp, but my trained ear tells me you have unrealistic beliefs and demands that Liv *should* agree with you; that she *must* denounce the Catholic Church; that you *can't stand it* when she doesn't respect or agree with your views. That might sound extreme, even unfair, but habitual beliefs are subconscious drivers of emotions and behaviours."

Rick gave Dr. Grey a sideways glance. "Liv *should* stop supporting an institution that does more harm than good in this world…in my humble opinion."

"Humble? When you talk about the Catholic religion, your voice is declarative. It's strident and preachy—pardon the pun."

"Seriously? Preachy? Is that how I sound?"

"That's how I hear it."

"So, it's finally come down to this: I'm a chip off the old block. Now what?"

"You *could* replace loaded words with milder equivalents—anger with irritation or annoyance; fear and anxiety with concern; depression and sadness with disappointment."

Rick stretched in his chair. "Okay, fine. But I think of myself as a writer, so if I say my anger is oceanic, I'm conveying its hold on me. If I say it's simply regrettable, I'd betray myself—the self that thinks in prose, if that doesn't sound too bombastic."

"Not at all. I've noticed your sophisticated way with words…your thoughtful ideas. And you're right; there isn't a direct correspondence between every word we utter and the feelings and behaviours that follow. But the *habitual* use of strong words, and the tone and body language that accompany them, concerns me. After all, the people I work with are in therapy."

Rick tapped his index fingers together. "Like me," he said, with a tone of resignation.

"Ah, but unlike many people who muddle their way through life, you're looking for an elegant solution to your problems."

"Elegant solution…for inelegant beliefs," Rick put his hands behind his head and stared at the ceiling. *What would happen if I were to drastically change? Would my elegant solution leave the old me hanging in the abyss?*

"About Liv," Dr. Grey said, breaking a heavy silence. "I wonder if she found it hard to ask you to leave. Perhaps regretted it later. You implied that both of you were enjoying each other's company before *Spotlight*. If she had hopes for an exciting new romance, her disappointment might have been as unpleasant as yours."

"I was too indignant to see things from her closed-minded perspective."

Dr. Grey remained as cool as a cat staring down a yapping terrier. "Where is it written that people *must* always be open-minded? Is it in the Canadian Constitution?"

"Okay, okay, it's not written anywhere." Rick was clearly getting peeved.

"In our first session, you said your dad's behaviour made you hammer him into submission."

"Kee-riste! I had to defend myself—had nothing to do with this Ellis guy or my screwed up beliefs. How else was I supposed to react to his brutal attack? Calmly tell the dumb fuck his hidebound views make him act like a monster? As if that would've changed anything." Rick felt his face burning.

Leaning closer to her distraught client, Dr. Grey said, "I apologize. Your father's assault *was* illegal. An unexpected, violent attack, and you needed to defend yourself. I haven't forgotten that you peacefully left the family dinner table on Boxing Day—a reasonable way to cope with his hurtful insults. You said that the only time you and your father physically attacked each other was that night, so I assume you've responded sensibly many times over the years."

"Mm-hmm. All my life I've managed to control my urge to smack him upside the head."

"Children in similar circumstances sometimes develop a host of chronic problems—persistent, uncontrollable rage, drug abuse, depression, chronic anxiety, personality disorders—to name a few. You've been more resilient than many."

"Resilient? I wasn't resilient on Boxing Day and I'm having a hard time bouncing back from Liv's rejection. Did I tell you that I texted her an apology and she replied that the kindest thing we could do is wish each other well and move on? The final blow. I'm not boyfriend material."

"Be good to yourself. Isn't it natural to experience a range of emotions when our hopes and dreams are shattered? When self-doubt, sadness, or guilt won't leave us alone?"

"Sure, maybe for a few days, but not this long. I still think about Liv's rejection more than I should. Oops, *could*."

"In times of transition when we're stranded between hope and fear, or confidence and self-doubt, we all feel somewhat adrift. That's normal."

"I feel more than adrift about Dad. If I knew a better way to argue, maybe I could at least get him to be less arrogant—a *slight* personality change."

"I don't argue with people who are emotionally tethered to their beliefs. The more I try to persuade them they're wrong, the more they'll find reasons to bolster their side of the argument. Google is their best friend—confirms what they need to believe and supplies the ammunition to rehearse every detail of their position until they're more convinced than ever they're right. In extreme cases, they're easily indoctrinated by cults. Whether what they believe is true or not doesn't matter; what matters is what's subjectively true for *them*."

"Cults," Rick said. "The people I'm thinking of sometimes look like they're locked in a weird trance, except for messiahs, who know exactly where they are and what they're saying and doing."

"Are you thinking of someone in particular?"

"Yeah, someone we all know. A president who swindled the public with the promise of university degrees that turned out to be nonexistent, fake. Cheats and bullies others." Rick caught Dr. Grey's look of disgust before she changed the topic.

"Another short exercise, if you're willing. Sit back, relax, and take a moment to recall your earliest childhood experience. Stretch as far back as possible; let an early memory surface like a movie clip. Stick with what first comes to mind. No censoring."

Rick quickly complied. "When I was about six, Dad slammed the car door on my thumb. He barely assessed the damage, then yelled, 'That'll teach you to watch where you put your fingers getting in and out of car doors.' Somehow it was all my fault for not paying attention. He didn't even examine my thumb...or apologize."

"Not doing either made it worse. Can you remember how you felt when that happened?"

"Angry. Not sure...like a child in a crowded, noisy street whose father just let go of his hand?"

"Lost and alone," Dr. Grey said. "Perhaps frightened?"

Rick bit off a chunk of nail he'd been picking at. "Most likely all of that. Another time, at roughly the same age, I asked Dad if devils really had horns, and he said something like: Stop with the stupid questions! When I tried to stifle my tears, he told me to buck up, we don't need sissy babies in the family."

"How does your body feel as you tell me this?"

Rick rolled his shoulders as if to loosen the tension. "Tight. Angry."

"You say you feel angry, but you look sad."

After a lengthy pause, Rick looked up and said, "I've cried enough about all that—can't cry anymore."

"As a child, was it risky to have your own feelings and thoughts? Unsafe to ask questions?"

"Never thought of it that way at the time, but yeah, wherever we went, no matter what we did or who we were with, Dad's hurtful judgments tagged along. My hurtful feelings kept pace. I didn't realize that he saw my questions as challenges to his authority until I was much older."

"Was there a turning point when you knew you were as capable of understanding the world as your father?"

"Can't remember a particular moment, but I must've believed that because, in my late teens, I tried to prove that I wasn't a dumb adolescent by arrogantly confronting anyone I assumed had an insufficiency of brain cells…especially anyone who faintly resembled an authority figure. I'd quote famous authors from nonfiction library books to bolster my self-appointed reputation as an egghead, delusional as *that* was. Later, I loved university courses that taught me to question all ideas and theories, including scientific research."

"My hunch is that cognitively, you're ahead of the average adult. A skeptic and an independent thinker."

Rick said, "A liberated skeptic who belongs to no one. I question the facts, not the person. And I'm not a cynic. Not like Dad…suspicious of everyone's motives."

"What have you learned about your emotions?"

Rick flicked his thumb nail on his front tooth. "That's where I fall short. My feelings sometimes run the show, without my permission. Maybe that's because—call it a missing memory—Dad never told me he loved me. Never came close to showing me anything that could be misconstrued as a hug. But he loved my sister, Joy—gave her affectionate hugs and a cute little nickname. Little Miss Joyful was his adorable one, the obedient one, the calm, easy-going baby so unlike me, who Dad says, 'Came into this world in a hissy fit that never ends.' Joy is everything I'm not."

"There's deep sorrow in your voice."

Rick exhaled loudly and slowly. "The feelings are still there. Nothing I do will ever be good enough."

"Recalling early memories can make us sad," Dr. Grey said, "but a long string of painful ones cause enduring sorrow. Your childhood recollections have themes of sadness, fear, doubt, and shame. As a kid, you likely thought bad things would happen no matter what you did because, like all children, you were physically small and inexperienced, with limited cognitive development. Adults were bigger, smarter, and more worldly than you. You might have concluded that since adults treat me badly, *I'm* bad. Perhaps you also assumed that every mistake was all your fault…*all* of you was worthless and blameworthy. You wouldn't have articulated it as such, but you may have believed you were unintelligent, undeserving, and unlovable—reasonable beliefs given your age and experiences."

"Fascinating. I can't remember what, if anything, I concluded, but I know I felt unloved. And stupid. Spent lots of time in my room, especially when Dad was home."

"What was that like?"

"Lonely. But safe."

"There you were, a defenceless little kid, all alone and without the cognitive development to accept your mistakes as a necessary part of growing up…of being human. I'd hardly expect you to think along these lines: Gee, I lucked out with my father, but I'll just hang out here until I'm old enough to leave home and put Dad's bad parenting behind me. I'm plenty good enough just the way I am."

"I'm sure I didn't think *that*!" Rick exclaimed, then sat back and chuckled.

Dr. Grey waited. "Today, when you make mistakes, are you still putting your thumb in that car door?"

Rick said, "I only know that I dump on myself when I screw up. And ruminate…a stupid thing to do because, as someone once said, if we stand with one foot in yesterday and one foot in tomorrow, we piss all over today."

Dr. Grey grinned. "It's like that, isn't it?"

"Like what?"

"I take it to mean we shouldn't dwell on the past, but learn from it…not obsess about the future, but plan for it. Right now, I'm still thinking about your early recollections that may have shaped much of your present personality."

Rick looked up at Dr. Grey. "Isn't it common sense that childhood memories influence who we become?"

Dr. Grey spoke in a soft, almost velvety voice. "Yes, but looking for themes in early memories isn't so common. From the millions of events we've experienced in childhood, the few we vividly recall in adulthood aren't random. They've shaped narratives about ourselves, others, and the world. You're here today, partly because of the stories you told yourself as a kid. Problems may occur when childhood narratives become patterns of thought and expectations that persist in adulthood. Does that sound reasonable?"

Rick took time to ponder Dr. Grey's suggestion. "But we all have childhood memories of unhappy or frightening events. Has a client ever recalled only happy memories?"

"No. Clients' early memories are often unpleasant—that's largely why they're in therapy."

"So, the memories I just gave are telling," Rick said.

"I think so. I'm assuming that you grew up believing the world is a dangerous, frightening place. People aren't to be trusted; they'll hurt me. I'm stupid and unlovable. Other kids grew up believing the world's a fun, beautiful, and exciting place to be. People are kind and helpful. I'm smart and loveable."

Rick stared hypnotically at Dr. Grey. "I never seriously considered my early experiences from that angle."

"Little kids are keen observers but poor interpreters. They act as if their views are correct and unalterable." She tucked her hair behind her ears. "You didn't recall any happy memories with childhood friends."

Rick puffed out his cheeks. "I was a shy, uptight little kid who no one wanted to play with, except for one year when Earl Wilson and I became friends. That summer, we spent hours on our bikes, and in the winter, we played in the rumpus room of the Wilson's big home. I remember thinking how nice it'd be to have a dad like Earl's—a dad who'd affectionately hug me when he got home from work. At the time, I didn't understand that male to male hugs, even fathers to sons, were repugnant for homophobes like Dad."

"Do you and Earl keep in touch?"

"No. His family moved to Toronto when we were twelve and he never contacted me like he promised, but I'm sure he was busy adjusting to a different school and making new friends."

"Still, some good, lasting memories," Dr. Grey said. "Before you met Earl's dad, do you think you assumed all fathers were like your own?"

"Can't remember—most likely. Don't all kids?"

"Most children don't develop the ability to think abstractly until their teens, so unless they're exposed to a variety of parents throughout childhood, their world is *the* world."

As Rick and Dr. Grey delved into childhood memories and feelings, Rick's father was in an Irish pub ruthlessly criticizing Simon, their newly hired employee who'd suggested the company try a technological change.

"I like Simon," Harry said, in the same wearisome tone he generally used with Dick. "He's bright and conscientious. Has good ideas."

Dick loosened his shirt collar. "Never mind. You don't see how critical he is."

"I never assume he's competing with me," Harry countered. "Cripes almighty man, don't be so touchy. It doesn't become you."

Dick stared at his pint of beer, then looked up at Harry and asked what he thought of last night's hockey game.

Harry smiled compassionately. "Missed a good one. Rose and I went grocery shopping after supper." The brothers talked hockey until Harry's right shoulder started twitching. "Time to head home—Rose has lasagna in the oven." He reached for his credit card.

"This one's on me," Dick said, then tossed his head toward the bar where an attractive woman sat alone. "I'm staying for another quick one." He waved his card at the waiter and as Harry grabbed his jacket, Dick mumbled, "Might consider what you said."

Harry firmly grasped Dick's shoulder. "Thanks for the suds. Take it easy."

Dick swaggered up to the bar and, despite several empty seats, slid in beside a middle-aged woman who put her phone down and looked up.

"Mind if I join you? I'm Dick Wright." He partially extended his hand as if to test whether she'd reach out to shake it.

"Just waiting for my husband," the woman answered, worrying the ice in her gin and tonic.

"You from Calgary, or here on business?"

"Visiting from Montreal," she said, somewhat abruptly.

Dick peppered the woman with increasingly intimate questions. "We're heading to the polls here in Alberta. Most westerners are die-hard Conservatives, not like you Liberals down east."

"Are you always this oily? Why are you asking such personal questions?"

"Oily?" Dick scowled. Having established that the woman didn't meet his criteria for a satisfying conversation, Dick signalled the bartender then glared at the stranger. "Forget my friendliness, ma'am. I've never laid eyes on such a…such a cold fish." Dick guzzled half his beer and left in a huff.

Across the city, Dick's son was having no problem answering his therapist's intimate question: "What about your father's childhood? Do you think memories of his early experiences shaped his personality?"

Rick dropped his arms over the edge of his chair and talked about the tragic circumstances of his father's childhood and the untimely death of both parents.

"Your father's early life was laden with disappointment and grief," Dr. Grey said.

"Yeah. He rarely talks about his parents or childhood, so I tend to forget that he truly suffered throughout his first eighteen years. Compared to Dad, I've been pampered." Rick tried to decipher Dr. Grey's Mona Lisa smile.

"Your persistence in trying to understand your father strikes me as very compassionate," she said.

"Compassionate?" Rick's brows nearly bumped into his hairline. "Never thought of myself as *that*. Surprised you have, especially given all my complaints."

"I think you have deep feelings for him. If you didn't care, would you be here?"

Rick stared at Dr. Grey, bug-eyed. Gaze softening, he said, "Dad's life was hell on Earth, but I'm sure he convinced himself that if he raised God-fearing little Christians and prayed for forgiveness, he'd be rewarded in the afterlife."

"To me, it's understandable that if your dad was a fearful child, he'd readily adopt beliefs that he assumed would ease his suffering. Protect him."

"But countless people have rough home environments without becoming hoodwinked into accepting fanciful biblical stories and conspiracy theories as absolute truths. Something extraordinary must've made Dad who he is."

"It'd be unprofessional and unethical for me to say anything that smacked of a diagnosis, but people with backgrounds different from your father's, people born with loving, emotionally stable parents, are generally more accepting of themselves and others. More broad-minded. Normal levels of biochemicals and neurotransmitters are also part of the mix."

"I'll try to remember that, especially when Dad starts pontificating about some screwy conspiracy theory."

"As I see it, the best way to cope with headstrong people is to change our attitude toward them...assuming they don't violate human rights or the laws of the land."

"That attitude stuff is the hard part. Still, maybe you're right. And maybe I care more about Dad than I let myself believe. Or feel."

The room was perfectly quiet until Dr. Grey said, in a meditative tone, "I'm thinking of someone else you care a great deal about. You asked if I thought *you* ruined the evening with Liv. Here's my best guess, but I might be wrong: Your early childhood experiences and unreasonable beliefs shaped your emotions, behaviours, and strong words. Let's both take a moment to reflect on that."

Rick slowly worked at tearing another piece of skin from his bottom lip. "I see, I see. You're saying that my stupid expectations ruined the evening as much as, maybe more than, Liv. Her reaction was secondary. Inconsequential."

"Exactly. Hard hitting, but something you might consider between now and our next session." Dr. Grey looked at the clock. "But we have a bit of time left."

"Good. There's something I'd like to mention before our time's up."

Dr. Grey's smile beckoned.

"Last week I started my English assignment, an all-consuming short story that's becoming quite an outlet for years of hurt and frustration. Creeps into my idle time, like waiting my turn at check-out counters, or stuck in traffic jams during rush hour."

Dr. Grey cradled her face in the palm of her hands and thought a moment. "At heart, you really are a writer."

"Thanks to Mom, much of my childhood was spent with her and Joy in the library. We always came home with armloads of books, from kiddie lit to mysteries, classic novels, short stories, anything and everything. At sixteen, I'd read some of Hemingway, Munroe, Roth, Salinger, and other authors who have no idea how much they influenced my thinking. Mom bought me a leather-bound notebook one Christmas so I could stop jotting down thoughts and ideas on scraps of paper."

"What a gift she gave you—a love of reading and now a love for writing."

"Mm-hmm. Writing helps me face the hard stuff. Takes me deeper into myself, a little like Margaret Atwood, I think."

"Ah, yes, a special form of therapy. May I suggest you rewrite your story when you're fifty; perhaps again at seventy. Age expands our view of the past."

Rick smiled as if slowly warming to the idea. "I'll remember that."

"And I'll remember your answer to this," Dr. Grey said, narrowing her eyes attentively. "What means so much to you it's worth fighting for?"

"Relationships…with Dad and Liv. And a PhD in English. If I have to wage war against myself to get those, I'll damn well do it."

"What about you, Rick? Are you worth fighting for?"

Rick grinned. "A heroic battle."

Dr. Grey said, "We battled it out in here today. How will you know when you've had enough therapy?"

"When I stop fighting myself. When I become what I need to become." Rick slid to the edge of his chair. His eyes darted around the room then locked onto Dr. Grey's. "I'm a son, a brother, a student, and a novice writer. But here's what I'm not."

He reached for his jacket as Dr. Grey looked at him with patient anticipation.

"I'm not much of a man."

Chapter 6

Rick checked his phone and inhaled deeply.

Hi Rick,

With mixed feelings I reread your candid apology. Thank you for remembering me fondly.

I've seriously thought about your indictment of the Catholic Church and agree that the entire institution needs to fess up to its cover-ups. Those priests should be tried, convicted, and jailed. But I still believe in an omnipotent, omniscient God—the church is simply a meeting place where members share that conviction, whatever form it takes.

Can we meet for coffee? Best we avoid the topic of religion, no?

Short notice, but any chance you're free tomorrow morning, 10:30, Caffeine Castle near you?

Rick gave a shout of pure joy. The power and possibility of one little text, he thought, then reread Liv's message and tapped a quick reply.

Great to hear from you, Liv. Yes, I look forward to seeing you there and then.

Rick

P. S. Happy to leave religion in the churches.

Nervous anticipation played out its own exquisite drama as Rick awaited Liv's arrival at the café. He slowly stirred his coffee and surveyed the clients, most of whom worked on laptops, checked their phones, read newspapers, or chatted with friends. Within minutes, Liv arrived, bought a bran muffin and espresso, and smiled as she approached Rick's table.

Rick stood to greet her. "Nice to see you again, Liv. Have a seat by the fire," he said, pulling back a chair and helping her with her coat.

"What a cozy little place for a wintry day," Liv commented, settling in at their table. "Is the new semester in full swing?"

"Back at it, I am, and classes are going well," Rick said, then added what he cautioned himself not to. "So is therapy...I think."

"Therapy?"

"Yeah. My fight with Dad on Boxing Day and my attack on your religion were key motivators to the couch, so to speak, not as cushy as my worn leather one at home. What I'm learning from Dr. Grey, my therapist, is more thought-provoking than anything I'm learning in my university courses—she's helping me better understand Dad, and I've stopped hiding from things I need to face, like my tendency to overreact to beliefs I'm more than a little passionate about."

In a jocular tone, Liv said, "Oh, I think we're both capable of overreacting. As for me, I'm sorry I told you to..." She shook her head. "Can't even say the words now!"

Rick's laugh lines made their own statement. "No problem. Simply telling me to leave wouldn't have had the same impact. I'm sorry too, for being so...ruthless. Before we move on, I'd like you to know that I do believe in a consciousness that transcends the physical brain. A thread that connects all organic life—call it religion, spirituality, mysticism, neuroscience—they all have unique stories that help us grapple with life's mysteries."

Liv stared at Rick's concrete jaw. "You sound more broad-minded than you did a couple weeks ago, but I'll now stop what I suggested we not do."

"Fine by me. Religion is now officially off the table."

"Can we put politics on?" Liv didn't wait for an answer. "As you may know, the writ's been dropped and the race is on. Did you hear that I've won the candidacy I told you about?"

"I've been so immersed in my courses and part-time job that I forgot about your nomination," Rick lied. "But after I got your message, I Googled our constituency and was glad to see you'd won it. You must be excited."

"Excited, but stressed to the max. We only have a few weeks until the election and I shudder to think of the work that's piling up. I'm grateful for the volunteers I have, but need a few more if I'm to pull this off. Part of the reason I contacted you was to see if you'd be interested in getting involved in politics—my campaign, to be exact."

Rick sipped his coffee and seriously questioned whether getting him to volunteer was the only reason Liv contacted him.

"I'd like to help but the timing couldn't be worse…course assignments, part-time job and all."

"I understand," Liv said, pushing back her cuticles.

"And I'll think about it," Rick said, then thought about it for ten seconds. "I'm overdue for some political action, so yeah, I really should help our constituency's best candidate win."

Liv put her sparkling white teeth on display. "Wonderful!"

Rick sipped his coffee. *Seren-fuckin-dipity. Liv and I can make a new start, one that benefits constituents, the province, and us. To think that a short while ago*—his fantasy faded when Liv interrupted.

"The candidate's priority should be personal contact with the electorate, which means I'll need volunteers to help me knock on every constituent's door between now and E-day. With a population of about 50,000, that's a lot of doorbells to ring."

Rick softly hummed a few notes of an unrecognizable song.

Liv said, "But door knocking can be intimidating for beginners, which is why John, my office manager with several campaigns behind him, has put together a short script."

"Good idea. You wouldn't want volunteers to misrepresent you or the party."

"Right. Tomorrow, friends, colleagues, and three or four people from the church are coming to my campaign headquarters for a one o'clock meeting. We'll door knock after and reward ourselves with beer and pizza at the office when we're finished…about five o'clock. Might you be up for that?"

Rick laced his fingers together. "I'm a bit apprehensive about knock, knock, knocking on strangers' doors. Aren't most of your constituents Conservatives, with vicious attack dogs?"

Liv discreetly laughed. "Nope. Many of them are loyal supporters of Dean Shields, the four-term Liberal MLA who's stepping down. He's so well-known and highly respected that die-hard Conservatives voted for him, not so much for what he's done, and he's done a lot, but for who he *is*—a politician with heart and brains. And integrity."

"Yeah, Shields. I voted for the guy. Met him at the annual river clean-up and was impressed with his sincerity. Seems different from most politicians—trustworthy comes to mind."

"Yep, he's the real deal," Liv said. "And get this—he assured me that his board members and former volunteers would help with door knocking and campaign expenses. Without his substantial support, I wouldn't have accepted the nomination."

"If I agree to door knock, could we go together for my first time out so I can get the right rap, so to speak? Do you have brochures?"

"Yes, brochures are ready to go and I'll make sure John puts us on the same team. Remember, I'm new at this too. We both have much to learn, so I'll welcome whatever help you can give, but I also understand if you're pressed for time."

"Wait. Given our unfortunate blow-up over *Spotlight*, I'm wondering why you'd want me to door knock. I obviously lack social manners when I discuss religion. How do you know I won't be an arrogant jerk about politics?"

Liv moved her face closer to Rick's and almost whispered, "Given your apology and willingness to go for therapy, I'm betting you won't be." She kept her eyes on Rick as she sipped her coffee.

Rick felt good about Liv's sensitivity and honesty, then covertly wondered, *how many residents would toss the brochures in the recycle bin without reading them*? He smiled at Liv and said, "I'll do what I can between classes and work, but slave labour will have to replace hard cash."

"Slave labour's just what we need now, mainly on the doors. But if you prefer, you could be my Communication Director—wouldn't even have to come into the office."

"I could hone my writing skills by helping with social media updates, so sure, I'll give that a brief go between classes."

"I'm pumped!" Liv covered her mouth and lowered her voice before she and Rick talked more about politics and the campaign. After furtively checking her phone, she said, "Oh damn, I'm meeting someone in fifteen minutes. Can I look for you at one o'clock tomorrow?"

"I'm slowly gearing up, but still not sure about door knocking. What's the dress code?"

"Warm! Especially head, hands, and feet." Liv gave Rick the office address, and as they left the coffee shop, he nudged her and said, "After every bedtime story Grandma Davidson told me and my sister, Joy, her wise eyes would smile as she said, 'And this story isn't over.'"

"Which meant?" Liv waggled her eyebrows.

"See you tomorrow!" Rick said and gave her a quick hug and peck on the cheek.

Throughout the rest of the day and into the night, Rick intermittently toyed with Liv's intentions. *Is she romantically interested? Did she welcome my peck on the cheek? Have we fully reconciled?* On it went until he mumbled aloud, "Fuckit! Stop ruminating!"

Enthusiasm ran high as volunteers arrived at Liv's campaign office and chatted over fresh coffee and blueberry muffins that helped camouflage the stale odour of a room previously vacant for months. Rick liked the gender parity and multicultural mix among the fourteen volunteers—eight women, including Liv; six men, including himself. Most of them looked close to Liv's age, except an attractive, elderly woman who told entertaining stories from her years of door-knocking experience to a paunchy man with a thick head of wavy, salt-and-pepper hair.

John studied a large wall map that outlined the borders of each poll in the constituency, some colour coded to indicate they had been canvassed or were of top priority. Rick had one probing question: "John, can you assure me you'll put Liv and I together for this, my first time out?"

"Yes," John said, "You and Liv will work one side of the street while a veteran doorknocker, paired with an inexperienced volunteer, will canvass the opposite side."

Rick submerged his pure delight beneath a look of serious concern as he watched Liv step to the front of the room and open her arms wide, as if to hug everyone.

"Thank you for coming…for all your help in this, my first political campaign and Liberal victory," Liv said, then briefly outlined party strategy, after which John explained campaign goals, door-knocking procedures, and the introductory script, "designed to keep everyone on message and bolster confidence in novice doorknockers."

In her strongest voice, Liv piped up. "Yes, consistency of message is important."

By four-thirty, Liv's team had knocked on every door within their designated poll boundaries. Tired but cheerfully optimistic, Rick said, "I'll tweet about today's successful canvass, then post a blurb on Facebook and the website. Tweeters among you, please retweet my comments."

Liv gave Rick's shoulder a hard squeeze. "Thanks! I'll look for that."

Partway through their celebratory pizza and refreshments, Liv thanked the doorknockers and announced that John would lock up since she had to leave for a friend's thirty-fifth birthday celebration.

Rick was disappointed that he and Liv wouldn't spend a romantic evening together, but consoled himself with the thought that, *we'll have plenty of private time throughout the campaign…unless Noah accompanies her to that birthday party tonight.* His feared fantasy vanished when Liv walked over and said, "Thanks for joining us on such short notice, Rick, and posting to social media."

Rick smiled as only the genuinely smitten can. "I'm getting the hang of it, and yes, more time on the doors should make experts of us all."

"Now there's something you could write about," Liv said. "I know I'm pushing the limits, but might we do this again soon? We're going out tomorrow afternoon."

"I've planned a brunch date with Mom, but will text if I'm able to catch up with you and the team later. Maybe a five o'clock canvass next week, barring death, disaster, or rush-hour traffic delays."

"Thank you," Liv said, then firmly hugged Rick before walking out.

No kiss on the cheek? Rick stopped brooding when John thanked the remaining handful of volunteers, walked over to him, and said, "Have you heard about SAL—the Students for Alberta Liberals—at the University of Calgary?"

Rick's eyes lit up. "No. Should check that out. Who's heading it up?"

John's phone was where it always was—in his left hand. "I'm texting you the organizer's contact info," he said. "Brittany's a law student who might bring a team of volunteers for next Saturday's door-knocking blitz."

"I'll text her," Rick said, which he promptly did before pulling out of the parking lot.

By the time he got home, Brittany had replied: *Welcome Rick! Next Friday, 4 p.m. The Den, back corner.*

Rick felt good about the world and everyone in it. He phoned his mother.

"Hey Mom, I've cooked up a plan for tomorrow. Just checked the weather forecast and it should be perfect for what I have in mind."

"Perfect for skiing?" Dorothy asked.

"Nope, I'm taking you for brunch. Just you and me, when you get home from church. Is that a crazy idea or what?"

"Not crazy, delightful! But what about Dad? He'll be upset if he's not included."

"Just tell him we're overdue for some mother-son quality time. If he protests, assure him that I'll take him for brunch next week."

Dorothy said, sounding apprehensive, "I'll fix him a big breakfast and call down when we get home from church. Hope he doesn't get in a snit."

"If he does, ignore him and come downstairs. We can handle this."

Dorothy knocked on Rick's door and stepped inside. "Let's go," she said, nervously. "Dad's puttering around in the garage. He's upset that we're going without him."

"Maybe he'll give some thought to why that is," Rick said.

Katie's Kitchen was filled with the sounds of chatty customers and aromas of breakfast. The hostess escorted Rick and Dorothy to a window table where Rick helped his mother with her coat and scanned the room.

"I like the feel of this place," he said. "Hope the service is good."

"I'm in no rush," Dorothy said. "Just glad we're spending time together." She passed Rick a menu.

"I could go for the Bottomless Mimosa and Vanilla Bean Pancakes Smothered in Blueberries," Rick said. "Top of page two."

Dorothy closed the menu and smiled. "For this special occasion, I'll have a mimosa too, and Classic Eggs Benedict."

Waiting to place their order, Rick said, "I've been wanting to tell you about therapy with Dr. Grey—once a week for six sessions, then I'll take a breather to work on changes we've discussed."

"It's going well?" Dorothy asked, smiling with unusual intensity.

"Yeah. She seems to understand me. Is very supportive, but doesn't shy away from confronting my stinkin' thinkin' that gives Dad power over my emotions. In a nutshell, I've learned that I can soften my reactions by telling myself different words—words that will make me less angry." Rick gave a couple examples and said, "Watch me stay calm as I slay the dragon within next time Dad insults me or goes off on a tangent. You can grade my performance."

Dorothy smiled. "I'm so glad you're telling me this. Sounds promising, but how are you going to pay for it? Even if Dad covers half of your therapy bill, it's expensive."

"He left me without a shred of dignity in my earlier years...be damned if I'll let him shred what I've since earned on my own. I don't need his begrudging charity. Besides, not getting help would be costlier in the long run."

"I think Dad's intentions are good, but it's hard for him to have a normal, give-and-take conversation. Gets all steamed up if someone questions him. Especially you. Then you overreact and...well, Lord knows professional help could benefit him too. And me. Family therapy isn't a bad idea."

"Yeah, but we know what he thinks of therapy. We also know that even if his intentions are good, the effect is not. His facial expression, his tone of voice...he might think his lectures are for my own good, but they feel condescending and judgmental. Controlling. After all, I *am* 28." Rick raised his mimosa. "But enough about that. Here's to us, Mom. To better days ahead."

"To better times," Dorothy said, and took a sip. "I like this drink. Could make it at home when you, Joy, and I have a special get together."

"Speaking of special times, when we chatted briefly at the kitchen sink after my first therapy session, I asked you how you've coped with Dad's irascible moods all these years and you said that someday you'd tell me about it. So...."

Dorothy plunked her elbows on the table and folded her hands. "Shouldn't have said that."

"Why not? Was curious then; more so now."

Rick's words hung heavy in the air until Dorothy picked up her fork and said, "Recently, I've asked myself why I've put up with Dad all these years. Did my stern father make me submissive to men? Your Grandpa Davidson was the strong, silent type, and I knew not to cross him or there'd be hell to pay." Dorothy closed her eyes and rubbed her forehead as if trying to block a painful vision. "Dad's eyes...no matter what I was doing, they followed me. But he never *saw* me."

"Sounds like you married your father," Rick said, then wished he hadn't.

"No, like a total doofus I married someone *worse* than that. Little did I know that before our first wedding anniversary, the real Dick Wright—your father—would come out like phlegm from his white linen hankies I washed and ironed every week."

Rick aborted a snicker as Dorothy quickly apologized for her "crass comment."

"The signs were all there before we married, but I was in that love-struck stage of denial. I wanted to take care of him, but how could I take care of a man who knew everything and needed help with nothing. Before long, I was heartbroken. Or simply broken. But that was then. This is now, and things have changed."

"Good!" Rick said, exuberantly. "Tell me about it."

Dorothy hemmed and hawed. Rick waited. For the first time he realized that his father wasn't the only man who'd eroded his mother's self-confidence; reduced her to a self-effacing jellyfish. *Mom was needlessly apologetic long before she met Dad.*

"What I'm about to say will shock your socks off," Dorothy said. "Not sure you want to hear it…if I should even tell it."

"Mom, maybe I should stop seeing you as a long-suffering saint."

"Saint! What in the world of grief do you mean? I'm anything *but* saintly."

"In the world of grief," Rick chuckled, "please tell me what you're up to."

Dorothy's eyes darted around the room as if searching for hidden microphones or ears the size of small cabbages. She nervously twisted her wedding band, then took another sip of mimosa. "This isn't easy, but, you see…two years ago a wonderful man came into my life. Efner. Yes, that's his name, and he's quite the gentleman."

Rick stifled a howl. "Efner? Unless you're a stand-up comedian, what can you do with a moniker like that? What did kids in the schoolyard do with it? And who in their right mind would name a baby Efner?"

"Norwegian parents, that's who," Dorothy said, in a stern voice that Rick and Joy flippantly referred to as the mother mode.

"How do you spell it?" Rick asked, thinking how coincidental it was that both he and his mother were attracted to someone of Norwegian heritage.

Dorothy slowly spelled Efner. "Remember, don't judge a book by its cover."

"Okay, but my imagination's running wild. Where'd you meet this guy?"

"He volunteers at the hospice, which already makes him special; most are women." Dorothy looked at her mimosa, then Rick, then back at her mimosa. "It felt like we were instant soul mates."

Rick's thoughts ricocheted from belief to disbelief. With an alert re-entry into the moment, he asked, "What else do I need to know? Where's he from? Where does he live? Is he married? Are you having an affair with this guy? Will you divorce Dad and marry…Efner?"

"Where to start with all your questions." Dorothy took a swig of mimosa. "Efner was born in an isolated village in Norway. He might have a couple relatives there but, like me with my kinfolk, he's lost touch. His only son, Dorvald—no daughters—is thirty-two. I met him once when he picked up Efner at the hospice, and what little I saw of him I liked. A confident, thoughtful young man, just like his father."

Rick tried not to sound overly concerned. "I've a feeling there's more to tell."

Dorothy nodded. "After every hospice shift, Efner and I have a glass of pinot noir at the hotel two blocks down from the hospice."

Rick's mimosa went down the wrong way. He sputtered, "Hotel! Can hardly believe it. Efner must be some kind of special."

"That he is! Kind and respectful…with a zany sense of humour. Can't tell you how happy I am every Wednesday morning just knowing we'll rendezvous later that day."

Rick's eyes narrowed. "I hope Dad doesn't have the slightest inkling about this."

"I could move my wedding band to my left nostril and your father wouldn't notice. Neither has he caught on that every hospice day I prepare casseroles in advance…ones he especially likes, just in case I'm late."

"And he believes the meeting excuse? No questions asked?"

"None. If supper's a bit late, he happily gets another beer. But here's the bad part. Without going into detail, it happened. Both of us, married to someone else, slipped into a full-blown affair. Aren't you glad you asked?" Dorothy said, lowering her chin and raising her eyebrows.

Agog, Rick said, "Slipped? As in slipped between the sheets?"

Dorothy giggled in a giddy, girlish way as Rick hid his unease behind a mouthful of pancake and worried that if remorse wasn't yet stalking his mother, it soon would be.

"Being with Efner is like being in a peaceful meadow, filled with the scent of colourful wild flowers. It's as if we're in Rose's Church of Kananaskis."

Rick smiled, overdoing it. "How poetic. Has there always been a bard lurking within?" For the first time, Rick saw his mother as an attractive woman with thoughts and dreams far beyond her little family, but as Dorothy's tension subsided, his own grew. Haltingly, he said, "I'm happy for you, but scared. How long will this last…without getting caught, that is?"

"Whatever twists and turns lay ahead, I think Efner and I will last a long time. But please know that this isn't easy for me. I have my moments—difficult moments."

Rick twirled his fork in the air. "What's the age difference? Hope he's not old enough to be my grandfather."

Dorothy sighed. "It doesn't matter a hoot that he's eight years older than I am. At fifty-three, I'm attracted to different qualities from those I thought important at thirty."

Rick said, "I'll try to remember that if I'm attracted to a woman who's eight or ten years older. Still, I'm worried. Maybe even a bit scared."

Dorothy slowly circled the rim of her glass with her finger. Misty-eyed, she said, "That's understandable. I won't try to justify behaviour that, according to the Church, is flat out wrong. Sinful."

"But Mom! The so-called sanctity of marriage has kept you in a bad one for thirty years. Thirty years! Maybe betrayal is legitimate justice. Have you thought about that?"

"Yes, a big chunk of my life has been a constant struggle, all because I've been too afraid of God's judgment, the Church's judgment, my kids' judgment. I've spent so many years putting God, the Church, and family first that I almost lost track of who *I* was. Until Efner.

Silence fell heavy until Rick said, "People stray for different reasons. I suspect boredom is a big one, but years of disrespect and abuse certainly lead to affairs, right?"

"That they do," Dorothy said. "Your father has never physically abused me. No visible bruises, but constant verbal abuse is every bit as bad…never heals."

"I've seen it all—the years of insults and silent treatment when Dad would go for days without talking to you. Somehow I always trusted that you were both intelligent enough to solve your problems, but I now think intelligence isn't the key player in ruined relationships. What can I say? On the one hand, I'm glad you haven't let Dad stand in your way to happiness, but I'm also afraid he'll find out."

"Please, don't worry. I'm being careful." Dorothy leaned her head against the back of her chair. "I can't tell you how relieved I am—relieved that you aren't angry." With a faraway look in her eyes, she added, "Still, to be fair to your father, he does have moments of genuine kindness. I've seen him give spare change to the homeless, and he donates generously to our church and the Alzheimer's society. Here's something else—something you don't see. He *can* be affectionate with me."

"I'm guessing those moments are as rare as cat insomnia," Rick said, smiling wickedly.

Dorothy laughed uneasily and furtively observed the people at nearby tables who were obviously engaged in their own private conversations. "According to your father, I sometimes talk in my sleep, which terrifies me. What if, in the middle of the night, I sigh through Efner's name?"

"Don't worry, Mom. Dad will chock it up to a mangled vulgarity."

Dorothy laughed so loud she could've drawn the chef's attention. Then she crossed her arms in a manner that told Rick she was sliding into something else. "Your father made it through a difficult life. Growing up without the love of parents and having to practically raise Harry wasn't easy. Imagine the years of resentment he's harboured."

Certainly has a more generous understanding of Dad than I do. Rick vigorously scratched his head. "Maybe the abuse Dad heaped on me was a mere shadow of his own, but that's no excuse. Don't let him off the hook. Let's get back to you and Efner—much more intriguing. How's his marriage?"

Dorothy's voice faltered. "Efner claims his affair with me isn't the issue. Years of underlying problems led to his infidelity, but despite their ongoing struggle, he's going to give his marriage one more go."

"Does that mean your relationship with him is winding down?"

Dorothy sighed. "Perhaps, but I'm grateful for his emotional and physical affection even if tomorrow, it all ends. Even if we become only fruvers."

"Fruvers! Really?" Rick's chuckle turned serious. "Is that a momism?"

Dorothy grinned. "Efner's zany humour. Means more than friends, less than lovers. Good grief, am I really telling you all this? Must be something about you that brings it out in me."

"Mom, I'm honoured—sounds strange, but that's the word— honoured that you've let me see the real you. You're not the one-dimensional woman I took for granted over all these years. How many mothers would tell their children about their sexual affair, least of all their sons? It would've been sad not to know this special side of you, the joyful experience you've kept secret until now."

"My kind, thoughtful son, there's so much we don't know about family—things we deliberately keep hidden. But thanks to you, my worst secret's no longer festering." Dorothy closed her eyes, sighed, and leaned back in her chair.

"That's why we need more brunches," Rick said, checking the time on his phone. "We should probably leave soon but before we do, can I tell you about someone I've met?"

"Yes, yes, of course!" Dorothy's entire face lit up. "A new woman?"

Rick talked about meeting Liv and his agreement to help with her election campaign, then added, "You'll be happy to know she was raised Catholic. *Is* Catholic."

"Catholic and…her name sounds Norwegian," Dorothy said.

"Mm-hmm. Liv and Efner might be distant relatives. How strange *that* would be."

"Ask Liv if she knows how to roll out lefse—famous Norwegian flatbread that Efner brings to the hospice at Christmas. Or lutefisk—cod first soaked in lye. Apparently it tastes good, but stinks to high heaven."

"I'll ask Liv if she's heard of them."

"But Ricky, and this is very important, please don't utter a word to anyone about Efner and me. No one, including Liv."

"Trust me, not a word. Promise."

"If Liv asks how you know about lefse and lutefisk, just say they're traditional dishes your mom talked about. Or dishes you've read about."

"I'll figure it out. On another note, would you consider helping Liv win by door knocking with us?"

Dorothy shook her head, saying, "I wouldn't be good at that, and it's the last thing your father would want me to do…well, second last."

Rick's grin widened as he hailed the waitress and reached for his wallet. "Didn't think I'd be good at going door-to-door either, but it's easy. Interesting and fun. You'd come with Liv and me…watch at first. I know you'd be a natural."

"We'll see," Dorothy said, voice withering. She plunked two $20s on the table. "I absolutely insist on paying. Dad won't know. Call it my contribution to your therapy."

Rick started to protest, then simply said, "Thanks, Mom."

"I hope I haven't made things too awkward for you," Dorothy said. "Confided too much."

"Never!" Rick lightly tapped his fingers on the table. "Makes me realize the little crosses parents silently bear...pardon the biblical reference."

Dorothy pressed her hands together and tapped her fingertips. "We're so blessed to have each other."

Rick nodded. "Genetic bonanza, I'd say. Happy to share the winning ticket with you."

Dorothy payed the bill and Rick followed the willowy wisp of his mother to the exit. As he held the door for her, he glanced back at the room that now held special meaning.

Katie's Kitchen. Good for intimate brunches.

Chapter 7

Rick pulled into the driveway and pointed to the large bay window. "There's Dad, sitting in his usual chair, probably swilling beer and watching wrestling."

Dick was doing exactly that. For the past hour, he had continually checked the driveway for Dorothy's return, and when she stepped out of the car, he promptly opened the front door, tapped his watch, and shouted across the lawn, "Lard Jayzuz, woman, it's the middle of the afternoon. Are we having toast and Cheez Whiz for supper?"

"That voice; how I hate it! Told him before I left that I had dinner all planned."

"I'll come in with you," Rick said.

"Not a good idea. I can handle this."

"Okay, but don't take any crap. I'll go in the back door and listen at the landing. If Dad gets combative, I'll come in and defend you...not physically. Don't worry."

Where's my head? Of course he'll be combative. Rick scurried along the side wall to the back door and stopped on the landing, pressed his ear to the kitchen door, and listened for his father's interrogating voice.

"Kindly refresh my memory, madam. Why did you and Ricky exclude me from your private lunch?"

Rick heard the rattling of dishes, then everything went quiet. He imagined Dorothy standing in front of the cupboard, staring vacantly into it. More rattling. *She's probably reaching for that big metal mixing bowl,* Rick thought, his sensory memory flooded with the smell of pure vanilla drops being mashed into butter and flour.

"Well, Dorothy, do I need an appointment to get an answer?" Rick couldn't see his father slowly circling the kitchen table, shoulders stooped and hands tightly clasped behind his back, but he could hear his mother's emboldened voice—a voice that sounded like it belonged to someone else.

"Look! Ricky wanted alone time with me. That's all. Had nothing to do with you. Can't you understand that without getting all grouchy and suspicious."

"You'd be grouchy too if Ricky and I went for a three-hour lunch that excluded you."

"Haven't you noticed that he isn't comfortable around you? Why would he spend time with a father whose contempt sours everything?"

"Contempt! What about *his* contempt?"

Dorothy's confidence billowed. "You and Ricky need to have a sensible talk about Boxing Day because both of you are stuck in something dreadful. Have you even asked him how his therapy's going?"

"Listen, Dodo, I'll talk to him when I'm good and ready."

Rick cringed at his father's insulting nickname, one he'd heard only once, years ago when Dorothy backed into the front fender of Dick's truck.

"Listen, Dicko!" Dorothy said, cranking up the volume enough to create a little perturbation in the relationship they called marriage. "What are you going to do about your violent temper? Your anger's getting out of control. For too long, I've been tiptoeing around the insults you hurl at me…Dodo being the most recent example."

Rick felt like cheering wildly. *Didn't see that one coming. Mom's teaching Dad something different.*

"Shush!" Dick said. "Stop entertaining the neighbours. They'll think you've lost your senses."

Dorothy plunked herself down at the table. "I don't care what the neighbours think, here's what *I* think. You need professional help for your anger. Ricky's doing his part, why not do yours?"

Rick wanted to nudge the kitchen door open enough to confirm his new image of Dorothy: eyes radiating heat, hands on hips, solid stance.

In his gentler, baritone voice, Dick said, "Here's what I need help with. Today you went on a date with Ricky. Who'll it be tomorrow? Some hunk at the library? And who was behind that private call display the other night…the man who phoned and hung up?" Dick pulled a chair next to Dorothy and let his arm graze hers.

Rick heard the plea in his father's voice. *God help her if she stumbles into a veiled confession.*

"I want you to stop being so hard on Ricky," Dorothy said, half choking on her words. "He's a grown man with ideas of his own, but you treat him like you did when he was six years old. It hurts me that you can't see…won't accept the wonderful son we have. Even though you had a terrible childhood, that's no reason to be a heartless, cruel father."

"Heartless? Cruel?" Dick's voice sounded strangely forlorn. "That's unfair. Don't you see how Ricky turns everything I say into an argument? The only time he respects me, as in keeps his mouth shut, is in front of our employees."

Like a mother bear protecting her cub from a pack of wolves, Dorothy protested. "Respect? I've yet to see you give Ricky any. I'm glad he stands up to you, and it's high time I did the same. I don't question most things you say or do because I'm afraid of your anger, but I'm done with fear. Done with being quiet. In fact, I'll make a little noise right now."

Dick's voice took a sharp turn to sarcasm. "Ya got my full attention, madam."

Dorothy pressed on. "You need to quit drinking."

"And you need to quit blathering! The truth of the matter is, I'm in full control of my drinking!" Dick stomped to the fridge and reached for another beer. "The wrestling finals are on."

Rick waited a moment, then cautiously opened the kitchen door and thrust two thumbs up. In the loudest possible whisper, he said, "Bravo, Mom!"

Dorothy stopped at the end of the table and gave Rick her signature, little-kid farewell. She kissed the tips of her fingers, made two sweeping circles with her arm, and quietly said, "Catch a kiss," then flung her hand forward and added, "Mwah."

Liv's door-knocking team was having their coffee break and planning a marathon canvass when Rick, still somewhat preoccupied by the family drama, joined them. Lively chatter filled the corner of the room as Rick drafted a short press release that invited the media to walk, talk, and film Liv door knocking.

"Hey team, how's this title for next week's outing?" Rick asked. "Liv Janson Meets Mount Vista Residents."

Liv stared into space as Brittany shouted, "Nah. Needs some spice. How about 'Day of a Thousand Knocks'?"

People nodded enthusiastically. "Great title, Brittany!" Liv said, face glowing as she looked at the poll map on her phone. "Fifty more knocks should mark the end of another good day on the doors."

Rick sat staring at his feet until Liv nudged him. "You look a bit...lost."

"Too much on my mind. Need to head home soon."

"Hi there," said Dr. Knowles, motioning Rick to have a seat. "I remember you from our first class. What's your name, and are you a psychology major?"

Nice welcome—not what I expected, Rick thought, seating himself. "Rick Wright, English major. Psychology's appealing but I'm determined to be a writer. This semester, my Creative Writing assignment is a short story. No title yet, but my main character has a mind like the bed in the guestroom; always made up, seldom used. Is that a personality trait or what?"

A smile stretched across Dr. Knowles' face. "Quite the metaphor." He propped his feet on a small cabinet beside his desk and leaned back in his leather recliner. "Are you hoping Personality Theory will open our minds about those that are closed?"

"Yeah, my mind's open to that idea," Rick said, smiling in anticipation.

"Off the top," Dr. Knowles said, brushing a chunk of hair from his eyes, "perhaps what most separates open- from closed-minded people is those who can tolerate ambiguity, and those who can't. Those who need definite answers; those who don't."

Rick opened his laptop. "Do you mind if I make a note of that?"

"Not at all, but is that what you came to see me about?"

Half nodding, Rick evaded the direct question. "I'm pretty sure you're describing my father, who isn't stupid, but once his mind's made up, he refuses to see things any other way. Is that because he can't tolerate ambiguity? Whatever it is, he sounds dumber than he really is."

"I won't discuss your father since I don't know him, but I will say that closed-minded people aren't all intellectually dull, uneducated, or lazy. We'd be naive to assume they are. However, I think it's safe to assume that most of them don't value cognitive effort because…" Dr. Knowles peered into Rick's eyes and raised his bushy eyebrows.

Rick pondered the probe and ventured a guess. "Because they already know the truth about everything?"

"Good answer. Questioning their beliefs would cast doubt on what they know to be true, which makes them anxious because they'd have to confess, at least to themselves, that they might be wrong. As they see it, being wrong means they'd lose something they desperately need. Since you're on a roll, any thoughts on what they'd lose if they were wrong?" Dr. Knowles flashed an expectant smile.

"Beats me," Rick said.

"They'd lose social respect and dignity—both necessary for self-worth. Humans are social animals; they need reassurance that they're valuable members of the tribe."

Rick stared at a shelf crammed with bulging file folders kept in place by a hard copy of the *Diagnostic and Statistical Manual of Mental Disorders*. "Going back to cognitive effort for a moment, I'm thinking of someone who spends hours delving into conspiracy theories. Isn't that proof that he values cognitive effort?"

"Effort yes; values, no. We don't have the time or inclination to specialize in many big ideas, so we rely on the opinions of authority figures, especially those with emotional appeal. For years I've studied people who adopt beliefs without question—beliefs of authoritarian parents, perhaps, or leaders who don't value delving into more than one side of an argument. They love to cite studies on the Internet that haven't been tested by the scientific method—still the best way to approach truth despite cynics' attempts to devalue it."

Rick said, "On the other hand, a mind half open helps them get by…saves a lot of time."

Dr. Knowles smiled with a nod of recognition. "But, as theory goes, hasty generalizations become stereotypes that some people believe with absolute certainty. Stereotypes simplify the complex…they eliminate ambiguity and reduce free-floating anxiety. They also prevent more spacious conversations that could enhance knowledge. And personal relationships."

Rick took a few more notes, and said, "Simple-minded certainty. Hmm…would they prefer poems that rhyme? And concrete art like…say, a bowl of apples on a table? Nothing abstract—six-year-olds can do better."

Dr. Knowles gnawed on the end of a yellow highlighter. "I haven't considered their literary or artistic preferences, but social scientists have demonstrated that rigid, indisputable certainty readily finds a home in political tyrants and religious proselytizers. Certainty defines them. Certainty consoles them. Beyond a shadow of doubt, certainty will save them."

"Whew! Like Dad. When I ask him why he blindly accepts a belief, especially religious or political, he doesn't have a good answer."

"Unlike open-minded people who can tolerate ambiguity and discuss their inner contradictions, the closed-minded fervently latch onto beliefs that *feel* right, then instantly dismiss all opposing views as irrelevant or wrong…fake news in today's parlance. Absolute, self-righteous certainty is like an addictive drug. It feels good. Unfortunately, it also hijacks rational thought."

Rick's fingers attacked the keyboard like a swarm of flies on roadkill. He stopped and looked up. "Some of us are so sanctimonious, so intolerant of immigrants, the mentally ill, the poor…people unlike themselves. Is narrow-minded thinking hard wired?"

"Good question, the hardest kind to answer but the best place to start. Genes and biology aren't destiny, but it helps if babies come into this world with fairly consistent, balanced levels of neurochemicals. Some are born with excesses or deficits of neurotransmitters that predispose them to intense emotions like anxiety, depression, anger, or mania. If these children are then raised by authoritarian parents, they begin to view the world as frightening and punishing. Hostile and dangerous. Others grow up feeling relatively unflappable, safe, and optimistic."

"Ah, ha! I've heard that children are keen observers but poor interpreters."

Dr. Knowles said, "Yes, we'd hardly expect them to tell their authoritarian parents: Gee, Mom and Dad, if you use the threat of punishment to force your beliefs on me, I'll be chronically anxious, which will hijack my capacity for intelligent, open-minded thinking and I'll grow up spouting your closed-minded truths."

The two shared a good laugh and after the professor gave a few more nuggets to ponder, Rick said, "My father makes a spectacle of everything you've talked about."

"How so?"

"Can't stifle his need to educate people. Rambles on with so much detail about everything he has an opinion on that no one knows how to respond. And he's condescending…says things like, 'Oh, c'mon, the truth of the matter is….' Or how about this doozie, when people agree with him: Congratulations!"

"Excellent examples of how *not* to communicate," Dr. Knowles said. "Good communication bridges the gap of understanding between people; poor communication is the wobbly bridge that widens it."

"Shoot and reload—that's Dad's style. He shoots his spiel and appears to listen, but behind the scene he's reloading to lecture the person or shoot down their argument."

"Good metaphor for people who talk *at* others, not *with* them."

"He loves to rant about the Liberals…libtards, as he disdainfully calls them."

"Have you tried paraphrasing your father's ideas to show that you want to better understand him?

"Mm-hmm, I've tried summarizing his views, with empathy, but that only expands his free airtime to torturous lengths."

"What about searching for a common concern buried in your father's monologue? When he rails about the economy, for example, you could say: Yes, unpredictable economic swings worry me too. Might he feel less confronted? Less defensive?"

"I've also tried the common ground approach, but it isn't long before he segues into rapid-fire, extreme declarations about all the evils of money, the deep state, yada yada. He ends up offending, not impressing, me."

"Ah yes, we humans have an amazing capacity for self-importance and self-deception."

"What to do with the wreckage," Rick said, exhaling a long puff of air. "I remember a former prof who was so enamoured with her own research that one day in class, she sneered at a student who questioned her, and said, 'Surely you're not serious!' She might as well have added: you feebleminded moron. Someone, somewhere said that academic disciplines make progress one funeral at a time."

"There's a bit of truth to that. Some professors are worried that a collaboration of ideas would threaten their own…rob them of their need for respect and dignity. I say *need* because on a continuum, need is more urgent than preference, want, or desire. Need is anxiety driven. That's why—"

A colleague tapped on the door and announced, "Department meeting in two minutes."

Rick closed his laptop. "You have a meeting and I have a class." He stood and shook the professor's hand. "Thank you for your time. I'll consider everything you've said…and edit everything I've written."

"Glad you came by, Rick. Feel free to drop in anytime during office hours."

Over the lunch hour, Rick phoned Joy. He wanted to hear her lively personality, her confident, playful sass, and the direct, easy way she answered personal questions. He also wanted to test her sibling support, which he'd always assumed was tinged with the guilt of being her father's favourite child.

"Yo, Bro, what's up?"

"I'm staring out a corner window killing time in the library," Rick began, but Joy interrupted.

"And I'm catching up on housework," she said, breathlessly. "Good to hear from you. I've got a story to tell. I know you don't like gossip but—"

"Gossip's useful if it teaches us to reconsider our own behaviour, assuming we're tolerant enough to learn—"

"Forget it. What's on your mind?"

"Sorry, I'm being pedantic."

"The word pedantic is pedantic," Joy giggled, "but let's not fuss about it."

"Come to think of it, my therapist said it takes a lifetime to see and say the simple things."

Joy paused a moment and said, "You sound…melancholy. Are you lonely?"

"Not really. Need a break from a heady meeting with my psych prof." Rick highlighted a couple points from his visit, then described the *Spotlight* fiasco with Liv, downplaying his emotional hangover. Unable to interpret Joy's silences, he recalled how, in his early adolescence, she urged him to embrace the Church rather than leave it.

"The most intense argument we ever had was when I told you Catholicism was a pack of lies," Rick said. "You accused me of not listening to you; not respecting our differences of opinion. Remember?"

"Yep, I remember saying how arrogant you were."

"Sheesh! I probably was, but help me out, Sis, because here's what I don't get. Why do intelligent women like you, Mom, and Liv stay loyal...no, *devoted* to a Church that doesn't practice what it preaches?"

"I know how you feel about the Catholic Church, so let's not rehash that stale argument. After our last trek through the Bible, I felt crappy. As hard as this is for you to understand, when I'm in church, the glory of God's presence inspires me to be more loving and kind, more peaceful within. It's impossible to explain, but I think you get it because you told me how moved you were when you visited the Notre Dame cathedral in Paris."

"You mean that bit about statues looking like they could come alive any moment and shake my hand? And Renaissance paintings with eyes staring down at me as if waiting for a confession?"

"Yeah, and Handel's Messiah. You said it moved you to tears...made you feel connected to humanity from all the ages."

"I remember that well," Rick said. "But do you remember your reaction when I said nothing inspired me to believe the Bible is the word of God? Says who?"

Joy snapped, "Hey! We're doing it again! I'm beginning to think you're obsessed with the evils of religion. Did you call because you're feeling bad about your argument with Liv and want me to agree with you?"

"Not in so many words. Anyway, Liv and I made up over coffee, so forget it."

As if she hadn't heard Rick's last comment, Joy said, "Please try believing this about Mom, Liv, and me. Being Catholic doesn't mean we're dumber than a tube of lipstick."

"Okay, okay," Rick said, listening for that familiar, unforgettable clucking sound Joy makes when she's distracted or annoyed.

"How's it going with you and Al? Give me the straights."

"We're good. Why that question now?"

"Just watched a woman push a stroller through the campus and thought how good it'd be if you and Al gave me a little niece or nephew to dote on."

"Must confess we argue about it from time to time but that's as far as we get. We love each other, but we both have histories of failed romances. His last was explosive, and remember Karl and me? So dictatorial, and if anyone knows what *that* means, you and I do."

"Totally!" Rick said. "I remember when Mom made you a nice birthday dinner and at the table, you started describing some study on aging and Karl sarcastically said, 'Listen up, everyone. *Joy* has something to say, and dear *Joy* is going to *university*!' Then he made that sickening, beckoning motion for you to continue."

"You winked at me from across the table, and Mom urged me to carry on as if I hadn't heard him. Thank God I woke up and left…without giving you a little niece or nephew to dote on."

"At least you had the courage to leave before that happened. How many people hang in there, thinking they can change their partner?"

Joy said, "Some begrudgingly put up with years of constant nagging—"

"They convince themselves they could never leave," Rick said. "for financial reasons, or they dread being alone. Maybe they fear their kids—even grandkids—will disown them."

"Or God will punish them," Joy added. "They stick it out to the bitter end. With Al and me, shift work and living apart solves most problems—gives us time and space to reconsider petty complaints, then woohoo! We reignite the romance next time we're together. Distance and kindness—good enough for me. Plenty good enough."

"Problem is men like me don't understand matters of the heart. Early crap gets in the way."

"Yep. Relationships…close ones are all a bit sticky. Are you talking about that in therapy? How's it going?"

"Can't put my finger on why it's working, but Dr. Grey's different from anyone I've known. Has a way about her. She listens."

"Gets big bucks to listen."

"It's more than listening. She seems to genuinely care."

"Gets big bucks for that too. How do you know she's sincere?"

"I don't, but it *feels* genuine. Listening is caring. Understanding. She helps me see things differently. Wish Dad had the guts to give therapy a go."

"Way too, way too," Joy said, as Rick visualized her swishing her hand back and forth in her usual manner. "Dad likely won't change, but remember this…for always and ever. You have me and Mom. We'll love you, no matter what."

"Ah, thanks, Sis. You and Mom…my best support system. Love you both. I've got another class in ten."

"Have a good one! Glad you called."

"It's been a joy, sister!"

After their Creative Writing class, Rick and Gabe did the usual—strolled into The Den and found a quiet table near the back.

"Have you given Doc Knowles the pleasure of your company yet?" Gabe asked, ogling two lively, attractive students who walked past their table.

"Yes, and guess what! I've done a 180 on him. You're right. The guy's good—damn good. Gave me most of his office hour, and lots to think about…stuff I can apply to fictional characters. And Dad."

"I thought you'd like him. Can I ask what you talked about?"

"Pig-headed people in general. Listen to this copy of a scene from the book Knowles is writing." Rick pulled a piece of paper from his backpack and waved it in front of Gabe.

"Lay it on me," Gabe said.

Rick opened his binder as Gabe, who'd heard many stories about Rick's tempestuous father, flashed back to a few months ago when he had picked up Rick to show off his new, second-hand car. Dick had stepped out on the porch to take a look, and when Gabe walked over to say hello, he told Dick that Rick was the brains in his class. Dick said that he hadn't seen any proof of that, a retort Gabe kept to himself.

Rick waved the scenario Dr. Knowles had written. "Get a load of this! Knowles asked me to imagine, *vividly* imagine, Dad calling me into the living room tonight."

Gabe leaned back and closed his eyes. "I've got the picture…you and your dad."

Rick read the scenario as if he were in New York, auditioning for a leading role in a Broadway play.

"Ya know what? I'm beginning to think I'm quite closed-minded. Maybe if I were less uptight and definite about everything, I wouldn't get so pissed off with people who won't admit that I'm right and they're wrong. After all, what's so wrong with being absolutely wrong? And what's so right with being absolutely right? Maybe there's a lot wrong with being absolutely right. If everyone lightened up, we might be easier on ourselves. And others. More open to different ideas."

Gabe burst out laughing and said, "Holy fuck, man! There'll be traffic lights in the Sahara before our dads say something like that."

The two of them hooted like old buddies reminiscing around a campfire. "Far-fetched, yeah," Rick said, "but it makes the point that people like Dad are too busy trying to impress everyone with their knowledge that they don't see how they turn people off…and get what they least want—the big brush off. Zippo respect."

"Why is admitting we're wrong such a big deal?" Gabe said.

"Doc Knowles said it's because people whose identities are tied to being right would see being wrong as a shameful blow to their insatiable egos. We could ask them what kind of evidence it would take to change their minds, and if they said something like 'Absolutely nothing; my mind's made up,' we'd have a good idea of *how* they think, which is more important than *what* they think or believe."

Gabe thought for a moment. "I could ask Dad that when he goes on about how everyone hates cops. Or the lack of respect he gets from the rest of the force when he pushes for the return of capital punishment. Then again, I might just do the usual— change the topic or make a lame excuse to leave. Can't argue with a stone."

"Yeah, but there's a big difference between your dad and mine. Daddy Dick is out-and-out abusive, but I've said all I need to about that. Here's something else Knowles suggested: try questioning strong words they use that suggest extreme thinking. Simply repeat words like: Everyone? Nothing? Always? Never? Who knows, in the privacy of their closed minds, our dads might think about what we've said."

Gabe bit into a mouthful of yam fries. "Hey, what's that student's name...the magnet in the front row? Burgundy hair—one side's shaved, the other hangs down her back. Sandals and heavy socks in the dead of winter. Always looks happy."

"Haven't a clue who you're talking about," Rick answered, then asked Gabe about his Creative Writing assignment.

Gabe's eyes shone. "I'm writing about Rex, a mangy street dog Dad brought home from Police Services a few days ago." He began sketching the comical plot, then stalled for words.

"I like it; tell me more," Rick said, then sat back and did what any good citizen of the world would do. He listened. Fully listened.

As the two of them devoured the daily special, Gabe said, "Enough on that. What's up with you and your dad?"

"We're backsliding," Rick said to his empty pint glass. "I'm trying new ideas from the two Docs in my life, but everything's still gloomy. Fuckin' gloomy."

Having had one beer on a full stomach, and feeling restless, Rick stopped in at Joe's Bar on his way home. As he walked through the parking lot, he noticed Billy-Bob coming out the door.

"Hey, Billy-Bob. Happy New Year and all," Rick shouted, sprinting towards him. "How's it goin'?"

Billy-Bob looked like he'd been accosted by a robber. "Oh, it's *you*," was all he deigned to say.

"Apologies for my preachy sermon a few weeks ago. University students...a little education turns us into pompous assholes. Beer's on me next time...let's talk hockey, or movies."

Billy-Bob flipped the hood of his worn parka over his head and mumbled, "Whatever."

Chapter 8

Rick strode into Dr. Grey's office, awash in a mysterious glow. "I have a new memory for my old age."

Dr. Grey opened her hands to Rick. "Something remarkable happened?"

"Remarkable first timer for me! I carelessly traversed three lanes of traffic and cut off a large transport truck. The driver leaned on his horn and, at the next red light, slowed to a stop alongside me. His piercing glare could've honed a butcher's knife."

"Then what?"

"I put my hands together and bowed in a mea culpa, but he shook his head furiously and gave me the finger. You'd be proud of what I did…turned up the volume on my car radio and for the remainder of an interminably long traffic light, rested in pleasant but unfamiliar territory, as if I were someone else sitting behind the wheel, calmly waiting out the traffic light. I'll take myself there next time Dad pisses me off."

"The next time you *let* him piss you off?" Swiveling her chair, Dr. Grey softly added, "Can he make you angry without your permission?"

"Well, okay, but I didn't give that truck driver permission." Looking smug, Rick leaned back and patted the arm of his chair.

"A+ in Applied Psychology," Dr. Grey said.

"More good news. Since the *Spotlight* spectacle with Liv, we've reconnected and, to my surprise, she's tossed her hat in the political ring…the one that circles the constituency I live in. She's exceptionally determined to win, and I'm exceptionally determined to help her."

"Today, you're cheerful and confident—quite different from last week."

"Last week I was dead; this week I'm alive." Rick paused and added, "I'll now dial back the melodrama."

"A rapprochement with Liv?" Dr. Grey said, knowing Rick's fondness for her…and for bookish words.

"Mm-hmm. She'd reread my apology for slagging the Catholic Church and texted an invitation for coffee. That's when she told me about her campaign, and I agreed to door knock. Later, I worried that she'd manipulated me into canvassing."

"Did you enjoy being part of her team?"

"Yes. Meeting strangers at the door was less intimidating than I had imagined, and I felt good doing something for Liv and the people she wants to represent."

"If you enjoyed yourself, were you manipulated?"

Rick toyed with the idea. "Interesting way to look at it. Still, I wish I knew if she feels the same about me as I do her. Thoughts of heartache and sorrow never leave me. Stupid, eh?"

"First heartache, then stupidity—a double whammy. What will you tell yourself if Liv makes it clear she doesn't want a romantic relationship?"

"I'll tell myself it's…unfortunate. That's all—unfortunate and disappointing. No more torturing myself. Are you preparing me for the worst or testing me on last week's therapy lesson?"

"Perhaps a little of both. I truly hope things work out for you and Liv."

"Thanks. I'm optimistic," Rick said nervously, then quickly segued into a description of the brunch date with his mother, and his father's uncharacteristic, sensitive reaction to Dorothy's assertiveness.

"Your dad was honest and vulnerable toward your mom?"

"Yes, but he soon veered to tough talk…as if any show of sensitivity or gentleness scares him. Emotions are enemy number one. What you said about not being able to sustain contact is bang on. He's skittish."

"What if, deep down, your father is worried that your mom's growing assertiveness threatens their marriage? What if he's also worried that his brother incurred the wrath of God by not going to Christmas Eve mass? Is that possible?"

Rick fumbled for an answer. "I doubt it. Dad's too busy fighting his war against the world to worry about such things. When he's around, it feels like the whole family is mired in a deep trench—the Wright family's Maginot Line."

"A sad story. Perhaps showing his true feelings would expose or embarrass him. Anger is a safe place to hide. A way to save face."

"Whatever it is with Dad, I don't give a damn."

"You don't give a damn? I thought you wanted to understand him."

Rick squinted hard. "I'm so tired of trying to figure him out. It's too…exhausting."

Dr. Grey said, "Throughout our sessions, I've sensed an ambivalence about your dad, which is understandable given your personal history, but I wonder if there's something else you aren't comfortable saying."

Rick's mind had creatively wandered elsewhere. "I have an image of Dad standing alone on the shore of a small island shouting to everyone he cares about as they sail away: Come back! Come back!"

"A heart-wrenching image," Dr. Grey said. She waited, then broke the lengthy silence. "I'd like to hear more about you, Rick…a man who values self-reflection. Insight."

Rick said, "Why else would I pay for therapy?" He leaned back in his chair. "Apologies. That was brusque. But I'm curious, why *do* people pay for therapy?"

"They have their own reasons. Some just want to talk to a therapist who'll listen; others want confirmation of their specialness, or reassurance that somebody or everybody else is wrong. Many have inner contradictions that burden them with chronic anxiety or guilt about all the things they should've or shouldn't have done…or said. Others are searching for meaning in their lives."

"I'm cool with the idea that there is no meaning in life except the one we give it." Rick twisted his upper torso and hoped for some show of appreciation. "But I wonder how many of us are philosophic enough to ask the question, much less take the journey?"

"I'd rather not count people short, but here's what most of my clients have in common—crushing loneliness. Bewildering disconnection."

Rick searched for the meaning behind Dr. Grey's enigmatic facial expression. "You've been responsible for so many people over the years. How do you keep sane?"

"I don't take responsibility for my clients. If I took responsibility for those who get better, I'd have to take responsibility for those who get worse. At best, I'm an optometrist who hands them different pairs of glasses. They fill their own prescription."

"So, I alone correct my impaired vision?"

"Mm-hmm, a correction that makes peace with your contradictions. What are you at war with?"

Rick stalled for an answer. "Anger. Judgment. Myself."

"From your perspective, anger and judgment are your problems. Your battlegrounds. From my perspective, anger and judgment are mistaken solutions for a deeper problem."

Rick scratched his temple as if digging for the right words. "Stinkin' thinkin'—wasn't that what you said my main problem was? Mine and everyone else's?"

Dr. Grey smiled radiantly. "Yes, but please keep in mind that when I talked about reasonable and unreasonable thinking, I wasn't referring to people with psychotic disorders like schizophrenia and bipolar disorder, which you obviously don't have. Who decides whether the thoughts that drive *your* anger and criticism are reasonable?"

Rick answered carefully. "I do. I decide."

Nudging him deeper, Dr. Grey gently asked, "Have your major decisions helped get you what you want?"

"Course not. I simply want Dad to respect me. Love me. I'm his son, and I'm doing the best I can despite my limitations...and his disappointments."

Dr. Gray nodded deeply, as if commenting would add clutter. Following another lengthy pause, she said, "Not being able to accept one's own son *is* a major limitation."

"Mm-hmm. How am I supposed to accept *that*?"

Dr. Grey said, "How are you supposed to accept your dad's inability to love and respect you the way you want him to? Maybe he can't, for his own reasons."

Rick stretched and crossed his lanky legs then looked up at Dr. Grey who seemed to him like she was in her own world. "Before I forget," he said, "I was thinking about Mom's mother, my Grandma Davidson, when I left your office last week. After every bedtime story she told Joy and me, she'd close the book, look over her silver rimmed glasses, and say, with a twinkle in her eye, 'Now remember, my Grandies, this story isn't over.' I can still hear the sound of her voice, like a lullaby. But I didn't grasp the meaning of her comment until I was much older."

"Ah, those wise Grandmas. Yours lingers in the background in case you need her. And now? What does her story ending mean now?"

Rick took his time answering. "Our lives are little odysseys of trials and triumphs, then death snatches it all away. From the time I was a little kid, Dad made my life a series of trials…a long, sad story that isn't over."

"Trials that you've survived. Did you…do you ever feel triumphant?"

"Now that I'm older, I let Dad win the mini battles so I can win the major war by cornering him with logic. Must confess, I've enjoyed my little victories, but I'm beginning to see how much I lose by winning."

"If you changed, you'd leave those victories behind."

"Maybe that's what my ghoulish nightmare was about the other night." Rick told Dr. Grey about wandering through a cemetery and stumbling on his own grave.

"Lying in a sarcophagus…hmm," Dr. Grey said. "Symbolically, it could mean you're dead or dying. Emotionally cold. Socially suffocating."

Rick cleared the lump in his throat. "Ah, here comes the deep psychoanalysis."

Dr. Grey leaned back and massaged her neck. "I'm not big on dream interpretation. I'd rather ask you straight out how a lifetime of father-son drama influenced you; your career choice, for example."

"Strange as it sounds, I've wondered if writing novels about other people's conflicts would move my own to a bigger stage. Is that what you mean?"

"Yes, and a bigger audience. The artistic, gentle side of you wants to be a writer. What about the spirited side?"

Rick stared at a small hole in the heel of his stocking. "My embattled side wants to fight its own little war on an imaginary battleground. Conquer it by writing about it."

"Very insightful. Yesterday's choices help us understand today's. I've seen clients become exhilarated when they react differently to troublesome situations."

After a moment's reflection, Rick said, "I've waited a lifetime for Dad to love me. On Boxing Day, I abandoned all hope at the dinner table, and I've since wondered if I provoked his attack to justify hating him. Justify retaliating."

Dr. Grey arched one eyebrow. "Was justice delivered?"

"No. A load of guilt was delivered. And haunting flashbacks." He pressed his fists to his temples and began to tremble.

Dr. Grey waited. In hushed tones, said, "Loss and regret are painful."

Rick wiped his eyes with the sleeve of his sweater and choked on his words. "These are tears of shame, Doc. Shame and disgust!" He reached for a tissue on the table. "Like I've said before, I wish I could...I wish I could love Dad, but I can't. I just can't. There've been times when I wished he'd drop dead."

"As a kid, you never felt good enough. Wasn't it natural to protect yourself from your father's abuse by hating him?"

"But...well, didn't I also tell you that Dad has some good points."

"Ah, yes, you did, so hate is perhaps too extreme. Still, something's stopping you from feeling less bitter?"

"*He* is, dammit! Drives me crazy." Rick sighed and immediately corrected himself. "Oops! Someone taught me last week that no one can drive me crazy. My inappropriate beliefs and words do that…single-handedly."

Dr. Grey smiled and said, "Your facial expression changed as you said that, and I've noticed something else—something quite remarkable. Your father's always with you. He's with both of us now, here in this room."

"Not in a good way, and I resent that. Didn't you say in one of our sessions that if we understand why people behave the way they do we're less likely to let them upset us? I wonder what you think of Dad now that I've given you more background information about him. About us."

"My sketchy impression of him is someone who likely felt insecure and anxious as a child. A lonely little kid without deep, loving relationships."

"Lately, that's how I'm trying to see him—an anxious, child-like adult."

"Perhaps he's learned to fear intimacy because it threatens too much need."

Fuck, this isn't easy. "I don't get it—the threatening too much need part."

"For people with histories like your father's, needing others symbolizes pain. Best bury it. Perhaps what your dad most needs from you is that which he most fears…intimacy."

"And that which I can't give. Sheesh, that's a lot of guilt to unpack!"

Dr. Grey forced her shoulders back like a soldier ready for inspection. For a moment, Rick thought she either didn't know what to say or simply felt uncomfortable.

"Except for heinous crimes, I'm not big on guilt," Dr. Grey said. "How about replacing it with softer, kinder regret? Can you imagine regretting your behaviour?"

"I like that. Regret…and forgiveness."

"Not big on forgiveness either," Dr. Grey said. "Forgiveness is based on judgment; in some cases, self-righteous condemnation of someone.

Instead of forgiving people, getting angry again, forgiving them again…round and round it goes, I'd rather work at understanding them. Then again, maybe I'm too picky about the meaning of the word."

Rick's eyes were brimming. "But you're a psychologist. Understanding comes easier for you than the rest of us."

"Possibly, but compassion and kindness are important too, if that doesn't sound too pious." Dr. Grey lifted the water jug, filled two glasses on the table and passed one to Rick, who said, "Before I booked my first appointment with you, I asked Dad to consider a joint counselling session—family therapy. His reaction was swift…vulgar and dismissive. Then I realized that if he's so certain he's right about everything, the very thought of therapy would imply he's wrong." Rick looked pleased with himself.

"Good point," Dr. Grey said. "But aren't there times when we all close our minds to understanding different ideas? Myself included? You?"

Rick gave a slow nod of recognition. "I'm convinced I'm quite right about Catholicism—but I might be wrong." Rick shook his head as if to ask: what did I just say? "If I'm too certain about religion, or anything else, it's because I've learned it from Dad."

"Oh, I see. It's all *his* fault?"

From the tone of Dr. Grey's question, Rick assumed she didn't like his answer to her question; judged it badly.

"Okay, that's a copout," Rick said, voice fading. "I'm the one to blame."

Without hesitation, Dr. Grey replied, "Now it's all *your* fault? Are you going to feel guilt-ridden about that?"

Scalding comment. Can't win. With renewed energy and a whiff of indignation, he said, "Not guilty. Plain and simple."

Dr. Grey relaxed her facial muscles as Rick sank in his chair and stared out the window at his close friend—pitch-black darkness.

"I'm thinking there might be regret on both sides," Dr. Grey said.

Rick's head dropped. He swiped his hand across his forehead. "Too much to process…need to decompress." He walked to the window and stared out at the traffic below. Dr. Grey waited until he returned and settled into his soft chair.

"Today, we're halfway through six sessions," she said. "What thoughts have you had about our time together? What's been helpful? What hasn't?"

Not wanting to be misunderstood, Rick again deliberated. "Early on, I questioned the usefulness of therapy, but I now think it would be riskier to drift along hoping that, by chance, a special someone would rescue me. Someone who'd make my life easier and happier."

"Interesting fiction, your serendipitous someone. How would that help you?"

"It wouldn't," Rick said emphatically. "I'd be endlessly stuck where I am."

"Were you hoping I'd be that someone who'd rescue you? Always support you? Avoid the hard conversations?"

"No. Maybe. I dunno. Too many words bouncing around in my head…searching for sensible sentences."

"Change is stressful," Dr. Grey said, "but over time, repeating the familiar might be even more stressful than trying something new, which is why I'll question that which I think is keeping you stuck."

Rick breathed so deeply his nostrils narrowed. "I'm trying to put the pieces together but they're all broken…nothing fits."

Dr. Grey checked the wall clock. "I don't think they're broken, but I'd like us to work a bit more at piecing them into an integrated portrait of Rick Wright. This was a heavy session. I was provocative."

"For sure." Rick slid to the edge of his chair. "Cognitive calisthenics," he said, with a curt nod, then reached for his jacket. "Where do we go from here?"

"Round four next week?" Dr. Grey asked.

Rick flashed an infectious grin. "Are we talking boxing? Golf?"

Dr. Grey volleyed. "Par for the course!"

"See you in a week," Rick said, smiling through half a wave and salute.

Driving home in light traffic, he thought about Dr. Grey's demeanour—*attentive, challenging, pensive, serene. Does she have an intimate partner? Do they enjoy each other's company? Sex? Silliness? No. Sharp wit."*

Later that evening as he worked his way through the last of his store-bought roast chicken and Greek salad, Rick made a few notes for his therapy file and drafted another short story scene. An evening of mild restlessness had left him feeling pleasantly exhausted.

Curious, amusing restlessness—maybe that's the good life.

Rick poked his head out from under his duvet and yelled, "Who is it?"

"Who else would come knocking at this time of day? The tooth fairy?"

Rick cringed at the sound of his father's inimical voice. *What will he go on about now? I don't have the energy to deal with him.*

Another loud knock. "Bad news, Ricky."

"One sec!" Rick stepped into his pants, opened the door, and tried but couldn't manage a smile. "What's wrong?"

Dick assumed his usual pose: hands on hips, chin and shoulders braced for attack. "You left your lights on. Battery's nearly dead."

"Dim like me this time of day. Thanks for noticing."

From the front porch, Dick watched as his son tried to start the crippled engine. When the Mustang gave a dying gasp, he shouted, "Can't flog that dead horse. My jumper cables are in the garage. Give me a minute and I'll boost the old nag."

Dead battery, new beginning? Amazing, Rick thought. *Dad's starting the day like a normal, civilized father.*

Dick attached the jumper cables and when the V8 snorted back to life, Rick lowered the car window and yelled, "Thanks, Dad. Can I buy you breakfast at Katie's Kitchen? I'll meet you there."

Dick dropped the hood. "Save your money," he said, walking toward Rick. "There's a big pot of fresh coffee in the kitchen and toasted blueberry bagels always hit the spot with me." Jerking his head toward the house, he added, "C'mon in and have breakfast with Mom and me."

"You sure? Not Katie's Kitchen? The old mare needs a good run."

"Let 'er run where she is. See you inside."

Confident that his father's counter-offer meant reconciliation, Rick sprinted up the front steps and into the kitchen where he affectionately hugged his mother. "I offered to take Dad to Katie's Kitchen…my way of thanking him for boosting the battery, but he insisted I come in for breakfast. Imagine that!"

"How nice! Dad's in a good mood. Maybe he's thought about a few things, and maybe now's the time to tell him Marg and I will door knock with you and Liv." Dorothy immediately texted Marg as Rick reached for a coffee mug.

"Wonder how he'll react when you tell him you're going to help the Liberal Party…he hates to have you out of sight." Rick winked and added, "How foolish of him."

Dorothy giggled and covered her mouth like a young schoolgirl sharing secrets. "Shh. He's stomping up the back steps."

Dick ambled into the kitchen. "Got an extra bagel for Ricky?" he asked, rattling the keys in his pocket.

Dorothy playfully shook the bag of bagels and put another one in the toaster, then smiled alluringly at her husband. "Ricky and I were just talking about a top-notch Liberal candidate, Liv Janson, who's running in our constituency for the upcoming election. We're going door knocking with her."

Dick heaved a guttural sigh and stared at his foot as if fungus had sprouted through his socks. "God help us," he bristled, "the lady of the house is dead serious about helping the pinko party." He walked over to the counter and poured himself a coffee.

Dorothy looked at her phone, then Rick. "Marg just replied that she'll door knock with us this weekend."

"Fantastic, Mom!" Rick said, with enough enthusiasm to straighten the ruffles on the kitchen curtains.

Dorothy put a plate of toasted bagels on the table, sat down beside Rick, and looked at her husband. "The Liberals are fighting for the up and coming generation and I want to help our candidate win."

Dick took his usual seat at the head of the table, reached for a bagel and, in a quieter voice, said, "You've changed, Dorothy. You're swirling down the drain on me. A stranger in my house…my bed and arms. What's come over you?"

"Maybe I'm just being forthright and honest for a change," Dorothy said.

Ignoring the poetic sadness in his father's voice, Rick said, "Don't have a coronary casualty over us door knocking for a pinko—a slur on all Liberals who believe strong social programs *and* equally strong business communities are important for a healthy society. Liv Janson—"

Rick might as well have stomped on a wasp's nest.

"Don't preach to me about libtards," Dick bellowed through a spray of spittle. "And don't you dare bring a scrap of literature into this house. No goddamn lawn signs either. The neighbours don't need to know that *some* people in this family have gone to the dark side. As for me, I'll vote Conservative. Mallore's the only guy who can solve all our economic problems."

Rick struggled to stay calm. "The *only* guy who can solve *all* those problems? What kind of evidence would it take for you to even consider voting Liberal?"

"Nothing. You're outta your mind if you think I'd do something that stupid!"

Dick's blistering reply affirmed Rick's new learning. To stifle his frustration, he did what he often did—stepped over to the kitchen window and stared out at the sobering Rockies. *Dad can't talk about Liberals without a gob of foam narrowing the corners of his mouth.* He turned and faced his father. "Point taken, Dad. I'm done." To Rick's surprise and immeasurable relief, Dick filled his coffee thermos, picked up the other half of his bagel and, with a patronizing smile, said, "Carry on you two. Time for me to hit the road."

"Thanks for the battery boost," Rick said, quite sincerely.

Dick didn't reply and when Rick heard the front door close, he leaned toward his mother and said, "I'm so glad you held your ground. An adventure into political activism will be fun…think what you can tell Efner."

Dorothy grinned and said, "Regardless of what I tell Efner, it's time to step up and fight for a better province. I've been too politically complacent—an easy out that gets us nowhere. Well, truth be told, I've been too scared to politically disagree with your father."

Rick thrust his fist in the air and shouted, "Right on, Momma!" then hugged Dorothy and slipped out the door. En route to the university, he silently thanked Efner for the powerful influence he's had on his mother's growing assertiveness and independence.

What love can do, Rick thought. *Romantic love—the all-embracing agony and ecstasy; the pride and humility.*

That afternoon in Rick's Political Science class, the professor said, "Historically, presidents and prime ministers driven by power and dominance have extended their reach to colonize nations that posed no immediate or foreseeable threat to their own. Authoritarian leaders, including some teachers and parents, need to aggressively control others. Reminds me of a recent family gathering when a relative of mine said, 'Some kids just need a good whuppin'!'"

Collective sighs rippled throughout the classroom.

"Only a century ago," said the prof, scanning his students, "your sighs would've been replaced by nods of agreement. In *The Authoritarian Specter*, a Canadian psychologist, Bob Altemeyer, cites his research that shows adults who score high on his Right-wing Authoritarian Scale significantly agree with this statement: Obedience and respect for authority are the most important virtues children should learn."

Rick made an addendum to his class notes: *Evolution hasn't stamped out the rot. Laws help, but….*

Later that week, Rick was thrilled when Gabe said he'd "check out the scene" at the Students for Alberta Liberals meeting. They had often talked politics over a beer and a bite, but neither had ever been politically active. That all changed when they met the following Friday in a far corner of The Den, and the SAL group coordinator asked members to introduce themselves. Waiting for someone to speak up, Brittany looked directly at Rick.

"I'm Rick Wright, English major, here on behalf of Liv Janson, the candidate for the university's constituency. She and her team are revved up and I'm hoping to recruit a few volunteers to help her win with a clear majority."

Gabe arrived, introduced himself, and pulled up a chair beside Brittany, who said, "Earlier, a few of us reviewed the university's political boundaries and talked about Liv Janson—a strong candidate in a winnable constituency."

Rick had the energy of a toddler with a new toy. "Liv's campaign has organized The Day of a Thousand Knocks for tomorrow afternoon, one o'clock. Best part, beer and pizza after. She needs all of us. Who's in?"

Brittany and four others readily volunteered, and Rick gave the group the campaign office's address and John's contact information.

"Great location," Brittany said, "she'll have people walking in from the street to volunteer."

Rick texted Liv: *At students' meeting in The Den. Animated! Bringing at least four volunteers tomorrow.* He then placed an order for two large nachos, which the group savoured over political strategizing that later drifted into socializing about various student concerns. Through it all, Rick's thoughts strayed to Liv and the exciting campaign that lay ahead.

The group exchanged contact information and as they walked out together, Brittany said, "Remember, layered clothing!"

Outside, Rick inhaled deeply and recalled an echo from the not-so-distant past. "Ah, the fresh, pure fragrance of winter air."

Chapter 9

A theatre of optimism had taken centre stage at the campaign office as Rick introduced Liv to Brittany and three other students who arrived for the door-knocking blitz.

John walked over to greet the new volunteers. He nudged Brittany and said, "Glad to see you're ready for another round of canvassing."

"Ready with bandages...for bleeding knuckles," Brittany joked. Glossy strands of raven black hair spiralled down from her red toque, nicely complementing her flawless complexion and prominent, dark eyes.

John held out his hands. "Let's do a pre- and post-knuckle test," he said, flirtatiously examining Brittany's knuckles. Liv, Rick, and Gabe looked pleasantly amused when Brittany said, "By the end of today, these knuckles will be flaming red."

As the group chatted lightheartedly, Rick noticed Gabe staring at Brittany, trance-like. He tapped Gabe's shoulder and whispered, "Has Brittany transported you to that mysterious zone that melts men's hearts and primes the male anatomy?"

Gabe leaned into Rick. "Those Bambi eyes are mighty appealing... let's just say my male anatomy is aroused, but my romantic heart's frozen. Don't get ideas, man."

"Ah hah! That's what we all say until *it* happens. Then we're goners...making out like bunnies and performing random acts of kindness. Give Brittany a try."

"Hey, life's never that simple. I can't just toss Sally out like so much wilted lettuce. We've had a lengthy run at it."

"Didn't mean to be insensitive," Rick said, sounding contrite.

"Captain Brittany," John announced, "the boundaries for Poll 8 are ready for download."

Brittany waited for the poll information as her team familiarized themselves with the sizeable wall map and gathered bundles of pamphlets and lawn signs. To Liv's delight, newly retired MLA Dean Shields strolled in, giving credibility to her campaign. A family physician and former government appointed medical officer, Shields had been arbitrarily fired for criticizing government policy—an injustice that prompted a public outcry and moved Shields from the field of medicine onto national TV screens and into the jaws of politics.

"Lovely to have you join us, Dr. Shields," said Liv. "Let me introduce you to my volunteers."

"Just call me Dean," Shields said.

Rick noticed his lanky frame, wavy brown hair, and weathered face, which he imagined fully bearded and crowned with a black, silk top hat. "Lincoln reincarnated," he whispered to Liv, having slipped in beside her.

At the first few constituents' doors, Liv watched as Shields, within seconds, had residents leaning into the door jamb, talking politics. She marvelled at his conversation skills, which she fervently hoped to emulate.

Rick had also observed Shields, now lagging behind the other volunteers. *How does he so easily engage constituents?* he wondered. *Next time, I need to be paired with him.*

When the team broke for coffee, Rick turned to Shields. "As reputation has it, you work magic on the doors. What's your secret?"

Shields smiled and addressed the group. "Ask, then listen—with an open-mind."

"I'll include that in my speaking guidelines," John said.

"Students, seniors, the unemployed, single moms—they all have different concerns that I want to hear about," said Shields, "even if their political views and policies clash with mine. Before I ring the doorbell, I scan the home and yard for toys, wheelchair ramps, vehicles…anything that suggests possible issues. I also notice the person's gender and approximate age before introducing myself and asking what most concerns them about the upcoming election."

"Nice start," Gabe said.

"Remember folks," Shields continued, "after hearing their biggest concern, briefly mention one of our policies that best addresses it, and somewhere along the way, a conversation might begin. And always thank them for their time." Shields scanned the group and smiled. "End of Door Knocking 101."

Liv said, "Thanks for the great tips, Dean. If you knocked on my door, I'd feel like you really cared what *I* thought. Was your bed-side manner as winsome as your door-side manner?"

Dean chuckled. "It's important for all of you to do what Liv just did—give candidates and volunteers a pat on the back when you notice them saying or doing something you like. This is a tiresome slog…a word or two of encouragement works wonders." Reaching for his jacket, Dean said, "I should be leaving. What a pleasure it's been to work with you."

"Liv!" Rick said jubilantly. "A reporter from the CBC just texted that she's on her way to do a short video of you door knocking." He looked at Shields. "Any chance you can stay a few more minutes, Dr. Shields…Dean?"

Shields agreed to be videoed with Liv, after which he shook Rick's hand and said, "Good work, Rick. In one day, you've moved Liv from a hundred doors to thousands of living rooms."

With only a block of town houses left, the team soon returned to the campaign office for pizza and refreshments. Brittany shouted, "Gabe, time for a beer?"

"Thanks, but I need to make a call first." Gabe looked at Rick and said, "Sally's wrath or Brittany's charm?"

Rick grinned. "Aw shucks man, you can handle both."

In a quiet corner near the door, Gabe gesticulated while he talked with Sally, then looked back at Rick, rolled his eyes, and caught Brittany's attention before giving both a wide, departing wave.

People mingled over refreshments and snacks as Edna, a newcomer who'd walked in earlier from the street and offered to door knock, ardently tried to convince a small circle of volunteers to change their pitch at the doors.

"Hey, guys, don't be so polite to Conservatives," Edna proclaimed to her team members. "Call them on their reckless policies."

Having overheard Edna, Rick joined the group and noted her sour expression and snappy, extravagant gestures. *Even her hair looks anxious.*

"What do you suggest we say to Conservatives, at the door?" Rick asked.

Edna raised her voice and jabbed her index finger at phantom enemies. "Tell them no intelligent, decent person would vote for a party that cancels school lunch programs and cuts funding to valuable social services. They need to know that Conservatives would privatize huge chunks of health care and education!"

Rick softened his tone. "Do you ever start by asking constituents for their concerns, or how they'd rate the current government's performance?"

"Absolutely," Edna said, looking smug. "After I educate them about Liberal policies."

"Educate? Sounds sanctimonious to me," said an older volunteer. The air was tense; conversation, halting. A young male volunteer asked Edna, "Would you be so kind as to tell us how you *educate* them? I don't think all Conservatives are ignorant; in fact, similarities exist among Conservatives and Liberals."

"I agree," Rick said, before Edna could respond. "I also think every political party, most certainly our own, has some members with vice grips on narrow-minded ideas. Just listen to panel debates at election time." Rick then politely excused himself, walked over to Liv and in hushed tones, said, "Edna's the kind of person who makes compassion difficult. I don't think her head's in the game. She'd be more useful ramming signs in the ground than politics down people's throats. You might want to talk to her."

Liv waited briefly, then joined Edna's group to take the social temperature. "Don't let me interrupt you," she said to Edna, who was still holding forth.

Edna's cheeks flushed as she flamboyantly continued answering another question. "Anybody with a pulse knows that Conservatives only care about low taxes and getting re-elected."

With veiled disdain, a younger woman asked Edna, "Has anyone ever slammed the door in your face?" Controlled snickers rippled through the group.

No longer oblivious of the obvious, Edna impersonated a Wagnerian opera conductor. "Why's everyone so upset? It's clear to me that Mallore could say all Liberals should be jailed, and his gullible little fan club would cheer wildly."

With a look of consternation, Liv faced Edna. "I'd like all of us to follow the script and, more importantly, remember that at the door, voters' opinions are more important than our own—a conviction that gave Shields four consecutive wins."

Edna's tone was bitter. "Okay guys, I get it. Some days I'm the pigeon; today I'm the statue." She turned and marched over to John, who listened briefly then handed her a copy of the script before calling for everyone's attention.

"Next Friday, seven o'clock, Mount Vista gymnasium, first panel debate," John shouted. "Liv needs our wild applause. Other candidates will have their supporters out too…let's show 'em what we've got."

Liv applauded John's enthusiasm. "Hope to see all of you there!" she said. "Once again, thanks to each of you for your generous time and support today—means everything to me." She smiled pleasantly at Edna, who had her hand on the doorknob.

People lingered to discuss campaign strategy and help tidy the office. When everyone had left, including Gabe and Brittany who walked out together, Liv, John, and Rick sorted the scattered election materials into neat piles.

Liv caught Rick's attention, smiled, and pointed first to him, then herself, then the door.

Rick winked and nodded once. Exactly once. *I've hit the jackpot,* he gleefully concluded. *No baby kisses tonight.*

Liv's signal to Rick did not go unnoticed. John scratched his stubble and said, "You've had a busy day. I'll organize next week's schedule and lock up if you like."

After giving John a quick hug of thanks, Liv looked at Rick and said, "Time to pack it in, Mr. Wright. I'll walk out with you."

As they ambled to the parking lot, Liv's sultry voice stirred something deep in Rick's romantic chambers. "The evening's still young," she said. "Are you free to come to my place and edit my debate speech? It's already making me nervous…don't want to fall flat on my ass."

"Best park it on a seat in the legislature," Rick said, quite seriously. "But yes, happy to help with your speech—content and tone…even delivery, if you like. As the saying goes: Fake it 'til you make it."

"Follow me," Liv said, her voice floating across a winter breeze that cooled the heat of the moment. Rick trailed Liv as far as her nearby liquor store where he bought what he hoped would be a lucky bottle of Chardonnay.

Liv was at the kitchen counter when Rick arrived—the same counter where, a couple weeks ago, he'd torn a strip off the Catholic Church. Tonight, he wanted to strip off the track suit she had changed into.

"Nice wine, Rick. Thanks. Did I tell you Dad's coming down from Edmonton tomorrow to door knock? Would you like to meet him?"

"Great timing! Other than homework, which I'll have to attack tomorrow night, I'm free to meet the father of my future MLA."

Rick poured two glasses of wine as Liv assembled a tray of cheese, crackers, and grapes. "Here's to our success on the doors," she said, hoisting her glass and tossing Rick a beguiling smile. "Let's go to into the other room and take a look at my draft. Needs fresh eyes…an English major's in particular."

At her antique oak desk, Rick edited the first few paragraphs, sat back and crooned, "Some good stuff here." He reached over and gently squeezed Liv's forearm.

Then it happened.

Liv and Rick gazed into each other's eyes until the kiss beckoned—a long, lingering kiss followed by a series of increasingly passionate embraces. Liv burrowed her face in Rick's neck, then slid her hand into his and led him to her bedroom. Slowly and erotically, they undressed each other in a glow of silvery moonlight that streaked through the silhouette blinds. Liv's body quivered in response to Rick's mounting want, and for the next hour, the lovers stopped at nothing. One body, one breath, one pile of steaming, clammy flesh.

Damp with spent desire, Rick lay beside Liv in quiet solitude, magnifying every trivial detail of their first sexual experience. He thought about how he'd treasure this moment when Liv's at the legislature in Edmonton and he's in Calgary, missing her in this bed. Their bed. In his young lover's mind, it was unimaginable that tonight's passion could possibly dwindle down to complacency, boredom, or regret.

"I love caressing every inch of your soft skin," Rick said. "It's as if our strands of DNA are united in their very own double helix."

Liv placed Rick's hand on her chest. "That's either my heart pounding or a small earthquake."

Rick chuckled. "I'd say it's rhapsody."

"It's been a long time—thought I might need a dust buster."

Rick laughed, then kissed the hollow in her throat. "No need for a dust buster. You were nice and sudsy."

"Sudsy!" Liv hooted as she flung her head back and banged it on the cushioned headboard. "That's a new one!" she said, continuing the jocularity. "Put it in your short story. Er…maybe not. No sexual innuendos about your future MLA, please."

"Fine, that one's between you and me, madam Premier."

Rick enjoyed Liv's free-spirited, sexual savvy, which he briefly compared to his former lover's sexual prudery. His impulse was to assure her that he'd keep her forever safe, forever happy. *No. Too macho. Liv doesn't need anyone to keep her safe and happy.*

"One small matter," Rick said, his fingers fluttering across Liv's forehead. "How would you like to handle our relationship in front of campaign workers? I can curb my libidinous glances, but it won't be easy."

"Let's keep it private. Volunteers might see our intimacy as taking something away from the group." Partway through a capacious yawn, Liv added, "I need to get a handle on my speech. While you rest, I'll print a copy of what I've written and bring it in."

"Sure, I've had all the ecstasy I can take. For now."

Liv pulled a slinky nightgown from a small, knotty pine dresser and let it glide down her body, then affectionately pinched Rick's toes on her way to the den. Within minutes, she bounced back into the room with a lightness of limb and childlike excitement, switched on the overhead reading light, and tossed Rick an extra cushion. "Let's review this intro again?" she said, handing Rick her speech and hopping under the covers. "Read it out loud, please."

Rick propped up the pillows and read the first sentence: *"I'm running for the party that considers evidence-based ideas from the left, the centre, and the right, then develops policies that reflect an open-minded, progressive approach to government. The Liberal Party is not beholden to corporations or unions—it's beholden to each and every Albertan. Above all, it's beholden to the preservation of democracy and the environment."*

"Perfect start to a winning debate," Rick said, then continued reading her pitch for equal access to quality health care, daycare, and preschool programs. After reading her last sentence, Rick asked, "How will Liberals pay for all that without implementing a sales tax? Alberta still has the lowest taxes in the country."

"With better management of our resources, we can improve social services without raising taxes, according to some policy makers," Liv said.

"Not if we want small class sizes and fair salaries for teachers," Rick replied. "You've got nothing to lose by being honest about the sorry-assed state of our economy, daycare, public health and education, which a policy on tax reform could remedy."

"I forgot the tray in the den," Liv said, jumping up and adding, "Just mentioning the word tax hands the Conservatives a clear victory."

When Liv returned, Rick sipped his wine and cautioned, "Liv, I'll only say this once. Politicians surrender to the myth that any mention of taxes would kill their political futures. What about citizens' futures? I might be wrong, but most Albertans are more intelligent, financially responsible, and fair-minded than politicians give them credit for. I'll canvass hundreds of homes for any leader who introduces a consumption tax, or more levels of taxation for the very wealthy...not as punishment, but as their fair contribution for the disproportionate benefits they get from the common good—benefits our taxes pay for."

"Convincing spiel, Rick, but I'll only push for a sales tax if I get elected." Liv squarely faced Rick. "You sound like a veteran politician. Why not run for office?"

Rick shook his head. "Too hot-headed for politics...but here's another idea. You could single out one of your opponent's reasonable views and say: Given what you've just said, I'll reconsider my position. Then pause...show the audience you're open-minded; willing to collaborate."

"I like that suggestion," Liv said, running her fingers over the outer edge of Rick's hand. "Have you ever noticed this bulge just behind your pinkie...a lovely hunk of male flesh, albeit a distant second to that lower bulge?"

"The things you notice, Liv Janson. Should I finish reading your speech or would you like another romp?"

"No, no! Please carry on. With me, silliness hovers."

Rick smiled. "Keep it hovering. I love your playful sense of humour."

After fine tuning Liv's speech, Rick wrote a posting for her website then nestled under the covers and gave her slender throat one last, erotic kiss.

Liv patted Rick's arm and sighed. "Best day of the campaign. Thank God we didn't let our religious differences ruin our relationship."

"Yes, my lovely. And thank you for accepting me back into your life. If you hadn't, I would've understood."

Morning sunlight streamed into the bedroom as Rick snuggled up to Liv's smell of sleep. After tender lovemaking and a few minutes of dreamy languor, Rick said, "I'm looking forward to meeting your Dad today."

"He and I will have lunch and be back in the office by one o'clock, ready to hit the doors," Liv said, tossing the covers aside.

Rick enjoyed their leisurely breakfast together then drove home to shower, shave, and change into clean clothes for that all-important meeting. As he stepped onto the landing above his suite, he heard his parents' voices pleasantly chatting. He knocked gently, opened the kitchen door, and leaned in.

"Good morning, Mom and Dad. Am I too late for coffee?"

"Well, well!" Dick said, sounding cheerful. "Look what the backhoe unloaded."

Dorothy quickly intervened. "Good to see you, Ricky. Come, sit down. There's bacon and toast left. What have you been up to?"

Before answering, and with laser intensity, Rick scanned his father's entire demeanour. "Happy to report that an amazing woman, Liv Janson, who Mom and I talked about last week, has come into my life. And get this, Dad, she's a devout Catholic."

Dick shuffled to the counter for a second coffee. "Catholic, eh?" He swiped his index finger across his tongue and made a winning mark in the air. "Liberal cancels that out." Four little words suddenly draped the kitchen in hostility.

Rick calmly replied, "Look, Dad, I'm indifferent to your feelings about the Liberals, but I hope you'll come to know and like Liv because I do. A lot."

"If you marry her and I have a Liberal politician for a daughter-in-law, I'll…I'll—"

Rick's tone saddened. "You'll what, Dad? Disown me? You did that years ago."

Dick scowled as Dorothy injected a different tone. "How exciting Ricky—a new relationship with a budding politician." She passed Rick the plate of remaining toast. "I've heard good things about Liv from people at the hospice."

Dick thumped his hand on the countertop; his eyes narrowed to angry slits. "Dorothy, politics is blood sport! Stay out of it!"

"May I remind you," Dorothy said, turning in her chair to face her husband, "I am *not* a child. I told you last week that I planned to door knock with Ricky, and since fifty percent of the front yard is mine, I have the right to put a sign on my half."

Rick and Dorothy quickly exchanged looks of confidence as Dick shook his head in a manner that exercised his jowls. "Bloody hell you will!"

Rick tumbled into an emotional sinkhole. He stepped over to the large kitchen window, looked up at a clear blue sky, and waited, for what he did not know.

Dick was staring at his phone when Rick turned and said, "Did I tell you that Liv's taking on Ron Mallore, who lost twice to Shields— our Liberal MLA who's retiring after four terms?"

Hands anchored on hips, Dick fiercely defended the Conservative candidate. "Don't talk to *me* about Mallore. He's a successful businessman; just what this province needs."

"Dad, let's not start another blistering political quarrel."

"I see! Now that you've had your say, I can't have mine?"

Rick pressed on. "For once, can't we agree to disagree? What are we doing to each other? Surely there's a better way."

"If you'd just admit that I'm right and you're wrong, there'd be no arguing," Dick said, chortling.

"Okay. From now on I'll agree to everything you say." Rick's voice was flat.

Dick switched gears. "I like guys who firmly stick to their guns. Who don't sit on the fence and bruise their balls. Has crazy love softened you up?"

"Yup. Crazy love's the mysterious main feature in life's joys and sorrows—softens the toughest. Right now, I'm riding the joy train." Rick's grin widened; Dick's frown deepened.

"Hope yer not headed for a train wreck," Dick grumbled, then smacked Dorothy's backside as he passed by, spilling bacon grease from the pan she was pouring into a cup.

Rick jumped up and grabbed the roll of paper towels. "Jeez, Dad! Take it easy."

Dick stomped out of the kitchen and, without looking back, slammed the front door.

"Bet he thought that was a love pat," Rick grumbled.

"He's just upset...wasn't thinking," Dorothy said.

"I wouldn't be making excuses for him. But I liked how the mother who came out at Katie's Kitchen last Sunday came out again today...in her own. Keep standing up to Dad; your voice is strong."

Dorothy's hands assumed the prayer position. "I'm still conflicted about so many things."

Her son thoughtfully nodded. *Conflicted about what? Her husband? Efner? Her entire family? Are there times she wants to run away...leave it all behind?*

The campaign office was buzzing with activity as Liv greeted Rick's arrival with enough voltage to charge her fading phone. Clutching his arm, she steered him to her father. "Dad, meet Rick Wright," Liv said, and before she could say anything more, her father reached out to shake Rick's hand.

"Gunnar Janson. I've heard good things about you. Thanks for helping Liv become your new MLA."

He's got that Nordic, sing-songy voice, Rick thought. "Ready as ever. Liv's doing her best to turn me into a pro...even managed a few lawn signs. Are you a seasoned campaigner?"

"I volunteered for our Liberal candidate in the last election, but this one..." Gunnar put his arm around his daughter. "This candidate's easy to go all out for. My wife and I miss her; a win would bring her home."

Two hours later, when Rick, Liv, Gunnar, Brittany, and Gabe had worked their way through most of the poll sheet, they stopped at a coffee shop and warmed up over hot drinks and hotter topics. Rick knew that before retiring, Gunnar had taught graduate seminars in Military History. When he asked Gunnar if he knew what shaped political tyrants, his eyes lit up.

"I'm no expert in psychology or psychohistory, but many tyrants grew up with strict, punitive fathers whose sons became hungry for power and revenge. Call it payback. What goes around…you know the rest. It's likely more complicated than that, but that's a basic take on it."

"Hitler and his Nazi followers, two examples among many," Rick said, his leg bouncing like it wanted out.

"Right, but Hitler's handle on truth became the shovel that dug his own grave, and many of his sycophants paid a heavy price for their war crimes."

Gabe looked at Gunnar. "I'd bet box office seats at a Stanley Cup playoff that you've never voted Conservative."

"I'm afraid you'd lose, Gabe. I was a Progressive Conservative for many years but didn't renew my membership when the party took a sharp turn to the right. Reduce taxes and privatize health care?" Gunnar slowly shook his head. "I don't think so. I'm now quite comfortable in the sensible centre, working for my smart, sensible daughter."

"Politics…people have become too polarized," Gabe said.

Gunnar replied, "Political polarization—"

Liv intervened. "Dad, when it comes to politics, you'd talk the ear off an elephant."

Gunnar nodded, then stared out the window where, across the street, people filed out of St. Joseph's church. "Looks like someone either got married or buried."

"Buried, given their solemn faces," Liv said.

Gunnar turned to Rick, motioned toward the church, and asked, "Are you a believer?"

Rick thought his score on Gunnar's rating scale for a son-in-law was about to plummet. "I'm not religious in a doctrinaire sense, but I do go to Mother Nature's church at the foot of the Rocky Mountains—the one I call The Church of Kananaskis."

Gunnar gave a throaty chuckle. "If I lived closer to your church, I wouldn't miss a service."

Rick glanced at Liv, who looked like she was leading the parade of mourners across the street.

"We still have a few doors to hit," she said. "Best we drink up and finish the poll."

Twenty minutes into the final stretch, the wind picked up, the temperature fell, and snow blanketed the ground. After skidding down the front steps of a bungalow, Liv steadied herself on the railing and shouted to Brittany, "Let's call it a day."

Back at headquarters, Rick worried that his grades would suffer if he didn't cut back on campaigning and stop obsessing about Liv. Thinking that her political prospects and their relationship had moved into auspicious territory, he walked over to Liv and Gunnar.

"A good canvass today, Liv, and nice to meet you, Gunnar." Rick smiled lovingly at Liv and under Gunnar's watchful eye, said, "Madam Premier, I'll catch up with you tomorrow, if I catch up on homework tonight," then hugged her as tightly and long as he deemed discreet. *Fuck! This isn't the time or place for a hard-on.*

A cold wind sent scraps of paper airborne as Rick walked to the end of the parking lot where he noticed a shadowy figure in a black trench coat, tinted glasses, and red tie. *Looks like a detective*, he thought.

The stranger approached Rick and, with an outstretched hand and friendly smile, gushed, "Hi! I'm Noah, friend of Liv's. Are you with her campaign team?"

"Yes. Rick Wright, *good* friend of Liv's." His limp-wristed handshake was quickly followed by a terse, "Gotta run." Rick marched toward his car, spat on the ground, and, in a solitary game of kick-the-can, blasted a rusted tin can clear across the lot. *So that's Liv's old boyfriend*, he mumbled to himself. *What's he doing here? Get back on the Ark where you belong.*

Loosely moored to his mental faculties, Rick sped down a main thoroughfare and, within seconds, saw bright lights flashing in his rear-view mirror. Cursing loud enough to impair his own hearing, he pulled over, breathed deeply, and watched the policewoman get out of her car. *Nothing's a disaster. Not this; not Noah. Easy does it.*

In a quiet voice, Rick answered the officer's question. "Yes, officer. Sorry, I was speeding. Overreacted to an upsetting incident concerning my girlfriend. No excuse."

Rick handed the officer his driver's licence and vehicle insurance, then waited as she walked back to her car and dispatched the documents. *What if she noticed my Liberal signs and literature? Cops vote Conservative. She'll throw the book at me!* He berated himself until he finally stopped and said aloud, "Crazy! Where's the evidence?"

Finding nothing of consequence, the policewoman returned Rick's papers. "This time, Mr. Wright, I'll let you off with a piece of advice: If you calm down, you'll slow down…and keep your girlfriend."

Rick's smile could've coaxed the sap out of maples in mid-winter. "I promise to do that, officer. Thanks for the advice."

At home, Rick carried two garbage bags to the compost and recycle bins in the alley where he saw, in the distance, a man and woman embracing intimately in the front seat of a pickup truck.

Mom and Efner? What the fuck are you two doing? He quickly disposed of the garbage and went down to his suite where he frantically paced and listened for the sound of his father's truck pulling into the driveway. Soon, the back door closed. Rick hollered up the stairs, "If that's you Mom, come down. We need to talk."

As she descended the stairs, Dorothy told Rick, waiting at the bottom, "I think I know what's bothering you."

Rick frantically motioned his mother to come in and have a seat. Dorothy plunked herself down in her son's easy chair and sheepishly looked up.

In a strident voice, Rick said, "You and Efner? Embracing in the alley? Have you got a death wish or what?"

"I'm sorry you saw that," Dorothy said, slouching further down in the chair. "We do need to talk."

"And listen for Dad's truck," Rick said, then continued pacing. "Look Mom, parking and smooching in the back alley is a dead giveaway. When you told me about your affair, I was understanding, even happy that you've found real love, but I'm now thinking—and it's not my place to tell you what to do—it's just that…I'm frightened for you. The risks you're taking—they're bloody dangerous! Maybe you should end it with Efner or leave Dad, separate or file for divorce. I've given much thought to everything we talked about at Katie's, and I feel certain that you're not doing anything morally wrong. Might think differently if Joy and I were still kids, but you've already sacrificed so much for us."

In a manner too carefree for Rick's liking, Dorothy said, "You're right, we are taking chances, but I know what I'm doing." Dorothy went to the kitchen sink and poured herself a glass of water, took a few sips and stood with her back to Rick, who kept pacing. "Ricky, please, don't tell Joy you saw us."

"As religious as she is, she's not puritanical," Rick said. "She'd understand. But like me, she'd probably worry that in a weak moment, you'd feel so guilt-ridden you'd confess everything to Dad. That'd be suicidal. He'd accuse you of running the adultery alphabet—from Adam to…Zachary. God only knows what else he'd do."

"Don't be ridiculous, Ricky. I'd never confess." Dorothy gave a belaboured sigh that sounded like her last breath. "I need to get upstairs and fix Dad a nice supper." She then walked back to her chair, sat back, and crossed her legs as if she had no intention of leaving. As if she wanted to talk. "I told Efner that for the better part of thirty years, Dad and I have been play-acting at marriage. But we've also had thirty years of history together, with all the ups and downs of building a family and growing a business. I feel so…" Dorothy covered her face with her hands.

"Aw, Mom, this is hard on you. Sorry I mentioned the word guilt." Rick flopped down on the sofa and to his relief, Dorothy looked at him and said, "Forget the guilt. I'm sure you agree that we don't need any person or church to tell us who we can love. When guilt comes knocking, I no longer answer. Your understanding and Joy's is enough. And God's."

Rick felt a surge of renewed support for his beleaguered mother. "Life's too short to spend it trapped in a marriage where one plus one equals less than two," he said. "In a good marriage, shouldn't it equal three?"

Dorothy looked contemplative. "I like your math. One plus one equals four when Efner and I are together."

"What about his marriage? And his wife's health?"

Mother and son exchanged knowing glances. "Efner rarely talks about his wife, but he once said she's married to her cats. And get this, he's mildly allergic to them! I'm guessing he wakes up every morning sniffling and sneezing, wishing he were elsewhere."

"If his wife loved him, she'd divorce her cats," Rick said.

Dorothy's grin quickly vanished. "Your father, my husband…a man we've spent years with, acts confident and strong, but deep down, he's very insecure. Pitifully weak."

"An imposter." Rick went to the fridge and opened a beer, poured half of it into a small glass, and passed it to his mom. "But you don't let him push you around as much anymore. He's getting weaker; you're getting stronger."

"Efner has given me confidence. So has Marg and my good friend, the library." Dorothy tapped the cover of a library book on the table beside her. "Great novels have helped me see things differently…confront my beliefs. My fears."

"Ah, the library. While you love big ideas from big thinkers, Dad studies the business world. No wonder the two of you have so little in common."

Dorothy modestly blushed. "I remember how much you loved the stories I read to you and Joy."

"*Tom Sawyer* and *Gulliver's Travels* were my favourites," Rick said.

"You were so young, so fascinated by good literature. And good words." Dorothy glanced at her watch and said, "I hate to end our heart-to-heart, but I'd better get started on supper." She took a couple more sips of beer, stood up, and hugged Rick. "I'll think about everything you've said. I always do."

Rick impishly raised his eyebrows. "And stop romancing in back alleys."

Well into his evening studies, Rick intermittently fretted about the messiness of romantic relationships. Closing in on midnight, he fought the temptation to text Liv but decided that doing so would only expose his insecurities. He Googled but couldn't find the source for a quote that dropped in from nowhere: There's nothing quite so attractive as a woman who's busy on a Friday night.

How about a guy? Manipulative as that seemed to him, Rick texted Liv. *Sorry, too busy to help with your campaign tomorrow.*

Chapter 10

"Where would you like to focus those binoculars you talked about last week?" Dr. Grey asked Rick, rolling a small office chair across the carpet to her usual spot across from her client.

"My communication skills. Had quite the lesson from a successful politician while door knocking a few days ago. He simply repeats one key word or phrase from a resident's remark, then waits, and listens, without interrupting."

"A politician taught you communication skills?" Dr. Grey said, with a tone of disbelief. "In my experience, most of them are in such a hurry to knock on every door, give their spiel and dash off to the next unwitting victim, they leave people like me feeling unheard. And unimpressed."

"Yeah, they waste everyone's time and lose votes they might've otherwise had."

"Have you tried the one-word tactic with your father? Then listened?"

"With him, listening doesn't come easy."

Dr. Grey said, "Perhaps your heart wants to hear but your head won't let it?"

Rick glanced up at the ceiling. "Something like that, but here's the good news. Last week I told Dad I was tired of our endless quarrels and to my amazement, he didn't argue with me...simply said something about crazy love turning me to mush, then left for work."

"How did you feel after that surprising response?"

"Numb. No big deal," Rick said.

Dr. Grey ran her fingers across her chin as if checking for whiskers were a big deal. "Numb?"

"Um, that's not actually true. I felt good. Somewhat hopeful."

"Have you decided that since you can't change your father, you'll change your attitude to him?"

Rick drummed his fingers on the arm of his chair. "Maybe so. We'll see how long that lasts. He knows how to rattle my cage."

"Who has the key to that cage?"

Rick floundered. "Okaaay, I do. Slow learner."

Dr. Grey said, "Discussing sensitive, value-laden issues with people we care about requires attitudes and social skills the best of us lack. Or forget."

"Dad likes to start his sentences with: 'You need to understand that....' Or, 'Listen, people with half a brain know that the only way....' Uber arrogance! And when he's finished mouthing off, his face freezes in a very unattractive resting position."

"Ah, yes. We also hear with our eyes, sometimes better than our ears," Dr. Grey said. "Emotional and physical add-ons announce unintended meaning. We may think our genuine thoughts are hidden, but scowls, vacant stares, phone checks—they broadcast how we truly feel about an idea or issue. Like right now. Your auxiliary add-ons tell me you're familiar with all this."

"Yeah, the class practiced body language in Intro Psych and later, when I told Dad he looked confused, he shouted, 'Confused! What in the name of God are you talking about?' His face was redder than the sweater you're wearing."

"It's tricky alright," said Dr. Grey. "Commenting on someone's frown, for example, might elicit deeper frowns of annoyance. Also, if we presume to know how others feel by saying things like 'You're so anxious. Why are you angry? You're sulking,' we might *really* annoy them."

"I better not show my own frustration when I hint at Dad's."

Dr. Grey nodded. "I've found that when I say, somewhat curiously or light-heartedly, 'Looks to me like you're a bit annoyed'—I could also say 'distracted' or 'ambivalent'—I invite them to tell me how they honestly feel. The key is to use a milder emotion than the one I think they're feeling: annoyed, not angry; concerned, not anxious."

"Mm-hmm," Rick said, sounding somewhat unconvinced.

"Two weeks ago, you mentioned that in childhood, your father scolded you when you cried."

Rick stared at the small African violet on Dr. Grey's desk as if he wanted to befriend it. "Dad would order me to toughen up and stop crying like a sissy girl. In hindsight, that was harsh but good advice because I was bullied in elementary school...boys called me names: fag and wimp were faves." Rick talked at length about other abuses he'd experienced from classmates over the years.

"Do you remember how you felt?"

"Sad, sometimes angry but I didn't show it because I was too afraid guys would gang up on me after school. But things changed in Grade eight when the gym coach encouraged me to sign up for soccer. A growth spurt had given me enough confidence to join the team, and hours of practice paid off. For once in my life I felt I belonged with kids my age, but only on the soccer field. Even though I was a good defensive midfielder and got top grades, I was a nobody everywhere else."

"With all your accomplishments, you felt like a sad, lonely nobody. And today?"

"Today I have Liv. She's rescued my heart and I think we're doing well, mainly because I'm working on what you and Dr. Knowles, my psychology prof, are teaching me. I'm learning how to talk more respectfully when I disagree with someone."

"*Disagree* with someone? A fine communication point here, but what if you said *differ* instead of *disagree*? I differ with you. Or: We differ on that point."

"Hmm...differ, not disagree. To Dad, the difference would be as subtle as the *b* in subtle."

Dr. Grey readily smiled. "Perhaps, but here's another subtlety we could all try. Instead of saying: I'd *argue* that..., why not simply say: I *think* that...?"

"Disagree. Argue. Yeah, those words are a bit edgy."

"Back to you and your father. I'm still wondering if it's possible he'd like to connect with you at a deeper level but doesn't know where to begin."

"Hmm, he's too eager to impress—and too defensive, especially when I ask him to explain himself." Rick picked at a scab on his left wrist until it bled, then reached over and pulled a tissue from the box on the table.

"Much of what we say invites people in or shows them the door," Dr. Grey said. "Too often, without realizing it, we try to convince them, impress them, correct them…or needlessly defend ourselves."

"It's hard to invite people like Dad into a conversation they're unwilling to have. Phones and washrooms are handy escapes." Rick edged his way to the front of his chair. "Picture this: Like a traffic cop, Dad shoves the palm of his hand in my face and hollers, 'Stop right there!' Or, 'Now just you wait a minute!' You might think I'm exaggerating but I'm trying to be as straight forward and honest as I can…trying to give you an accurate description of him."

"It's hard to understand others if we can't let go of judgment and accusations."

"Judgment? How can I improve our communication when I can't ignore *his* rude judgment? Feels like we're still spinning our wheels…spraying mud in every direction."

"It takes practice. You have the basic communication skills and your varied interests could make you an excellent conversationalist if you practice something important; something we haven't discussed yet. Any ideas?" Dr. Grey waited.

Rick gnawed on his thumbnail. "Manners? Politeness?"

"Manners and politeness are important, but…." Dr. Grey's smile locked Rick in. "It's the all-important pause." Then she did just that.

"I know you're right because when I get going, when words are clickety clacking along, I'm so entertained by my own verbiage that I forget others might have something to say. Hate to admit it but I'm slowly becoming aware that, as Joy says, I jump in and mansplain every little thing. Like Dad, but not so condescending and preachy."

"In social situations, especially when we're with people we care about, it's crucial to pause after a few sentences to let others in…to ask for their opinions, particularly on topics you raise."

Dr. Grey again waited, as did Rick.

"I need to put my ego on the table and tell it to wait awhile."

"That's how you'll get second dinner invitations," Dr. Grey said, smiling.

"But what about people who think they've nailed truth to the mat, or brag about their accomplishments, or constantly interrupt to overstate the obvious? They're boring, boring, boring."

"Some people are like that," Dr. Grey said.

"Guys in the bar are like that. They brag about their accomplishments. I'd rather hear about their failures…their imperfections. And they drone on about stuff devoid of meaning, or stuff they know nothing about, especially politics."

"Nothing? Know *nothing* about?" Dr. Grey said. "How do you respond to their ignorance?"

"If they're not ready to listen, I change the topic or walk away."

Dr. Grey massaged her wrist and Rick imagined she was getting bored with him, feigning interest. The intonation of her voice soon proved otherwise.

"If they're not *ready* to listen? Really now. As if barroom guys *should* be ready to hear you. As if your ideas are of great importance. I hear cynical arrogance in that remark."

Rick moved his jaw from side to side. "Okay, so sometimes I'm arrogant, but sometimes it's justified."

"When is it justified to use a rough, aggressive tone of voice that says: Listen to me, you ignoramus, or remain stupid?"

Rick didn't answer. He turned and looked at the door, the plant, the table—everything except Dr. Grey. With contrived patience, he said, "When people are closed-minded and condescending—when they only see things one way. That's when it's justified…I think."

Dr. Grey's silence made its own statement.

Rick felt a strange undertow. Struggling against the current, he asked, "Are you saying I'm closed-minded? Arrogant?"

"What would you like to hear me say?"

"Open-minded, yes; closed-minded, no. Jeez doc! I want you to answer my question, not give me another one of your own."

"Fair enough. As I see it, you're very definite about religious beliefs. What would happen if you loosened your grip on such certainty?"

"Maybe that's just who I am."

"Would you lose faith—bad choice of words—in yourself if you changed your mind, or at least suspended judgment long enough to see what happens?"

Dr. Grey waited, then tilted her head sideways, keeping her eyes centered on Rick. "I see you as open to considering what others tell you…what they see in you and might have seen for some time."

"Maybe I am too definite, too judgmental, easily annoyed. Pious believers really get me going."

Dr. Grey said, "In social situations, if I'm flustered, I have a hard time putting things together. Even though I'm aware that all thinking occurs within a field of emotion, I'm not always tuned into my feelings, some partying a little louder and longer than they should."

Rick grinned. "I know what you mean. Since coming here, I'm trying to be aware of my feelings. Especially frustration."

Dr. Grey said, "What are you feeling right now?"

"Um, good, overall. Pleasantly curious; definitely not frustrated."

"Monitoring strong, negative emotions can reduce their impact—prevents them from bombarding our mid-brain and short-circuiting our higher order reasoning and analysis, the work of our neocortex."

"I get it. When I'm too emotional, I'm dumber."

"So the theory goes. What's your own best example of that?"

"Boxing Day," Rick said, without hesitation. "I was uncontrollably angry."

"What did your body feel like then?"

"Don't know. I was just angry."

"Had you been more emotionally aware, a cognitive skill, you'd have noticed the first, immediate sign of anger and named it; for example, I'm frustrated, annoyed at the sound of dad's voice. You would've then chosen whether to let it build to anger and express it, or let it go."

"Like my argument with Liv over religion. Only later did I realize how angry I was."

"Emotional awareness in the moment is the first step, Rick."

Rick sat back and closed his eyes.

"How *are* things with you and Liv?"

"Much better. She seems willing to forgive my shortcomings."

"Good relationships make room for mistakes."

"Yeah, Liv's given me space. Tomorrow night, she's on a political panel at the Mount Vista gymnasium, and on Saturday, I'll door knock with her team." Rick paused, frowning. "Hope her ex doesn't show up."

"What thoughts and feelings will you have if he does?"

Rick tapped his knuckles together. "Hard to say." *Expects some brilliant insight.* Rick's direct gaze radiated intensity. "Okay. I'll be pissed off, but I'll talk myself down to annoyed."

"And tell yourself it's not awful or terrible? You can stand it?"

Rick flexed his shoulders and glanced at the clock. "You haven't pulled any punches today."

"And you've noticed the time," Dr. Grey said. "I've tried to be straight, but fair. Hope I haven't been too teachy."

"Not at all. I'm here to learn."

Dr. Grey slowly pushed her chair back. "Our session has come to an end, but please know that I appreciate how honest you've been—cognitively and emotionally."

Rick smiled as he shook Dr. Grey's hand. "Likewise. See you next week for more of the same."

Rick anxiously eyed the clock as a steady stream of constituents arrived for the first all-candidates political forum. An air of anticipation accompanied the faint smell of sweaty gym shoes as people draped their winter jackets behind their chairs or simply dropped them on the floor before seating themselves under harsh, white lights. John and Rick hurriedly unstacked another tower of chairs to accommodate a surprising turnout of the politically curious.

A raised platform had been rolled in place at the front of the room and shortly after Liv took her seat behind her prominent name card, the petite moderator tapped the microphone.

"Welcome everyone to Mount Vista's first all-candidates debate, and thank you for taking an interest in the upcoming election. Tonight, a draw determined the speaking order, and the first we'll hear from is Ron Mallore, our Conservative candidate, then Liv Janson, our Liberal candidate, and Ruth Nordstrom, our New Democratic candidate." The moderator then outlined time restrictions and audience conventions before directing her first question to the panellists.

"Mr. Mallore, please tell us why you think constituents should vote for you on E-day by emphasizing three policies that differentiate Conservatives from the other two parties."

The sixty-eight-year-old Conservative kept his bulky frame seated at the table. "Thank you, madam moderator, candidates, and local constituents for attending tonight's important debate. I'm running for the Conservative Party because it's the only real choice for those who want policies that protect and preserve the Alberta Advantage. Unlike the Liberals and New Democrats, Conservatives believe that people with business smarts can manage social programs better than government bureaucrats. Education and health care can best be improved by allowing more private investment. We'll give voters choice in the quality management and delivery of children's education and family health care."

A slight rumble spread across the room as Mallore shuffled his papers and sighed, then continued his monotone message. "Conservatives believe that governments should not interfere with market forces. My party has a history of low taxes," he said, then compared Alberta's tax history with other provinces and promised further reductions for corporations and small businesses. He concluded his speech by supporting gun ownership. "Farmers and other Albertans are quite capable of protecting their own property," he said, amidst a cluster of boisterous cheers.

Despite his obvious lack of oratory, staunch supporters listened patiently and responded with their usual thunderous applause. Edna, who'd reappeared for the first time since volunteers criticized her door-knocking approach, sat two seats down from Rick, fourth row from the front. She leaned forward, caught his attention, and said, "Once again, Mallore's trying to wing his way to the legislature. I'd rather pick lint from my hairdryer than listen to the same old drivel."

Rick nodded fleetingly to Edna and responded with a version of Dr. Grey's comment. "Some politicians are like that," he said, then checked his phone.

"Thank you, Mr. Mallore," said the moderator. "Let's now hear from the Liberal candidate, Liv Janson."

Unlike Mallore, Liv moved her chair back, stood tall, and smiled as she scanned the room and rested her eyes on her most steadfast supporter. In a measured pace with modulated volume, she delivered the speech she and Rick had worked on. Liberal supporters gave key points a resounding applause; she gave them a conspicuous surge of confidence, then outlined three proposals for early childcare, education, and support for seniors that would distinguish Liberal policies from those of the other two parties.

"I'll end with this," Liv said. "Children are the future. Our greatest asset lies in *their* beds, not corporate oil beds. In *their* sand boxes; not the tar sands. Liberals will do what's best for all Albertans, especially children, by balancing environmental and social concerns with those of the broad business community. We will not fail to protect public services. Thank you."

Liv's campaign team jumped to their feet, clapping and hooting as the moderator turned to Mallore. "Do you think Miss Janson's policies give voters a clear choice?"

With newfound energy, Mallore thumped both hands on the table and said, "Clear choice, alright. The *wrong* choice."

Liv snapped her head sideways and scrutinized Mallore as he unabashedly exaggerated his numerous accomplishments on a prominent Canadian oil company's Board of Directors.

Thumper did its own special dance as Rick nervously scanned the smiling faces behind him.

Mallore said, "I'm someone voters can count on to do what's best for business, because what's best for business is what's best for all Albertans and Canadians. I promise to—"

With a surge of adrenaline, Rick leapt up, jabbed his finger at Mallore, and shouted, "No! What's best for all Albertans is quality *public* health care and quality *public* education. You'd privatize the air we breathe!"

A big, burly man who sat directly behind Rick, jumped to his feet and shoved his index finger into Rick's neck. "Put a plug in it, Commie!" he shouted, stunning the audience.

Rick spun around and unintentionally clipped his attacker's chin. When he started to apologize, the provocateur ordered, "Keep your fuckin' hands off me, you baboon, or I'll—"

"You'll what!" Rick demanded, exposing a mouthful of teeth.

A feral look crossed Mr. Burly's face as he twisted Rick's arm and said, "Do ya wanna talk outside, tough guy?"

The audience bolted upright in their seats as the moderator stomped down the aisle and, with a strong larynx, ordered, "Sit down, both of you and follow the conventions I gave earlier, or leave."

Mr. Burly slowly backed down the aisle toward the door. He curled his index finger in and goaded Rick, "Step outside and show me whatcha got, Commie!"

Flushed with searing rage, Rick shouted, "Make like a cockroach when the lights come on."

The audience laughed, booed, applauded, or sat quietly in disbelief.

Liv's eyes, like burning needles, pierced Rick's. He opened his palms in a manner that begged for mercy, but seeing none, listened to the loud voice in his head that told him to leave immediately and save face. He lowered his head and waited until the moderator restored order, then excused himself as he crawled over several pairs of legs and crept along a side wall to the exit. Rick gulped when he caught sight of Noah leaning against the back wall, feasting on pure schadenfreude.

Noah's mouth is too small for his fat head, Rick thought, feasting on pure contempt.

At home in the full brunt of misery, Rick sat crossed-legged on the carpet, his hands resting in his lap and gaze directed downward. *Mr. Burly is seriously troubled*, he concluded, then tried concentrating on his breathing but couldn't control intrusive thoughts. *What next? Self-indulgent poetry? A novel about heartbreak?*

Feeling defeated, he poured the remaining half of his beer down the sink and texted Liv.

I'm sorry.

Rick spent the remainder of the evening hyper vigilant for an incoming reply.

Nothing.

Throughout the sleepless night, his angst alternated between anger and sadness. *Why hasn't she replied? Still pissed off with me?* Rick couldn't stop imagining unpleasant scenarios of walking into campaign headquarters with his mom and her friend Marg. Deep in the middle of darkness, he anxiously checked his phone again.

Nothing.

The next morning, after barely opening his eyes, Rick checked his phone and flopped back on his pillow. "Shit!" he mumbled, then reframed his thinking. *Get up, dress up, show up.*

Partway through his second office visit with his psychology professor, Rick said, "I asked my Political Science prof and a retired historian about similarities among authoritarian leaders, tyrants, and white supremacists. I'd also like to ask you."

"Ah, yes," Dr. Knowles said. "Much has been written on the psychohistory of such people—the propagandists who claim to be open-minded, but scratch the surface of their posturing and they bleed bigotry or racism. I suggest they're much the same in that they categorize the unknown, unwanted others as 'them'—the vilified ones, which bolsters their ties to 'us'—the glorified ones, and strengthens their us-against-them, fortress mentality."

"And promotes hatred?" Rick said.

"Yes. The stage is set for such leaders, supported by populist movements of gullible followers, to commit grave atrocities in the name of national pride—pathological pride. They prejudge others, not out of curiosity, but out of a need to pigeonhole them in black-and-white categories of superior to me or inferior to me. Helps them determine, without question, where they themselves stand on a hierarchy of power and status."

"Dad does that. Like Pavlov's dogs, he drools at powerful presidents and billionaires, famous sports figures and contestants on reality TV shows—they're all automatically virtuous, no matter how they acquired their wealth or live their lives. It's embarrassing to admit, but he thinks the poor are all lazy bottom feeders who lack self-discipline...who deserve their lot in life. When he meets people, he wastes little time confirming their racial background, where they work, their residence. Even pries into their religious and political orientations. Sheesh, his judgments and my embarrassment are easier to read than tickertape in Times Square. I'm sure he's more than a little disappointed that he can't brag about his only son, the prominent lawyer...or brain surgeon."

"Your father's just one of many who are preoccupied with power and status. They give people they judge superior or inferior to themselves control of their own emotions—jealousy, awe, anxiety, disgust, anger, and fear—emotions that drive nationalism, racism, and discrimination."

Rick said, "But...but shouldn't powerful, wealthy people who rig the system and create huge economic gaps between themselves and the rest of us make us angry? How else will we change the system?"

"I agree. We aren't doing enough to stop psychopathic, corporate predators and hate-mongers from exploiting and marginalizing others."

"Are all tyrants psychopaths?"

"Most likely. They have that cold, predatory nature that makes us feel like something's being done to us, but we don't know what. And they lack anxiety, guilt, and empathy. We could catch them in a bold-faced lie and they wouldn't flinch. All they care about is using others for personal gain—the hell with cultural beliefs and values."

Rick said, "Ordinary citizens also have narrow-minded beliefs that make them prejudiced and mean spirited."

"Mm-hmm. Some of them we've met or are related to; others are partners we've loved and left, bosses and coworkers we've endured, or political candidates we've voted for, with later regret." Dr. Knowles smirked. "Never ourselves, of course."

Rick paused his busy fingers and asked, "Am I taking too much of your time?"

"Not to worry. I'll let you know when our time's up." Dr. Knowles flicked through a stack of papers on his desk. "In my opinion, a personality trait that's universally recognized but seldom mentioned is a serious, global problem. Few psychologists have studied it in depth, but its harmful, even deadly, potential is the thread woven through everything we've talked about in here. Any thoughts on what that trait might be?"

"Not sure what you're looking for...what the right word is. Narrow-minded? Opinionated? Isn't that what we've been discussing?"

"Right, but the trait I'm thinking of captures a broader range of features and, as far as I can tell, it isn't going away any time soon. Starts with the letter *d*." Dr. Knowles waited until Rick's uneasiness was obvious, then answered his own question.

"Dogmatism."

Rick's eyeballs were like those found on key chains. "Really? Dogmatism? Thought it only applied to religion...evangelical Bible thumpers."

"Yes, dogmatism disrupts the best intentions of religion, but it also scars the face of reason in science, politics, education, marriage, and parenting—all cultural belief systems that shape institutionalized ideologies." Dr. Knowles leaned back in his recliner and watched a mixture of relief and concern flash across Rick's face.

"So that's it," Rick's said, and immediately thought of people other than his father: former friends, ex-girlfriends, classmates, politicians, and...*holy fuck*, he thought, *my own face is at least scratched by dogmatism.* "What makes people dogmatic?" he asked.

"In addition to those influences I mentioned in our last visit, I suggest it's shaped by four innate needs, the first of which begins in childhood: the need to know and understand one's self, others, and the surrounding world. I've written a journal article that outlines my ideas on the topic—I'll give you the reference, which lists related studies."

Rick listened as Dr. Knowles explained the second basic need— the need to defend ourselves against inevitable anxiety and fear, especially in childhood. "Relentless anxiety stifles the child's need to know, and jeopardizes the third inherent need, the need for social connection. Think how difficult it would be for children who lack confidence and good social relationships to gratify their last basic need: the need for dignity. Are you with me here?"

"Let's see," Rick said, intermittently tapping his thigh. "Is this how it goes? Dogmatism is influenced by childhood anxiety that stifles the need to know and prevents strong social ties and...oh yeah, social ties necessary for dignity."

"You've got it!" Dr. Knowles said. "Are you sure you don't want to major in psychology?" Rick smiled. "I'll give that some thought. A psychology degree could help enrich character development in my narratives," he said, knowing full well he'd stick with English and assuming that three psychology courses and therapy sessions were likely enough for character enrichment.

"Keep in mind that my theory began as a narrative," Dr. Knowles said. "A story I told myself that emerged from questions, which went

something like this: I wonder why…. Or: What would happen if….
Those ideas gradually consolidated in my theory of dogmatism that
draws from related concepts and research. But it needs scientific
support from many studies—support within an acceptable range of
probability."

Rick's eyes were searching. "It needs proof."

"In academic domains, the words 'proof' and 'true' sting my ears.
I replace them with statements like: Cumulative evidence lends
scientific validity to the idea that…."

"How will I know if my book characters are dogmatic or simply
opinionated?"

"Dogmatism pertains to entire belief systems. We can be
opinionated about a person, a movie, or a book, for example, but
we're dogmatic about institutionalized, cultural belief systems. But
remember, without scientific evidence, my concept of dogmatism
lacks credence."

"Hmm, three years of university and none of my profs even
mentioned the word."

"That doesn't surprise me. Back in the 1950s, social scientists
wanted to know why reasonably well-educated people in western
civilizations committed the horrors of Nazi Germany and fascist Italy.
Milton Rokeach, a psychology professor at Stanford, pioneered an
assessment tool of dogmatism in 1960, but in his book, *The Open and
Closed Mind*, he said little about its psychological origins or specific
features. Related questionnaires exist, but the psychological nature of
dogmatism hasn't been robustly studied."

Perplexed, Rick said, "Yet so much of the world is run by people
with dogmatic beliefs. Dangerous beliefs." He wanted to raise the
topic of religion, but time was running out.

"Mm-hmm. Consider this," Dr. Knowles said, as if he'd read
Rick's mind. It's been said that religion piloted those planes on 9/11,
but I'd say the real culprit was grotesque, unbridled dogmatism that
found a home in religion. Some terrorists who belong to groups like
ISIS and the Taliban aren't even devoted Muslims; their loyalty and

idolatry to jihadis is borne of instant group acceptance and respect, especially from the leader. Imagine the power of a group that replaces the pain of alienation and insignificance with dignity and glory."

Rick sat quietly, then asked, "How about dogmatism in close relationships? Marriage, for example? The family?"

"I might be wrong, but I think arguments about money, marriage, sex, and parenting aren't the leading cause of divorce. Dogmatic preaching and pronouncements of arrogant certainty are the wrecking balls of intimate partnerships. There's no closing like the closing of a dogmatic mind."

Rick was mesmerized. He hoped for understanding when he said, "Maybe *I'm* dogmatic, especially about religion. I royally pissed off my girlfriend about the evils of Catholicism."

"It's easy to spot dogmatism in others while overlooking our own. Seems to me we all have shades of it, most certainly myself," said Dr. Knowles. "But to have the trait, we need to consistently portray several of the thirteen features I propose, which means we're not dogmatic on Wednesday, but open-minded on Friday. And even if enough features qualify for trait presence, we can't always predict people's behaviour. If you collapsed during a heated argument about, say, religion, there's nothing to suggest that your dogmatic, evangelical opponent wouldn't apply CPR, if necessary. People are more than a cluster of features that define a trait, but as history reveals, dogmatic leaders and their true believers have inflicted monstrous crimes against humanity."

"One last question, if I may. Determined protestors have made important social changes. Are they all dogmatic?"

"No. Passionate believers have sparked many civilian uprisings, but they're more rational and open-minded than their dogmatic counterparts who are extravagantly emotional, who rigidly seal their beliefs in separate compartments without connecting corridors. Whose dogmarrhea leaves us feeling ambushed."

With constrained amusement, Rick said, "Dogmarrhea? Is that in *Oxford*?"

"There's logorrhea, extreme talkativeness, but dogmarrhea is my term for the social fire alarm that sends people running in all directions." Dr. Knowles reached for a binder and handed Rick a chart. "This chart outlines thirteen features of dogmatism…might give you some ideas for your English assignment. I'll email you a copy if you like."

"Thank you," Rick said graciously, then briefly surveyed the chart, tapped it, and said, "How can our species progress when people in positions of power have these features?"

"Ah, yes. Neuropsychologists, evolutionary biologists, political scientists, historians—they'd all like to know how to soften the bark of dogmatism."

"The bark that bites," Rick said, with a satisfying smile, then added, "Rabid Rottweilers."

Dr. Knowles laughed wholeheartedly. "Let's hope they don't have pups."

Chapter 11

Money shouldn't be a barrier to improving mental health, Rick mused, pushing the remainder of a large pizza to the middle of his kitchen table and calculating the net cost of therapy. He opened his laptop and scanned Dr. Knowles' chart on dogmatism, then printed an enlarged, bold-face duplicate that he pinned over his desk, hoping someday his father might have cause to enter his suite and stumble upon it.

THE PERSONALITY TRAIT OF DOGMATISM

COGNITIVE FEATURES

1. Intolerance of Ambiguity
2. Defensive, Cognitive Closure
3. Rigid Certainty
4. Compartmentalization
5. Lack of Personal Insight

BEHAVIOURAL FEATURES

1. Preoccupation with Power and Status (seen in prejudice & discrimination)
2. Glorification of the In-group; Vilification of the Out-group
3. Dogmatic Authoritarian Aggression
4. Dogmatic Authoritarian Submission
5. Arrogant, Dismissive Communication

EMOTIONAL FEATURES

1. Belief-associated Anxiety and/or Fear
2. Belief-associated Anger
3. Existential Despair

Note: Dogmatism is a personality trait that combines cognitive, emotional, and behavioural characteristics to personify prejudicial, closed-minded belief systems, often pronounced with arrogant, rigid certainty. Theoretically, six of thirteen features are assumed necessary to determine trait presence: a minimum of three cognitive features, two behavioural features, and one belief-associated emotion.

Eureka! A black-and-white portrait of Dad, Rick thought, his eyes glazing over as he stared at the chart. He opened his notes from talks with Drs. Grey and Knowles, then sat back and did what he never tired of doing, what he excelled at. Rick linked dogmatism's features to his father, Billy-Bob, and Edna. They'd all score high on a dogmatism questionnaire, he concluded, except Dean Shields who'd anchor the low numbers on the scale. He also thought about the current polarization of major ideas, some of which are thought-provoking and productive, but support for dogmatic polarized beliefs is a problem. Big problem.

Rick put it all together in a manner that furthered his understanding of the trait, then drafted a letter to his dad. He reached for pen and paper, and in his most legible hand-writing began with the suggestion that his father's growing up with an alcoholic mother and largely absent father might've created a belief that adults couldn't be trusted; the world was unfriendly and unpredictable. Rick then explained how the impact of biology and early social relationships hindered his father's innate need to know others, the world of ideas, and above all, himself. With specific examples, he outlined how the features of dogmatism gave his father a false sense of safety and security.

Can't teach an old dogmatist new tricks. That was...is...me too, except for the early death of my parents. Rick concluded, then ended his letter with an appeal: At last my bitterness toward you is being replaced with a greater understanding of both of us. Can we please start over Dad? Can we?

Rick reread the letter. *Too academic. He won't get past the first sentence...will accuse me of psychoanalyzing him.* Rick closed his laptop and reflected on his own tendency to dogmatically proselytize beliefs he cherished, including his newfound conviction about the evils of dogmatism. Moved by gratitude for all he'd learned, he emailed his psychology professor.

Hello Dr. Knowles,

Special thanks for your chart on dogmatism, which I now see as the bottleneck on freedom's horn of plenty. Knowing why and how people become dogmatic strikes me as a crucial first step in understanding and solving serious problems in the world.

I've opened my mind to the idea that it's more closed than I care to admit, but thanks to you, I'm trying to listen and fully hear people with different beliefs, especially beliefs I most care about.

Thanks too for giving me a huge chunk of your office hours.

Sincerely,

Rick Wright

Exhausted, Rick shuffled to his bedroom, crawled under the fluffy duvet and thought about Liv. And sex. With acute longing and a short burst of fresh energy, he re-opened his laptop and titled a file: *Dogmatism and Sex.* The last two sentences of a brief introductory paragraph summarized his thoughts: Rigid sexual beliefs create anxiety and guilt that roam under the covers and punish the body with sexual frustration. Dogmatism in the bedroom leads to divorce in the courtroom.

Needs revision. I need the sleep of a hibernating grizzly.

Late the following morning, Dr. Knowles replied.

Hello Rick,

Thank you for your thoughtful message. Remember that the chart is simply a laundry list of dogmatism's 13 features that scientific studies will hopefully validate as more or less useful.

Keep prying your mind open as widely as possible and you'll do your bit to help remove that bottleneck you mentioned. To quote Charles Taylor, "Understanding the 'other' will pose the 21st century's greatest social challenge."

Best wishes for a post-graduate degree in Creative Writing. Perhaps you'll publish a rousing story about a protagonist who softens the bark of dogmatism to a faint whimper.

Woof.

Jack Knowles

Rick laughed at Dr. Knowles' novel suggestion, then quickly dismissed it. *How could I write a story about dogmatism? Who the fuck would read it?*

Head lowered, Rick led Dorothy and Marg into campaign headquarters where he caught sight of Liv, who tossed him a confusing head shake and immediately resumed studying the large wall map. When two volunteers began approaching him, he dashed over to meet them.

"About my rude disruption last night…I'm sorry," Rick said. "I'd rather my mother, standing over there, not hear about it. Let's talk another time." The volunteers gave a subtle nod of understanding as Rick smiled and walked back to introduce his mom and Marg to Liv and John.

"Today I bring new, dedicated help," Rick said, somewhat self-consciously.

"Dedicated but inexperienced," Dorothy quipped, as Liv stepped closer to welcome them.

Rick smiled at Liv and opened his hand toward his mother. "My Mom, Dorothy Wright, and her friend, Marg Mason, have come to door knock with us."

Liv simply nodded at Rick, who was obviously squirming. "Nice to meet you both," she said, shaking hands with them. "Thanks for volunteering to help with my campaign. I look forward to canvassing with you."

Dorothy said, "Ricky briefed us on what to say at the door. We'll be sure to tell constituents that you're campaigning with us and ask if they'd like to meet you. If they'd rather not, we'll try engaging them by asking what changes they'd like to see in the next government. Oh, and get their contact information so we can update the poll list. What else?"

"Excellent! If they sound supportive, ask if they'll take a sign," Liv said, then handed Dorothy and Marg the script guidelines. "You can come with us for the first few doors to get the hang of it before we leapfrog down the street. Marg, will you please go with Rick? Dorothy and I will campaign the other side of the street."

"Certainly. Glad we can watch the experts at work before plunging in," Marg said.

Rick's relief was abruptly shaken when Noah strode into the office, shoulders back, chin thrust forward, head held high.

"Noah!" shouted Liv. "Perfect timing! We need a recorder for our group of four. Now that you've got that job down pat, will you join us?"

"Happy to do so," Noah said, with a tone Rick deemed controlled exuberance.

Liv introduced Noah to the group, and Rick was thankful that he said nothing about their previous meeting in the parking lot, or the debate debacle.

As Noah helped Liv gather the necessary supplies, Rick leaned into his mother and whispered, "Noah is Liv's ex. His garish comb-over and pouty little mouth remind me of someone."

Dorothy gave Rick what he and Joy dubbed the killer glare. Rick gave Noah another inquisitive glance.

"We're off," Liv said, stepping into the front seat of Noah's new Lexus van while Rick, Dorothy, and Marg climbed into the back.

Driving to the poll boundary, Noah trumpeted his win at the annual realtors' golf tournament. "Hey, Rick," he said, flicking his head in the direction of the back seat. "Are you a golfer?"

"Haven't got the balls for it," Rick harrumphed, then reprimanded himself for his boorish answer. No one laughed or commented, and for the rest of the trip, Rick's stomach made the most noise in the back seat.

Door knocking progressed uneventfully for the next two hours. Rick signalled Noah information to record, and without a coffee shop in the poll district where the team could take its usual chatty break, it was easy to keep a safe distance from Liv's ex. Distancing himself from Liv was painful. Walking back to Noah's van, Rick heard Dorothy and Liv burst into gales of laughter. "Hey, Mom and Liv," Rick said, trailing behind the group. "Sounds like you've got a story to tell."

Dorothy motioned Rick to catch up. "You should've seen it! A tough old bird took one look at me and screeched, 'I wouldn't vote Liberal if my life depended on it,' then slammed the door in my face. I was rattled, but to my surprise, the old crow's neighbour, an elderly gentleman, not only invited me in, but took a lawn sign. And would you believe it? He gave me a bag of cookies he'd just bought to support some charity." Dorothy reached into her shoulder bag, pulled out the bag of cookies and gave it a shake. "On our way back, it's cookie time!"

As Noah drove the team to campaign headquarters, people nibbled on cookies and chatted about their various experiences. Rick tapped Noah on the shoulder and faked friendliness. "So tell me, Noah, aside from golf tournaments, how are things in the real estate business?"

Noah chortled. "Real estate prices have made a comeback and I now make more money in an afternoon than I made in a month this time last year. That makes me a happy dude."

Exudes narcissism. If Liv wants the dude, I don't want her. Rick leaned forward and said, "I suspect no matter how much you make, it'll never be enough." Chiding himself for making yet another cutting remark, Rick began an interior monologue. *Fuckin' fell off the rails again. Why can't I accept others as they are without exposing their faults? Without teaching them a lesson.*

Noah brushed his hand across Liv's knee as he reached over and turned up the volume on the radio.

Liv turned it down and looked back at Dorothy and Marg. "How long have you two known each other?"

Dorothy explained, "Marg volunteers at the library check-out counter and, to our surprise, we discovered that we live a couple blocks from each other." Dorothy looked at Marg and continued, "Was it during our last morning coffee that you said you'd be willing to try door knocking for Liv?" The three pleasantly chatted until Noah pulled into the parking lot.

Dorothy nudged her son. "We should probably head straight home, Ricky."

"Ricky!" Noah exclaimed, looking like he'd been hit with the stench of rotting fish. "Thought your name was Rick."

Rick bit his tongue and helped Dorothy and Marg step down from the van, then forcefully slid the door closed with a resounding bang. "Ricky's my family's term of endearment," he shouted to Noah.

Liv stepped over and sincerely thanked Marg and Dorothy for their kind help.

Rick listened with anticipation, then silently grumbled. *No thanks for my help? Fuck you!*

On their way home, Dorothy and Marg talked about how good it felt to work for a candidate who'd chart a better course for children and seniors, a candidate who'd earned their respect and commitment to door knock for the remaining Saturdays. After Rick dropped Marg off and drove the couple blocks home, Dorothy put her hand on Rick's shoulder and said, "You look tired, honey."

"Just a lot on my mind, Mom. Nothing serious."

"Hmm," Dorothy said and let the matter slide. As she opened the car door, Dick, who'd been watching their arrival from the living room window, opened the front door, beer in hand and jaw clenched.

Dorothy clenched the door handle. "I don't like the looks of this, Ricky."

"I'll protect you if I have to," Rick said firmly, then slipped around to his private entrance. Before descending the stairs to his suite, he paused on the landing and, hearing his father's belligerent voice boom in from the living room, nudged the kitchen door open.

"Listen, Dorothy," Dick said, "I don't like you knocking on strangers' doors, and I certainly don't like you convincing them to vote Liberal! What's gotten inta ya?"

Dorothy calmly said, "Please, Dick, go back to whatever you were watching and let me get dinner ready. I don't want to talk about this."

Dick slammed his beer down on the coffee table and snarled, "We'll talk about this now!"

Rick marched into the living room and stood tall beside his mother. "Dad, stop hounding Mom," he said calmly. "She has a right to door knock with me, and since we always go out in teams of four or five, there's no need to worry that she's off on her own somewhere."

Dick stomped his foot. "That's enough outta you…the one who started all this."

Rick positioned himself between his parents. "And that's enough out of *you*, especially since you've been boozing all afternoon."

"Ricky," Dorothy said calmly, "please, let me handle this."

Rick stepped back and faced his mother. "Okay, Mom, but one more thing and then I'm done." Rick looked sternly at his father. "I see the rage in your eyes, Dad, and I'm afraid you'll attack Mom next." Voice rising with resentment, he added, "If you ever raise a hand to her, you'll have me, cops, the padded van, and a judge to deal with. Then time in the slammer for—"

"Lower your voice, I'm not deaf!" Beer spilled onto the carpet as Dick wildly gesticulated. "You know goddamn right well I've never raised a hand to your mother. I'm just worried that…that a deranged whacko will assault her."

"Seriously, Dad, how many whackos live in this constituency?" *I'm looking at one. Bonkers. Flat out bonkers.*

Dick pumped his finger toward Rick and with blistering intensity, said, "Lots, and that's fer sure! The truth of the matter is, too many immigrants…drug pushers, thugs—"

"My question wasn't an accusation; a simple answer would do."

"Oh ya? A simple answer?" Dick vigorously rubbed his arm and stepped closer to his son. "You always want me to quote some high fallutin' research study."

"I'm not evaluating your intelligence," Rick said. "I just want credible facts."

"Oh c'mon!" Dick said, then elbowed Rick hard enough to push him into his mother.

Dorothy stumbled then steadied herself. "Don't get me calling the police on you two!" She reached for the phone in her purse.

Dick's face turned white. He looked at Dorothy and said, "I don't feel so hot, maybe I…." His voice trailed as he gasped for air, clutched his chest, took one wobbly step forward, and, with a resounding boom, crashed to the floor.

"Dick!" Dorothy shrieked and dropped down beside her husband. "Call 911, Ricky! Dad's had a heart attack!"

Within minutes, a team of Emergency Medical Services arrived and promptly diagnosed Dick with cardiac arrest. Dorothy and Rick looked on in terror as two paramedics worked on him in a manner Dorothy later described as violent. After resuscitating him, they lifted Dick onto a stretcher and slid him into the ambulance.

"Foothills, we're taking your husband to the Foothills Hospital," one shouted back to Dorothy now standing beside Rick and watching from the sidelines.

Rick rested his head on top of his mother's and groaned, "This was all my fault."

Dorothy pulled away and gasped. "Don't go there. Just don't."

As the van backed out of the driveway, siren blaring and emergency lights flashing, Dorothy said, "Phone Joy. Tell her we're on our way to the hospital."

In the hospital's emergency waiting room, Rick intermittently paced from his chair to the window and back again while waiting for information about his father's condition. When the nurse arrived, she explained how Dr. Salib, the cardiovascular surgeon, had successfully opened a blocked artery to restore normal blood flow. "Your husband needs to rest quietly and allow our experienced team of medical staff to continuously monitor his heart for any signs of bleeding or abnormal function. I'll take you to his room for a short visit, but please remember that visitors—family only, at this time—must be calm. Dr. Salib will try to drop by and update you on his condition."

"We'd like to give my husband a few minutes of quiet, loving support," Dorothy said, taking Rick's arm to steady herself. As they followed the nurse through long hallways filled with soft-spoken, blue-gowned medics, Rick recalled how ten years ago he had walked this hospital's halls to visit his mother as she recovered from a hysterectomy. This time, the air felt heavy with medicinal odours and solemn concern.

In the Cardiovascular Intensive Care Unit, Dick Wright lay under crisp white sheets. Rick noticed his chalky complexion that contrasted sharply with heavy dark circles under his eyes.

"Looks more like a corpse than a sick man at rest," Rick whispered to Dorothy, who walked over and enveloped her husband's hand in both of hers. "Ricky and I are here for you, Dick." She closed her eyes and wiped her blotchy cheeks.

Dick slowly opened his tired, filmy eyes and gently squeezed Dorothy's hand, then looked at Rick and let his head flop to one side of the pillow.

Rick stepped into the hall and repeatedly tugged at his shirt collar, then texted his Uncle Harry. Feeling lost in an oppressive fog, he leaned his forehead against the wall where he stood motionless until Dorothy came out and patted his shoulder.

"Let Dad know you're here for him...that you're worried."

Rick didn't budge.

"He's your father, Ricky, the flesh of your flesh." Dorothy waited. "Ricky," she pleaded, "for all we know Dad's time is almost up."

Rick lumbered into the room and stood at his father's bedside. *Looks defeated*, he thought, then studied his father's slack jaw and listened to sporadic moans that sounded like small branches cracking in the wind. He twitched his nostrils at a faint smell of...vinegar? Disinfectant? On the verge of nausea, Rick rested his hand on his father's shoulder. Words that troubled his mind, thickened his tongue. "You'll pull through this, Dad. I'm betting on you."

Dick looked at his son with a lingering facial expression Rick couldn't decipher, then closed his eyes again. Rick briefly hovered over his father before walking to the window and absorbing the soothing colours of a sky tinged with wide streaks of pink and smatterings of yellow. *Who was it that warned us to be careful what we wish for? Can't make sense of anything.*

Oblivious of the physician who had entered the room, Dorothy sat massaging Dick's hand in a repetitive motion, as if she were wringing her own.

The surgeon stepped close to Dorothy and spoke softly, "Hello, Mrs. Wright, I'm Doctor Salib." He shook her hand and looked over at Rick. "Are you Mr. Wright's son?"

"Yes, I'm Rick Wright. Thanks for coming by."

Dr. Salib smiled. "Your father's main artery was blocked, but we've managed to widen it and increase the blood flow—a common procedure." He looked back at Dorothy. "We'll carefully assess your husband's progress throughout the night, and tomorrow morning we'll test the results of surgery. Rest assured that professionals at the nursing station will keep a very close eye on him."

"Will he...what are his chances for a full recovery?" Dorothy asked.

Dr. Salib rested his hand on Dorothy's shoulder. "Since everything went as planned, we expect your husband will fully recover."

Haltingly, Dorothy said, "Thank you, doctor—thank you for giving Dick the best possible care."

"Yes, yes, of course, but he needs plenty of rest, so please make your visit brief. We'll welcome you back tomorrow any time after nine o'clock."

Having smelled Dick's rancid beer breath, Rick followed Dr. Salib into the hallway and quietly said, "About this time of day, Dad would be staring into his second or third mug of beer, then pretty much finish a bottle of dinner wine."

"Thank you, Rick," Dr. Salib said. "Important information."

Rick and Dorothy chatted quietly about their confidence in Dr. Salib and the strangeness of seeing Dick in a hospital bed, asleep but breathing heavily.

A short while later, Dick half opened his eyes as Dorothy leaned over him and kissed his forehead. "We'll follow the doctor's orders and keep our visit brief. Sleep well, my dear. I'll see you tomorrow morning."

Dick started to respond, but Dorothy put her fingers to his lips. "Don't try to talk; you need to sleep. There'll be time to visit after you're well rested and feeling better. Just know that we're all praying for you."

Rick patted his father's shoulder. "I've texted Joy, who's at work, and Uncle Harry. We'll all drop in tomorrow, after you've had a good sleep."

Rick and Dorothy had barely stepped in the door when Joy phoned. "Just finished my shift…didn't get your message until now." Rick started to assure her that their father was in good hands, but she quickly interrupted. "Can Al and I pick up an extra-large pizza and come over?"

"Please do. See you soon."

At the kitchen table, Rick and Dorothy detailed what had happened as Joy and Al, listening intently from their medical perspectives, asked questions and gave opinions about Dick's prognosis. "Based on what you've said, Dick's condition is serious," Al said, "but modern medicine should have him home soon, provided his heart returns to normal functioning."

Questions followed, many unanswerable, as did lengthy silences. Joy reached over and grasped Rick's arm. "Hey Bro, you look done for the day."

Rick patted Joy's hand. "It's been a difficult one. Can we decide who's going to the hospital tomorrow and at what time?"

The family planned their visiting hours and when Joy and Al stood up to leave, Rick put his arm around Dorothy. "Will you be okay tonight, Mom?"

"Yes. We'll all get through this together." Dorothy looked at Joy and Al and smiled. "We're so lucky to have a nurse and paramedic in our family."

Alone in the kitchen, Rick gave his mother an extended goodnight hug, then went downstairs and turned on the TV to check the local news. Thoughts turned to Liv; his fingers, to the keyboard.

Dad's had a heart attack. In Foothills Hospital. Will put canvassing on hold for now. CBC news reported Mallore's lead dropped 4%. You're a close second. Terrif!

Dorothy and Joy picked up Rick after church and the three of them settled in for lunch at the hospital cafeteria. In a nearby corner, a family of four appeared burdened with sadness. Rick leaned into Joy. "Those teenagers at the back table look like they've just lost the family pet...or worse."

"I hate this place," Joy said. "Even the walls look sad."

"Funereal vibes," Rick said.

"Which reminds me, Ricky," Dorothy interjected. "Joy and I were moved by Father McFarland's sermon about the gift of life and finding meaning in sorrow. I think you would've liked what he had to say...very philosophic."

"Perhaps," Rick curtly replied.

Conversation waned as they finished their lunch and went to Dick's room, where Dorothy kissed her husband's cheek and reached in her purse for a comb to tame the remaining few tufts of hair around his temples.

Rick stood close by. "You're looking much better today, Dad."

"Better, but tired," Joy said, as if answering for her father while fussing with the bedcovers. "Uncle Harry and Aunt Rose should arrive soon for a short visit."

Dick scanned Dorothy's face, then Joy's and Rick's. "Thank you for coming. Don't know why I'm so tired. Haven't done a bloody thing...except think things over."

Dorothy nervously twisted her wedding band. "You couldn't sleep last night?"

"Too restless to sleep, strange bed and all. Need a stronger sleeping pill, and my woman beside me."

Moments later, Harry and Rose arrived with a vase of fresh flowers. "That hospital bed doesn't suit you," said Harry, smiling. "You look better behind your solid oak desk." As Rose rearranged the flowers and put the vase on the window ledge, Harry continued, "Don't worry about the firm. We'll keep a tight ship until your old self is back. Remember, I got through my heart attack; you can too. At least you don't need a bypass."

Dick smiled and gave a thumbs-up.

After a short interlude, Rick looked longingly at his father. "Dad, there's something I've been wanting to say...was foolishly waiting for the right moment." He pinched his nose and looked downward. "I'm sorry for all the angry arguments we've had. All the times I've pushed you away."

Those words, Rick thought, *disembodied for years.* Something within him was crying out to also apologize for his hideous Boxing Day retaliation, but the best he could offer was a stumbling compliment. "I liked your comment awhile back, that somewhere along the way...what was it you said? We took a wrong turn?" Rick looked at his father's grizzled face and hoped for some spark of affection. Stepping closer, he found it in his father's rueful gaze.

"I'm sorry too, son. Let's make a U-turn on that road." Dick smiled and added, "Two wrongs don't make a right—a Rick or Dick Wright."

Rick chuckled. "You haven't lost your sense of humour."

Dick spoke quietly. "But I haven't been the father you deserve."

Rick's eyes widened in disbelief. "I think you just became that father." He felt his throat constrict; his eyes watered. "And I haven't been honest with you. Anger was my disguise for sadness." Rick sniffled and looked deep into his father's eyes. "I desperately longed for—"

Dick interrupted. "Thought I needed to toughen you up for the hard knocks this world will give you."

Harry and Rose had walked to the back of the room to give what little privacy they could to the family. They stood beside a nurse, who leaned into Harry and whispered, "Best the family only make supportive comments. Mr. Wright needs rest if he's to repair his damaged cardiovascular system."

Harry violated polite social distance. "Right now, my brother needs to apologize if he's to repair his damaged relationships."

Dick slowly turned his sorrowful face toward Dorothy. "And you, my good wife. I haven't been the husband you deserve, that's fer sure. I pray to God for a second chance to prove I can do better."

Dorothy pulled her chair closer to Dick's bed and tried to meet her husband's eyes, but blinked and looked away. "I haven't always been a good wife."

Dick reached for her hand and held her eyes as if he knew she had dreams that didn't include him. As if he knew something hurtful was gnawing at Dorothy's conscience. "What good will regrets do, Dorothy? At least you can change whatever's tearing you apart. I might not be so lucky."

Joy gawked out the window as if seeing elephants flapping their ears in full flight.

Dorothy lowered her head, thought a moment, then looked up and, with a loving smile, said all she needed to.

The nurse walked to the door and looked back at the family. "I'll be monitoring Mr. Wright's vital signs and, with the rest of my team, we'll see that he makes a full recovery. May I remind you to keep your visit short."

Rick smiled sincerely. "Thank you for taking good care of Dad."

Harry chatted with Dick until he looked dozy. Ending her quiet vigil, Dorothy reached for her coat and leaned over her husband. "We should leave now, but remember dear, you're in our every prayer."

Dick gave a shuddering yawn and half opened his eyes. "Thanks for coming everyone."

Rick moved closer to his father. "I'll be back soon, Dad."

"Me too," Dick replied, "as in home. A couple of days in this joint oughta be enough."

Joy rested her hand on her father's arm and surreptitiously took his pulse. "I'm praying for you, Dad."

"Don't worry Miss Joyful, I'll be okay no matter what."

Harry and Rose wished Dick a speedy recovery and as the family walked to the elevator, Joy anxiously reported, "Dad's heart...not good; misses every other beat."

Rose glanced back and said, "Let's talk more about that over dinner tonight. I took a big tub of spaghetti sauce out of the freezer, hoping you'd all join Harry and me." Rose stepped closer to Joy. "Including Al, of course, if he isn't on duty. Six o'clock?"

"Thanks, Aunt Rose. A family get together is just what we need," Rick said, Dorothy and Joy agreeing.

Joy passed Rick her car keys as they walked through the parking lot and said, "Sorry I'm such a cry baby, but I'd have bet big money that you and Dad would never apologize to each other. Remember when you told me that if you ever weakened—at the time, I took that to mean apologize—I should check your marble bag? But tonight, both of you...."

"Even rocks change, Sis." Rick stepped into Joy's car and adjusted the rear-view mirror.

Between sniffles, Joy said, "I can't...can't shut off the waterworks."

Seeing his sister's face awash in tears, Rick glanced back at her. "Next Christmas I'll give you windshield wipers for your eyes."

"Good one, Ricky."

Everyone remained silent until, nearing home, Rick said, "Who knows what a near-death experience can jump start. 'Twas almost as if overnight, Dad wrestled his demons to the ground and there's now hope for the *possibility* of better relationships."

Joy said, "And Mom, after Dad said he wants to be a better husband, you said you hadn't always been a good wife. What was *that* all about?"

Dorothy sighed. "Nothing in particular, honey."

If Joy only knew, Rick thought, then intervened to rescue his mother from any further probing. "In the face of death, everything's so...what's the word I'm searching for, Mom?"

Dorothy thought a moment. "Poignant?"

"That's it," Rick said, pulling into the driveway. "Time for me to take a walk along the river."

Under a brilliant blue sky, Rick inhaled the sharp winter air as he meandered along the familiar river pathway and opened himself to his favourite teacher. With humility and awe, he studied nature's cycle of life—the snow that partially buried a wind-torn wasp's nest, the lone brown leaf that clung to a high branch as if refusing to surrender to winter, and tree rings that marked time just as age spots disclosed its passing on Dick's hands. Rick bowed his head to the snow-covered Earth and pondered how all living things are controlled by unelected, undemocratic, and ungovernable forces of life and death.

Later that afternoon, family members who had witnessed the run-up to The Incident seated themselves at Harry and Rose's dining room table. Except the patriarch. Throughout the meal, Rick was consumed by haunting memories of their last dinner together—the sound of his father's incensed voice, his thumping the dinner table, and failed attempts to quell the brewing storm, then footsteps stomping down the stairs. As he twirled spaghetti noodles around his fork, he wondered what others were thinking. *Will we ever talk about what went so wrong on Boxing Day? Have they forgiven me?*

After tea and cookies, Rose reached for an album of faded photos from an old camera. Harry looked long and hard at a graduation picture of himself and Dick, proudly standing with his arm around his younger brother who'd been awarded a Business Diploma with distinction. "That's a go-to memory," he said.

Dorothy tried to spot Dick in an old, yellowed photo of his young hockey team huddled together on the ice for a photo op. "That's him," she said, confidently pointing to a grim-looking boy in the front row. She looked up at Harry. "Wonder where you were when that was taken."

"Who knows, but when Dick was about eight—I'd have been six—we got skates for Christmas. He learned to move the blades well enough to play defense for Peewee and Bantam hockey leagues…but many penalties gave him the nickname, Sinbin Wright. When Dick was on the ice or football field, I'd cheer him on from the bleachers, or lose myself in some book at the town library. I remember the long, lonely weekends when Mom was hammered and Dad was either promoting show homes or doing God knows what with a willing female."

Rose gave Harry's arm a quick squeeze, then pointed to an old sepia photo and nudged Dorothy. "Remember that night before you and Dick got married…the four of us sat on the living room floor of your small apartment and got high on marijuana?"

"Whose idea was *that*?" Al asked, laughing through his words. "It was illegal then."

"Mine, of course," Rose said, with a tinge of pride. "And wacky tobaccy's back! Might make more of those Mary Jane muffins."

Harry grinned, and Dorothy watched her grown children laugh extravagantly. With tensions eased and memories surfacing, the family flipped through the remaining few pages until they came to the last leaf of the album. Rick tapped a picture of his grandfather Wright holding Dick as a baby. "Hey, Uncle Harry, you mentioned Grandpa Wright's car accident the night you and I had tea in your kitchen, but I'd like to know more."

"That memory is as vivid as yesterday," Harry said, staring into his lap. "Late one night, about three months before Dick's high-school graduation, I heard a heavy car door slam, looked out my bedroom window, and saw a police cruiser in the driveway where Dad usually parked. I ran into Dick's room and shouted, 'Get up! The cops are here!' We thought burglars might be prowling about, so we tiptoed downstairs." Harry looked lovingly at Rick. "Your dad stepped over to the front door and bravely hollered, 'Who is it?'"

Harry paused, then blinked rapidly and continued. "A friendly, middle-aged cop from the police detachment asked if he could come in." Harry looked directly at Rick and winked. "Incidentally, Dick I later found out that the cop's wife thanked your grandfather for selling their house by adding another freebee to his checklist of dalliances. In a small town, that's the kind of stuff people love to gossip about. Anyway, I remember the officer putting his hand on Dick's shoulder and telling us that he was sorry to bring us such awful news, but a short while ago, Dad was killed instantly in a head-on collision with a tractor trailer. The cop assured us that paramedics did everything they could to save him, but his injuries were too massive."

Rick shook his head. "What a terrible shock. Must've been hard to believe."

"We were stunned. I went totally blank until Dick shrieked, 'Dead? Dad's dead? Fuckin' goddamn world!' Pardon my language, but those were Dick's exact words, still as clear as the train whistle that roared through town every night about that same time."

"What did you do after that…after you got the news?" Joy asked.

"The cop wanted to know if there was anyone we'd like him to call, but Dick said he'd phone Ben, an insurance agent and good friend of Dad's. We really liked Ben…took us fishing a few times when Dad was AWOL. He came right over and helped us through the whole ordeal."

Rose topped up Harry's tea as he continued, "Dick has always had my back. Pushed me to further my education so we could start our own business. Covered half the down payment for our mortgage, eh Rose?" Harry scanned the faces at the table and said, in a tremulous voice, "Because of him, we're all better off today."

"Jeez, if only Dad could've talked about his wretched past," Rick thumped his chest. "With us! His own family!"

Harry looked as sullen as a grave digger. "He couldn't, for the same reasons I haven't been able to, until recently. After all these years, our childhood still haunts us. But Dick won't go there."

Rick twisted his mouth sideways and pointed to a photo. "In that one of Dad standing beside his dazed mother—" Rick's voice broke from the strain of stark imagery. "I glimpsed that same, frightened little-boy look on his face today."

"Only a week ago," Dorothy said, "Dick lived as if he had many tomorrows. Now this—a chance for all of us to think about our lives…regrets and sorrows."

"I'd rather think about the future," Rick said. "How Dad and I will try something different. Something new and exciting. But he'll have to stop drinking."

Dorothy gave a loud moan. "Rose," she said firmly, "let me help you clear the table."

Home again, Rick walked his mom through the front door and into the kitchen. "If you're up before I leave in the morning, can we have breakfast together? You could come downstairs and have breakfast with me for a change. Bagels and peanut butter. Cream cheese, if you prefer. My instant coffee's nothing to brag about, but I do have a special way of whipping it into shape."

Dorothy smiled then stumbled as if she were about to collapse. Rick steadied her and wrapped her frail body in his arms. "Always at your side, Mom."

"Thanks, honey," Dorothy said, then summoned the energy to stand alone. "Come up for breakfast and I'll grind us some fresh coffee beans." She took Rick's face in her hands. "Sleep well tonight, my one and only son. I love you with all my heart."

Rick squeezed his mom's hand. "Love you too, my one and only Mom, all the way to the moon and back. Remember how you told us that as kids?"

Dorothy's eyes watered. "What would I do without you and Joy, the loves of my life. I'm so blessed."

Rick's phone gently shook his pocket.

Sorry to hear about your dad, Rick. Sorry too about other things. You'll likely want to spend time at the hospital, but if possible, how about coffee tomorrow night, Caffeine Castle, 8:30?

Rick wondered what else Liv was sorry about. Telling him three strikes and he's out? Pinch hitter, Noah?

Chapter 12

Standing motionless in front of his living room window, Rick felt like he was in an altered state of consciousness. He inhaled the fresh midnight air and stared at the glistening streaks of colour in moonlit icicles that hung from the eaves. *What have I got to lose?* He tapped Liv a reply: *Nice idea Lady Janson. Meet you tomorrow night in the castle.*

Rick strolled into Dick's newly assigned room on the hospital's Day Unit and greeted his father, who was working his way through a bowl of tomato soup as his mother worked her way through the daily crossword.

"Hey Dad, do you feel as good as you look…in your own silk pyjamas, no less?" Silk was Dick's signature attire. Even at work, he usually wore Dorothy's choice of silk blend shirts, adorned with slim-cut silk ties, both of which she'd give him for Christmas and birthdays.

"Still exhausted," Dick answered. "Appetite's coming back and I'm sleeping better." He moved his empty soup bowl to the back of the tray and lifted the warming lid to uncover a thin slice of lean ham, plain green beans, and a small scoop of mashed potatoes with one pat of margarine. Beside the plate was a dish of carrot and raisin salad and a small, whole-wheat dinner roll. "There's never enough butter or salad dressing, and strawberries without chocolate sauce hardly passes for dessert." With that, Dorothy reached into her purse for a Ziploc bag that she placed beside Dick's supper tray. "I ran this by the nurse on my way in—your favourite fruit and nut bread. One slice every other day, but that's all. Doctor's orders."

"Dorothy, if you don't mind my saying so, you're a peach."

"Why would I mind a compliment from my husband?" Dorothy said, looking somewhat unsettled.

"Oh, women's lib and all. Thought the peachy part might be politically incorrect."

"Let's just say I'm glad you didn't call me doll face."

Rick gave a sly grin and placed the latest copy of a popular business magazine on the night table. "Some light reading for you."

"Thanks, both of you. Very thoughtful."

"I put in a full day's work and all's well at the office," Rick cheerfully announced. "Uncle Harry's at the front desk, odd as *that* looks…said to say hello and tell you the sail's up and HMS Wright Brothers is tacking to the wind."

"Hey, family," Joy chirped, striding in with a vase of red and yellow roses and looking for a spot to place them.

"Why thank you, Miss Joyful. Bring that pretty bouquet over and let me smell the roses—somethin' I've been too damn busy to do."

Dick closed his eyes and savoured the aroma as Dorothy reminded him how good she felt every Mother's Day when he gave her a dozen long-stem roses.

Did she really mean that? Rick wondered. *How's she handling thoughts of Efner as she sits bedside?*

Supper finished, Dick rested his cloudy blue eyes on his son. "Tell me, what's happening with that Liberal friend you've taken a liking to? What's her name?"

Astonished, Rick smiled as if he meant it. "Liv Janson. Her team's running a smart campaign and, judging by the reception she gets at the doors, we think she has a good shot at winning this one. But you'll be glad to know that at an all-candidates' debate, Ron Mallore spoke well. You'd have liked his opening address."

"No surprise there, but nice of you to say so."

"I used to think there was absolutely nothing good about the Conservative Party, but I've been rethinking a few of my ideas. Most people—Conservatives and Liberals alike—strive for a better world; they just differ on how to get there."

Dorothy smiled in the general direction of all humanity as she listened to Rick and her husband talk politics like a normal, caring father and son—like two mature adults.

"Does Ron Mallore have a website?" Dick asked.

"He does." Rick pulled out his phone and his father read Mallore's "About" section. In a strong voice, he said, "Mallore has my vote if I'm outta prison in time."

"Here's hoping one more day of recovery will do it," Rick said. "Democracy needs your vote." He tucked his fist under his chin and continued, "I'm reading *The Righteous Mind: Why Good People are Divided by Politics and Religion*—a book for all families that bicker about those topics. It's helping me understand why intelligent people vehemently argue about different views."

"And...?" Dick said, looking bewildered. "Your point is...?"

"Time to drop the pretenses. I don't have any answers to the big questions. But hey, humans have moved from the age of agriculture to industry and technology, the next better be the age of otherly love. If we can't do that, we're doomed."

In a measured tone, Dick said, "you mean brotherly love."

"No. Otherly love would include women; in fact, every person and group that differs from ourselves. Isn't that the Bible's main message?"

"Indeed it is," Joy said, smiling profusely at Rick.

Dick reached for his glass of water, smiled, and gave a conciliatory nod.

Rick felt a wave of inner gratitude. When his mother began idle chit-chat that ended with reference to the Calgary Flames' recent win, he highlighted the final plays for his father, who now had a TV in his room but had fallen asleep during the second period. In the final play of their visit, comfortable spaces blended with relaxed conversation until Joy patted her father's arm and took his pulse. "Your heart's ticking along, doing what it should, but it still needs lots of rest. As for me, I should pick up Al, but please keep this in mind," she said as she leaned over and kissed Dick's forehead. "I love you, Dad."

"I should be going too, Dad," Rick said. "Good to see you're in fine shape, given all you've been through."

Dorothy gave Dick a puckered kiss and awkward bed hug. "Sleep well, dear. See you tomorrow morning." Walking to the elevator, she nudged Joy and said, "Nurse Wright, did you manage to take Dad's pulse again?"

"I did. Don't want to alarm you, but his heart still misses about every eighth beat, according to my reading. We need to ask the doctor about that tomorrow."

Rick said, "I'll ask too, and we'll compare notes. Oh sheesh! Might have to pass on tomorrow's visit…busy time at work and I have an English assignment due." Rick winked at Joy and added, "I'm meeting Liv for coffee in twenty minutes."

Joy winked back as Dorothy asked, "What's your assignment about?"

"Transitions. How to move from one literary scene to another. I have enough trouble doing that in everyday life—from classes to work to door knocking and hospital visits. The warehouse supply most in need of replenishing is me, but don't tell Dad that. And don't tell him that I think what happened between us tonight was stranger than anything this side of the Twilight Zone. Bewildering, but beautiful."

Rick approached Liv's table at the Caffeine Castle and, as always, her smile took his breath away. "Good news," he said, pulling out a chair and hoping to set a positive tone for their meeting. "Dad's rallying. Yesterday we managed a few remorseful words that might've jump-started a new relationship. God knows our current one's more damaged than his heart."

"Sounds exciting; glad to hear that," Liv said as five boisterous teens burst into the coffee shop and sat within hearing range. Three of them talked over each other until the smaller girl of the two criticized their behaviour. "You're all acting like badass brats in the sandbox trying to out-do each other."

The tallest boy flung his hands wide open and blew a puff of air. "Meh, it's just the way guys are. Don't mean nothin' by it."

Rick moved his chair closer to Liv's. "What is it about guys who need to prove they're bigger, stronger, and smarter than everyone else? When will they get out of the sandbox?"

Liv rubbed her tense jaw as if she had a grinding toothache. Her expression hardened. "Weren't you in that sandbox when you jumped up and shouted Mallore down, then kicked sand in the guy's face behind you?"

Raising his voice above the teenage din, Rick said, "I wanted to support you, not piss you off. I would've sat down if that moron behind me hadn't jabbed me in the neck and called me a Commie. Didn't intend to hit him. Reflexes kicked in. Did you see how he baited me as he backed out of the room? Wanted to take me on outside."

Liv raised her eyebrows; said nothing.

"I knew by the way you looked at me that I had to leave." Rick drummed his fingers on the table. "I shouldn't have called him a moron. A woman told me on my way out that he's mentally ill. Apparently, he's had a string of arrests for disorderly conduct. Hope he gets the help he needs."

"Me too," Liv said, "but what if he or someone else starts another heated argument at the next debate?"

"Don't worry, I owe it to myself not to indulge someone's rage, but I'm glad I called Mallore on his ignorant comment. Whatever's good for business is *not* good for everyone. Privatizing health care and education would fatten the coffers of the wealthy and destroy public services that benefit the common good. That's us, Liv, and everyone else who pays taxes that give corporations the infrastructure to make their CEOs filthy rich."

"I agree, but you…you still sound angry."

Rick thought for a moment. "I am working up a lather, aren't I? Therapy's helping me with that."

Liv waited, as if she could tell by the way Rick answered that he wanted to take it further.

Pointing to the adolescents at the next table, Rick toned down his voice. "I was once like them. It's taken a while, but I'm finally learning better ways to communicate."

"Would that apply to Noah? You were quite condescending toward him."

Now it's Noah! For Chrissakes, gimme a break! Rick tried a show of patience.

"Has obvious insecurities, but he means well." Liv slowly stirred her coffee. "Six years ago, a close friend lost her fiancé in a car crash. Now, when people complain about someone, she simply says, 'You're alive; he—or she—is alive. That's all that matters.'"

"Yeah. Noah was just being…alive." Rick glanced at Liv, hoping for a show of comic relief, which was clearly absent.

"And you were just being you?" Liv's face suddenly softened.

Rick hoped for a flash of inspiration. "Liv, you're alive; I'm alive. That's all that matters." He gulped and briefly closed his eyes. "Can we move on? I'm going through a lot now."

Liv stared at her coffee as if she pitied it. "Sorry, Rick. I was insensitive to where you're at."

Rick saw the remorse in Liv's eyes. "What I like about you is your honesty. Your openness. Both of us can make thoughtless comments, but at least we talk things out. We take risks. I take risks…because I care. If I didn't, I'd take the easy way out."

Liv lightly rubbed Rick's forearm. "Well said."

Feeling like their quarrel had brought them closer, Rick rested his hand on Liv's. "I've missed being with you and the team. How's the campaign going, Madam Premier?"

Liv summarized her recent press interview, her munificent financial contributions from committed Liberals, and positive reactions from people at the doors. For their remaining time together, conversation was breezy until Liv asked, "I'm curious, but there's no need to answer this: How's therapy going?"

Rick half winked. "I'll spare you the tedious details and simply say that Dr. Grey's been confronting my mistaken beliefs—one of which is that I have a gift for diplomacy and personal insight. Duh!" Both chuckled as Rick added, "A couple more sessions, then I'll take a break and practice everything I've learned until I become God's specimen of the perfect male."

Liv smiled adoringly and once again, Rick felt short of breath just looking at her. "I'm glad we've cleared the air," she said. "Please don't feel obligated to door knock or update social media at this stressful time for you and your dad. If necessary, John and I can manage press releases and the website for the rest of the campaign."

"Thanks. I won't feel obligated, but will do what I can between work, classes, and hospital visits…or during them. Dad sleeps a lot."

Rick walked Liv to the end of a dark street where she'd parked her car, then gathered her in and kissed her with high-octane passion. "Sleep well, my dear." He ached for her, and although he sensed a slight withdrawal from her usual warmth, he plunged ahead. "How about some decadent delight—a little skin to skin?"

"Sorry, Rick. I'd like that, but I'm beat. Next time."

With hopes dashed for a romantic evening, Rick trudged to his car, snow crunching beneath heavy feet. *Love's so unpredictable.* He picked up the pace when he considered that he'd just experienced the intimate connection of openness, vulnerability, and honesty— qualities he admired. *Sex and a few spasms of orgasm. Exquisite pleasure, but less important. I guess.*

After a challenging English class, Rick and Gabe went straight to The Den, sat at the bar, and ordered a brown pop, Rick's term for beer.

"Hey Gabe, what's up with you and Sally?"

"I'm done with her, but she isn't done with me. Bears grudges. Her load of shit, not mine. I'm relieved, but don't like the way I ended things."

"If you're relieved, you made the right move, but that's only a guess. The Green Monster bared its teeth when I ran into Liv's ex in the parking lot outside her office and instantly assumed we were done. Was stopped for speeding on my way home but luckily, got off easy. Can't blame Liv or Noah for my stupidity; did that little number all by myself...on myself."

"That's what Sally did—jumped to conclusions that I didn't love her. Ruined whatever future we might've had by needing proof from the git-go that we were a committed couple. Don't do it, man. But hey, I'm hardly the one to give advice—the guy who's incompetent with women."

"Oh, but Mr. Incompetent, I noticed you and Brittany walking out together last week. Whazzup with you two? Are you hooked?"

"I'll let you know if anything *big* happens."

Rick returned Gabe's infectious grin. "That tells me all I need to know...for now."

"Put that bit about wild assumptions making us do dumb things in your short story," Gabe said. "Doc Evans will love it."

"Speaking of Evans, she gave me quite the feedback on what I've written so far. Said my story has the potential to morph into a full-length, epic novel." Rick threw his arms in the air. "Epic, no less! Damn near burst out laughing, then waxed philosophic about Camus' praise for writers who keep civilizations from turning to rat shit."

"What! Camus said that?"

Rick laughed. "I'm paraphrasing. Should've told Evans my story was largely autobiographical, especially the part where my romantic screw up ruined my best laid plans for getting laid. Some sex would've—"

A booming voice chimed in, "Sex? Did someone say sex?"

"Hey, Barney," Rick said, glancing at the wad of weed tucked behind his former classmate's ear.

"According to my ex, I know nothing about the finer details of fucking."

Gabe reached over and shook Barney's hand. "I'm Gabe. Rick and I are in the same class. Same election campaign team too."

"Oh yeah?" Rocking on his heels, Barney turned to Rick and boldly asked, "Who ya supporting?"

Without hesitation, Rick said, "Liv Janson. Liberal candidate for Mount Vista."

Barney plunked himself down on a barstool beside Rick, pushed his empty mug to the far edge of the counter and shouted to the bartender, "Pull me a pint," then swivelled toward Rick and Gabe.

Rick flashed back to a small gathering of fellow Political Science students who'd gathered in The Den where Barney so dominated the conversation with his hard-nosed ideas that Rick whispered to the student beside him, "Wright should've been Barney's surname. Middle name: Absolutely."

"Hope this doesn't fog your windshield," Rick said lightheartedly, "but I've heard you talk politics before, right over there." He pointed to a large table near the wall and added, "I get the feeling you're fifty shades of black and fifty shades of white…for the blue party."

Barney grimaced. "Huh? Face reality, man. Liberals would raise taxes and squander the revenue on frivolous social programs. We need more private delivery of health care and education, fewer taxes and tuition cuts, for starters." He pushed out his bottom lip. "The less government the better. Liberty and individual freedom are my motto. I'll vote Conservative unless some ballsy guy runs Independent."

"Or woman?" Rick said, in a subdued voice. "And I'll vote for the candidate who believes we're all in this together—a Liberal value."

Gabe sharply intervened. "Barney, how could people on minimum wages pay private companies for quality health care and education?"

"Listen, Gabe! People who have the work ethic should run this country; the rest of us have to step up and take care of ourselves and families. Government can't save us from incompetents and batshit crazies."

A hundred billion neurons in Rick's cranium screamed dogmatism. Putrid dogmatism. Still, he cautioned himself to be open-minded and respectfully listen. "Hey, Barney," Rick said, unaware that his grin had a hint of malice. "What would it take for you to change your mind and vote for a Liberal candidate this time around?"

Like a little kid with a temper tantrum, Barney flapped his arms. "Nothin', man! Fuckin' nothin'! Liberals can't manage their way out of winter underwear! Conservatives would put more money in consumers' pockets for goods and services, investments in the stock market, new business start-ups...anything that grows the economy."

Something dislodged in Gabe. "Try to get the hang of being human, Barney. There'll always be some people who can't make it. Are you a team player or just out for yourself?" Shifting to a jocular tone, he added, "Some of us haven't evolved beyond cave men thumping their chests around the campfire."

"Yeah, Barney," Rick said, "sharpen your pencil on *that!*"

Nostrils flaring and faintly wheezing, Barney said, "Whoa! Sharpen *your* pencil on this. You've both been taken in by the left-wing media's fake news and Social Science profs who teach stuff that doesn't mean fuck all! They're soft in the head."

Rick clenched his fists. "Jesus H. Christ, Barney, don't you see what's happening in this world!"

"What the fuck does the *H* stand for?"

"Damned if I know, but may I indulge your patience and tell you what our Poli-Sci prof and a retired History prof said about political tyrants?"

"Podium's all yours, sir," Barney said, bowing his head condescendingly.

"The first thing wannabe dictators do is hook people on idealistic promises." Rick looked down his nose and did his best imitation of Donald Trump. "I'll make this country great again! Reduce taxes. Create thousands of new jobs. End poverty."

"Kindly tell me, Rick, what's wrong with that?"

"Here's what's wrong," Rick said, recalling the A+ paper he'd written for his Political Science course. "Authoritarian assholes don't care about *any* of that. They only care about making false promises, creating chaos, and repeating propaganda that stokes fear in the vulnerable. Next up, malign your opponents and lambaste the media for spewing fake news, then shred the justice system—secret service agents, court officials, the rule of law...oh, and sack human rights, especially for minority groups. In short, attack everything democracy values by repeating vicious lies ad nauseam to brainwash the gullible. Presto! A narcissistic psychopath becomes an idolized hero. A cult is born." Rick sighed and proudly folded his arms across his chest.

Gabe grinned at Barney, pointed to Rick, and said, "Profound gravitas!"

Barney's eyes were a vivid shade of anger. "Relax, Rick! You're all steamed up about stuff that doesn't concern us."

"Listen, politics *should* concern us," Rick declared. "You need to understand that politicians who cling to their truths with adamant certainty, who don't question their beliefs because it's too uncomfortable, wade into a swamp of dogmatism." Rick snapped his fingers. "Poof! The promise of democracy vanishes in thin air. If people become too cynical or complacent to care about politics, that suits an authoritarian leader just fine." He waggled his eyebrows as if to establish his intellectual superiority.

Barney thumped the counter. "Well fuck me dead. I don't *need* to understand any of your crap."

Rick swept his arms open and swivelled his bar stool. "Look around you. Dogmatic rednecks are right here in The Den. Toss in hidebound bigots and science deniers and if any of them gain power, we're in trouble, man. Big time."

Barney kicked the side of the counter. "I'm no asshole bigot and I'm not dogmatic! Don't even go to church."

Rick's face was close enough to smell Barney's foul breath. "Hitler said, 'What luck for rulers when men do not think.'" He sat back and wallowed in his cleverness until the cursing in his head warned him he was preaching to a hardliner. *That dogmatist won't hunt.*

"Knock it off, Rick! Fuckin' call me the university's lunatic and be done with it!" Barney looked back at Gabe, whose facial expression seemed to say: What on Earth's happening here?

Gabe rested his elbows on the bar and massaged his temples. "Barney, sounds to me like you're one sentence shy of dogmatism, and Rick, you seem….” He paused, then deadpanned, “The two of you should write a book—a very short book. Call it *The Absolute Truth About Dogmatism.*”

Rick threw his head back and roared. “Can’t iron the wrinkles out of that irony! You’re more entertaining than parkour off the Calgary Tower.”

Barney let rip a monster belch, downed his last swig of beer, and gave his mug a hard flick of the thumb. “Thanks a little, Rick,” he scoffed, then stepped down from his perch, swiftly turned on his heels and marched to the back of The Den.

Gabe shot Rick a look. “Lucky me. My first lecture on dogmatism, complete with demo. Quiz to follow?”

“Lecture?” Rick recoiled from the word.

“Darwin could explain it better,” Gabe said, reaching for his phone.

Rick didn’t know if Gabe was bored, amused, or annoyed. Feeling somewhat chastened, he said, “A club in my hand and…well, hokay! From now on I’ll try to be more open-minded with the closed-minded Barneys of this world.”

Gabe slid his empty mug back and forth between the palms of his hands. “Barney was dogmatism at its finest, but you…you sounded like a smug, high and mighty academic.” He snapped his head toward the window. “For what it’s worth, nobody out there talks like that. You’re too brainy to get so bogged down in dogmatism. Doesn’t explain everything that’s wrong in this world—oceans are rising; bees are dying—and people aren’t thinking *together* to solve problems.”

“I know that, but—”

“Time to hit the road.” Gabe grabbed his jacket, flung his backpack over his shoulder, and walked out, leaving Rick tongue-tied. Feeling judged and misunderstood, he flamboyantly pushed his remaining beer to the middle of the counter. “What’s with him?" he muttered, giving his bar stool a hard spin before leaving.

Dick was having an after-supper snooze when Rick walked briskly into his room and came to an abrupt stop. Dorothy had put her index finger to her lips and was motioning Rick to follow her into the hallway.

"Good news," she said. "Dad's heart has stabilized and he'll be discharged tomorrow. The doctor put him on a strict regimen of exercise, diet, and medication. So far, he seems willing to follow orders."

"Here's hoping," Rick said, crossing his fingers. "I'm working tomorrow. Will you help him check out?"

"Mm-hmm. Come up for breakfast in the morning."

"Will do. Tell Dad I stopped by tonight but didn't want to wake him."

Later that evening, Rick decided that his run-in with Barney provided rich content for a dynamic chapter in his short story, one he'd title, Barney's Blarney, but before he started writing, he remembered Gabe's cutting words, his curt tone of voice and hasty departure.

Pissed off. Gabe was bloody pissed off with me. He then dug as deeply as humanly possible in search of the real motive for his pompous lecture to Barney. Minutes passed; how many he hadn't clocked. Digging his teeth into his bottom lip, he reached for his phone and sent a text.

Hey, Gabe, I'm in therapy to learn how to deal with Dad, but what I really need to deal with is that rotten apple at the foot of our family tree.

The following afternoon, when Rick got home from the warehouse he went straight to his parents' bedroom where Dick lay fully clothed on the bedspread, head propped on pillows and blankly staring at the TV.

"Welcome home, Dad. How does it feel to be back in your own bedroom?"

"Hungry and thirsty," Dick grumbled, then gave a melancholic shrug and muted the TV. "Can't have whatever I want any more—cold beer, steak with red wine, cake and cookies…the good stuff." He handed Rick a page that outlined his strict, daily routine. "Guess it's time to get serious about my health…exercise to begin with."

Who is this man? This rogue wave of reason? Did the spectre of death infuse him with logic? Rick scanned the regimen then looked up and smiled at his father.

"We could both use a little exercise, and this time of year, prices are slashed on treadmills, bikes, rowing machines—the whole shebang of workout equipment. I'll make room for a couple downstairs; you can work on one machine while I crank up the other."

"Remember," Dick said, sounding indifferent. "I've had a serious heart attack. Don't expect me to jog around the park in a few days."

Rick folded his arms across his chest and casually leaned against the dresser. Trying not to sound morbid, he said, "Ever since your heart attack, I'm curious to know if, like me, you think more about death; the inevitability of it and the dread of not knowing what happens after." Noticing the strained look on his father's face, he smiled provocatively. "Guess that's something we can't argue about."

Dick hesitated, then sighed deeply and said, "Life and death...it's simple. We're born. We put our time in. We die. Everything's on schedule, Ricky. Everything's on schedule."

Chapter 13

Later that night, Rick was digging into Rollo May's theory of Existential Psychology when Gabe's text arrived: *Serious flu. Hope to door knock this weekend. Rotten apple? Trash it. You'll be dead soon enough and long enough.*

Relieved to get Gabe's reply, Rick wrote: *Thanks for the upbeat text. Dad had a heart attack but is now home from Foothills and on the mend. Get better—dogmatic order.* ☺

Gabe replied immediately: *Sorry to hear that. Let me know when we can go skiing. Need crazy adventure. Will bring fresh apples!*

Rick spent the following day shelving and cataloguing supplies for the warehouse; tasks he was behind on but proficient at. Over lunch, his uncle confidentially mentioned a proposed buy-out of Wright Brothers. Lengthy discussions about the possible implications of selling the family firm made Rick feel special, a rare occasion in a setting overshadowed by his father's aura. In particular, he was deeply touched by Harry's suggestion that any potential buyer must agree to Rick's employment until he finishes post-graduate studies.

At the end of his workday, while stuck in traffic, Rick texted Dr. Grey: *Accident ahead. Traffic gridlock. Sorry, I'll be late.*

Rick arrived twenty-five minutes later for his scheduled fifth therapy session, apologized to Dr. Grey, and dropped his coat on the floor beside his usual chair. "I want to make the best use of our remaining time," he said, flopping down in his chair and twisting his toque in his hands. Teary-eyed, he summarized the week's events and delved into thoughts of death—his father's and his own.

"Lately, I sometimes feel like a mere shadow…or a dead leaf floating on a cold breeze. Can't find the words for life in the face of death. Feels like I'm on the edge of some shadowy force…standing outside the known world."

Dr. Grey looked lost in a thoughtful moment.

"Call it spiritual," Rick said. "Whatever *it* is that sweeps over me, I'm trying to make peace with it…remind myself that life's still beautiful as it is, despite the unknowns."

"A powerful journey into yourself and beyond. Has any of what you've described so movingly altered your view of your father as he struggles with what could be a terminal condition?"

Rick gnawed on his bottom lip. "I've traipsed around too many lost opportunities to tell Dad I'm sorry for my savage retaliation on Boxing Day…most of all, that neither of us has ever told each other, 'I love you.' During my last visit, I desperately wanted to say those three powerful words, but the best I could do was fumble with a flimsy apology for all the times I've argued with him. All the times I've pushed him away."

"What was that like for you, imperfect as it was?"

"Stifled my emotions in front of Dad, then wailed like a baby when I got home." Tears burned Rick's cheeks as he buried his face in his hands and visualized his father's smile—a warm, fatherly smile.

Dr. Grey gave him space until Rick reached for a tissue and said, "Sorry. Sadness took hold."

"Sorry for sadness? As I see it, the strong in you embraced the weak. The whole embraced the parts."

Another prolonged silence.

"My big fat façade finally crumbled enough to alter my view of Dad. Up until now, I couldn't see him as anything beyond a raging extremist. I now see how growing up in tragic circumstances chiselled the sharp edges to his personality."

Dr. Grey tapped her fingers together. "Hurt and loss. Isn't that what you both grew up with?"

Rick propped one elbow on the arm of his chair and curled his fingers into a tight ball. "In my reflective moments—more frequent since coming here—I've seriously questioned whether I treat Dad much the same way he treats me. It's now painfully obvious that we've both been barking up the wrong tree. A dogwood."

Dr. Grey's gentle smile was quickly replaced with a frown so deep her eyebrows almost met in the middle. "Is it possible that underneath your bluster, both of you, at times, are still frightened little boys with no friends on the playground?"

Rick squared his shoulders like a quarterback defending himself against a tackle. "I'm not a frightened little boy on the playground," he said, somewhat defiantly.

"I didn't mean to offend you. I merely wanted to suggest that on the surface, it looks like you're fighting each other, but beneath the anger, unpleasant emotions that make you feel powerless and vulnerable might be hiding out—fear, hurt, rejection, sadness."

Flicking his fingers one by one, Rick said, "I have Mom, Joy, Gabe, and now Liv, so although I *was* a frightened kid on the playground, that doesn't resonate with me now. But it applies to Dad. On the outside, he's a successful businessman; on the inside, he's a lonely misfit. He used to drop in at a sports bar for TGIF but he stopped going, probably because his pontificating left patrons thinking he was three beers short of a six pack. I doubt he's ever questioned why people abandon him."

Dr. Grey offered Rick a lozenge then unwrapped one for herself and rolled it around in her mouth. "All of us develop personal agendas that we hope will blaze a trail to friendship and respect…agendas we rarely articulate, but subconsciously believe will keep us from tumbling over the edge."

"Dad's dangerously close to the edge."

"Are you sure about that? Can you see the world from his perspective…a perspective that might've changed somewhat given his heart attack?"

Thumper started its annoying dance. "I need time to consider that."

"How about a week?" Dr. Grey said, smiling kindly and glancing at the clock. "I have another client in a few minutes, so we'll have to stop; my accountant will only charge you for a portion of this session. Before you go, I've noticed that lately you let our silences take you deeper. That takes courage."

"Thanks." Rick quickly grabbed his coat and said, through an enigmatic smile, "And this story isn't over."

"I look forward to the next chapter," Dr. Grey said.

With one hand on the doorknob, Rick looked back and said, "Chapter title: Rick stops playing the victim."

Rick walked to the exit and stopped in the lobby to phone his mom. "How's Dad?" he asked, flipping his keyring back and forth over his hand.

"Sleeping right now, but he's feeling out of sorts today. Spent most of it lying in bed watching TV and dozing off. Doesn't want to start exercising or dieting and he hates not being able to have a beer."

"Not good. I'll do what I can to cheer him up when I get home, then retreat to the privacy of mind and space and think about what I've learned in therapy today. Short session; heavy going."

At home, Rick was pleased to see his father fully absorbed in a football game. Pleased too, that a few words of simple pleasantries were enough to give him the freedom of a thoughtful night alone.

After the final all-candidates' debate, Rick and Liv savoured a chocolate Frosty at her kitchen table and rehashed the highs and lows of the evening.

"Tell me, Rick, what did you *honestly* think of this last go-round?"

"Stellar performance darlin'! You threw everything you had at it…showed the audience how calmly and cleverly you could think on your feet. Best part was the way you handled the NDP's energy policy."

"What do you mean?"

"Nordstrom looked pleasantly surprised when you said, 'After listening to your views on the oil industry and climate change, I'll reconsider some of my own.' Class act! Supporters of *both* parties applauded, but Liberals hooted and hollered like joint winners of a multimillion-dollar lottery. I had a multimillion-dollar desire to replicate my DNA."

Liv's eyes smiled. "*You* suggested that clever strategy, remember?" Under the table, she started a game of footsie.

"Compared to last week, this debate was a leisurely stroll on the beach," Rick said, then thought better of telling Liv that he'd spotted a broad-shouldered gentleman in the back row helping his mother with her coat—a man whose face matched the silhouette in the alley scene; a man whose husky build was that of a steer wrestling champion at the Calgary Stampede. He dashed over to satisfy his curiosity and when Dorothy introduced them, Rick said, in a shaky voice, "Nice to meet you, Efner." Before either of them could start a conversation, the moderator asked everyone to take their seats and welcome the candidates. Later, near the end of the debate and with mixed feelings, Rick glimpsed his mother and Efner quietly leaving.

"You look deep in thought," Liv said as she finished the last of her Frosty.

Rick shook his head. "Just bits and pieces going on upstairs."

Liv reached for his hand and changed the setting. She opened her bedroom window, then curled up against Rick and returned his long, melting kiss. "Here's my plan for tonight," she said. "Let's cuddle and dream…make love in the morning."

Rick tapped on the kitchen door and poked his head in. "Nice to see you're up and about this morning, Dad."

"I'm slowly gittin' there," Dick said, as Dorothy motioned Rick to join them for lunch. "Harry assured me things were quiet at work, but if you want to put in an extra half day here and there, I'm sure you'll find things to catch up on. Might drop into the office for a few hours tomorrow."

"Sounds good. Will check with Uncle Harry later about a full day tomorrow."

On the table was a deep serving dish of Dorothy's version of thick Moroccan bean soup, which she called stewp, and a basket of fresh homemade buns. She passed Rick a bowl and said, in a subdued voice, "Marg's up for door knocking this afternoon but she can't be gone much more than two hours."

"Great, Mom! I'll make sure we're back by three o'clock, or shortly after." Rick glanced at his father. "Will you be okay on your own for a while?"

Dick gave a loud grunt. "Do what ya gotta do."

Rick furtively winked at his mother and concluded, *Dad's practicing his second chance at becoming a better husband. Feels like the first day of spring.*

Dick said grace, quickly devoured his lunch, then gave a single nod to his wife and son before leaving to watch a televised sporting event.

When Rick, Dorothy, and Marg arrived at campaign headquarters, there stood Noah and Liv, talking excitedly to John as they surveyed the poll map.

"Nice to see you again, ladies," Liv said. "And Rick. We're deciding which polls the five of us can finish today." She smiled avidly at Noah, which gave Rick's stomach a jolt. "Noah agreed to be our recorder."

I'd rather have a prostate exam than door knock with that narcissistic blowhard. Liv knows how I feel about him...is this some kind of test?

"Leaving in five minutes," Liv shouted as Rick rushed to meet Gabe who breezed into the office.

"Gabe! Good to see you, man. Come over and say hi to Mom and her friend, Marg Mason." After their pleasant greetings, Rick said, "How about canvassing with us, Gabe?" He beckoned to Brittany to join their team, and as she sprinted towards them, Gabe winked at Rick and mouthed: nice work.

"Gabe's coming with me, Mom, Marg, and Brittany," Rick shouted to John, then looked over at Liv. "With five of us, you and Noah could join another team."

Despite looking flummoxed, Liv calmly said, "If that's what you'd prefer, Rick. John has your poll ready to go."

She's lost her lustre. Her voice sounds...edgy. Rick downloaded the information and announced, "We're off, team! I'll drive." For the rest of the afternoon, recording constituents' information helped tame Rick's wild imaginings of Noah and Liv canvassing together. Ninety minutes in and close to the campaign office, Brittany spotted a coffee shop, but since Marg had invited company for dinner, Rick, Dorothy, and Marg begged off early.

Leaning over the front seat, Gabe whispered to Rick, "Liv and Noah—things probably aren't as bad as you're making them, m'friend."

Rick shrugged. "And Bob's your uncle."

After dropping Marg off, Rick grew tense as he pulled into their driveway and heard the alarm in Dorothy's voice. "Well take a look at that! Dad ordered us not to put a Liberal sign on the lawn, but he let Mallore's team put a big one on the corner of *our* property."

Rick promptly replied, "Pretend you didn't see it, Mom. I'll put a sign on your side of the lot after Dad goes to bed tonight."

Dorothy looked amused. "The perfect opportunity for Dad to show—twice in one day—that he meant business when he talked about second chances."

"And the perfect opportunity to show the neighbours that the Wright family is politically tolerant of differences," Rick said. "Those who've met Dad will be thunderstruck." He then noticed a piece of paper wedged into the front door frame, jogged up the steps and grabbed the note. *Man collapsed in front yard. Phoned 911. Call me. Maria.* Attached to the note was Maria's personalized card.

Rick opened the front door and yelled, "Dad! Dad!"

Dead silence. "Mom, something's seriously wrong!"

Dorothy rushed up the steps as her son read her the note, then leaned against him while he called Maria.

Rick watched his mother's face turn ashen. He tapped the speakerphone and waited.

"Hello," came a soft voice at the other end of the phone.

"Uh…might this be Maria?"

"Yes, speaking."

"Rick Wright here. Thanks for the note you left in the door. Looks like something serious happened to Dad."

"Oh no, not your father. I'm so sorry. Was on my daily walk when I saw a man collapsed in your front yard and shouted, 'Are you alright, sir,' but he was unable to speak or move. I'm a retired nurse, so I checked his pulse and called 911, then did CPR until the ambulance arrived and went through their routine. They took your dad to the Foothills."

"Oh my God! Thanks so much, Maria. You might've saved Dad's life. Mom and I are off to the hospital now."

"Please give me a quick call to let me know if he's okay."

"I'll do that," Rick said, voice quivering. "Thanks again."

"Text Joy," Dorothy said, now pacing back and forth on the long veranda. "Tell her to meet us at the Foothills."

Dorothy clung to Rick who strode into the now familiar surroundings of the Intensive Care Unit where Dick lay, mouth slack and lips bluish-purple. She stared aghast at her husband, now looking nothing like the one she'd served lunch to three hours ago.

A nurse who'd been checking Dick's vital signs, introduced herself and said compassionately, "I'm sorry to say that Mr. Wright has had a serious stroke."

"How serious?" Rick asked. "I'm his son, Rick Wright, and this is my mother, Dorothy."

"I don't want to alarm you, but the damage appears extensive. The doctor on call tomorrow will go over his test results." She then explained the information she'd been given, and ended by saying, "Hope for the best, but prepare for the worst."

Hope for the uncertain? Dad would have a problem with that, Rick thought, then leaned close to his father's ear. "Dad, it's me, Ricky. We're in this together, for however long it takes." He reached for his father's hand and perched on the narrow bed. "Squeeze my hand if you can hear me." Rick waited patiently, then, with greater urgency, repeated, "Dad, squeeze my hand. Just a gentle squeeze." About to give up, Rick said, one more time, loudly and slowly. "Squeeze my hand, Dad. Please!"

Dorothy and Rick stared at Dick's hand until, miraculously, his thumb appeared to lower just enough to graze the top of Rick's.

Rick grasped his father's hand and breathlessly said, "Way to go, Dad! Mom, did you see that?"

"I did." Dorothy's confirmation sounded somewhat tentative.

Joy arrived as Rick exuberantly told the nurse, "Dad's going to make it! He might be on the ropes, but he's not down for the count. There's something I'd like you to know about Dick Wright: when he puts his mind to something, there's no stopping him. Healing might be tough, but Dad's tougher."

The nurse smiled and slowly stepped toward the door. "The rehab team will be glad to hear that. As Hippocrates said, 'It's far more important to know what person the disease has than what disease the person has.' Rest assured that a team of medics will monitor Mr. Wright's condition. Together, we'll take exceptionally good care of him. Please don't hesitate to call us if you need anything; the nurses' station is only a few steps away."

Within minutes, Joy arrived and solemnly listened to Rick's summary of the entire event and nurse report. She kissed her father's cheek and, in an effort to collect herself, disappeared into the small bathroom.

"A setback, Dad, that's all this is," Rick said, hovering over his father.

Dorothy nestled Dick's hand in both of hers and prayed aloud as Rick slowly acknowledged that a man who was so much a part of his personal history was in a battle for his life. *His body's collapsing in on itself.* He strode from one end of the small room to the other, stopping intermittently to stare vacantly at the floor.

Dorothy said, "Ricky, please text Harry and Rose." Rick stepped to the back of the room and discovered that his phone's battery was closer to death than his father.

Later, in the hospital cafeteria, Rick took his BLT sandwich to a corner booth, sat down beside his mom, and caught the inconsolable expression on Joy's face. "Ah, Sis, I feel the same," he said, then reached across the table and tenderly pinched her soggy cheeks. "Tomorrow's another day. Hopefully, for Dad too." Between mouthfuls of sandwich washed down with gulps of milk, Rick continued, "It's strange, but all my whining about Dad's difficult personality seems less important now. I almost feel sorry for him…the last thing he'd want. In the face of imminent death, do we see people differently? Does gratitude come easier? Understanding? Affection?"

Dorothy simply nodded as she picked at her macaroni and cheese. "Here's my take on Dad's condition. If he's going to live out the rest of his days like a vegetable, I'd like him to go now. Peacefully." She nudged her plate toward Rick. "Can't finish this."

Rick ignored the mac and cheese. "My sentiments too, Mom. I wouldn't want the Grim Reaper to slowly torture me; neither would Dad."

The three of them sat quietly until Rick broke the silence. "First the heart attack, now this. It's as if death's stalking him."

Joy worked at smiling. "Trust you to come out with the bleakest—"

"But Joy," Rick interrupted. "Considering Dad's health and age, I think he was right when he said, expectantly. 'Everything's on schedule.'"

"Peculiar comment," Joy said, her frown deepening.

Knowing there was little they could do, the family sat quietly with Dick for another hour then left for home. As Dorothy stepped into the kitchen, she stopped, hunched her shoulders, and said, "I feel a bit like that other Dorothy—the one who looked at her little dog Toto and said, 'I've a feeling we're not in Kansas anymore.'"

Rick chuckled. "We're right here, Mom." He stamped his foot on the tile floor. "Firmly planted on home turf."

Dorothy hugged Rick, then reached for the daily newspaper on the counter. "I love the precise answers in crossword puzzles." Two seconds later, she flung the paper on the table. "Today, they won't be so clear." She sighed and looked up at Rick. "I promised Marg I'd call if things changed."

Rick patted his mother's shoulder. "Do that, and I'll phone Liv."

Alone in his suite, Rick flopped on his bed and dove into his pillow, then he tore off the mask he'd hidden behind since childhood. There he lay for several minutes, curled up in the fetal position and weeping uncontrollably until, like a dolphin soaring up from the depths of blackness, he burst into the light. He promptly sat up, as if he'd experienced a rebirth. *If I heard the worst news imaginable, not a single tear could fall. My emotional hard drive's been defragged.*

Rick's phone awakened him from a deep sleep. "Ricky, how was your night? Hope I didn't wake you," Dorothy said.

"Dozed off and on. Hardly qualifies as sleep. Worried all night about Dad and wondered if we should talk openly with him about the possibility of his death—funeral arrangements, the service, cremation. Would he want the church choir to sing his favourite hymn? Should someone from the family read from scripture? Give a eulogy? That stuff. Also worried about upcoming midterms and Liv's campaign. And…what time is it?"

"Nine-thirty, but snuggle in as long as you like. Marg's here. We're having coffee and talking about a fascinating book she signed out for me. I'll tell you about it when you come to the hospital. You will come, won't you?"

"Can't make any decisions without a caffeine hit, but…yes, yes, of course. I'll catch a couple more hours and head over."

"I just called the nurses' station and Dad's sleeping peacefully, so I'll leave in about an hour."

Rick slept a solid three hours then leisurely completed his morning routine and left for the hospital. A heavy medicinal smell greeted him as he sniffed his way into his father's room, then stopped abruptly and studied Dick's fallen face. He leaned down and whispered in Dorothy's ear. "Looks like he's somewhere else."

Dorothy nodded knowingly as Rick ambled over and hugged Joy. "Thought you had to work today."

"Called in sick. You missed the doctor's review of test results. The news isn't good."

"Give me the worst first."

Eyes resting on her father, Joy said, "The stroke, more like an assault, damaged his brain and, according to the ECG, also his heart…takes long naps, then races to catch up."

Rick sat on the bed and lightly stroked his father's forehead. "Me again, Dad."

Not a flicker of response. Rick looked at Joy, who further explained, "The damage is largely in his left hemisphere, which controls language and reasoning, among other things. Even if he can hear us, he'll likely have a hard time finding meaning in our words."

"Hey, kids," Dorothy said, voice animated. "Listen to this! Things might not be so bad after all. Maybe—"

Rick soundly interrupted. "What do you mean? It's *worse* than bad if he can't understand us or speak."

Dorothy raised the book she'd been reading. "This is the library book I mentioned earlier, Ricky…can't put it down." She tapped its cover and said, "*My Stroke of Insight*, written by Dr. Jill Taylor, a neuroanatomist who describes her stroke and near-death experience. Listen to what she wrote."

Dorothy read slowly, highlighting key words and sentences. "Everything, including the life force you are, radiates pure energy. Your heart soars in peace and your mind explores new ways of swimming in a sea of euphoria. I loved knowing my spirit was at one with the universe and in the flow with everything around me. I was simply a being of light radiating life into the world. In the absence of my left hemisphere's negative judgment, I perceived myself as perfect, whole, and beautiful just the way I was. Most of all, I loved the feeling of deep inner peace that flooded the core of my very being."

Joy looked at Rick. "What if—just think for a moment—what if Dad's experiencing something like that? What if he's in some divine world of peace and beauty? What if he wants to stay there?"

Rick's mouth fell open. "Nah. But…a neuroanatomist? Amazing. What if…yeah, what if?"

Joy looked imploringly at her father and lightly gripped his shoulder. "We know you're in there, Dad, and we're out here, praying for you and watching you heal.

Come back to us." Rick said, "Psychologists, physicists, neurologists, eggheads on YouTube—they're all trying to explain consciousness, but so far, it can't be scientifically measured because—"

Joy snapped, "Cut, Ricky, before you sound like that pompous physicist on *The Big Bang Theory*." She tossed her brother a brief smile that quickly turned into a placating pucker.

Rick liked the sudden return of his sister's perky personality, her no-nonsense but good-humoured candour. He put his face close to his father's ear and carefully chose his words. "Dad, you look so peaceful. Sleep well. Your body knows how to take care of you." Seeing not a flicker of response, Rick stepped back and imagined his father absorbing that strange, beautiful world his mother quoted. Inaudibly, he began humming the hymn, *You've Got to Walk That Lonesome Valley.*

Dorothy sat quietly immersed in Taylor's book while Rick and Joy briefly chatted between intermittent phone checks. As mid-afternoon approached, the two of them went for coffee in the cafeteria while Dorothy stayed behind to continue reading. The afternoon dragged on until, seeing no change in Dick's condition, the family left for an evening meal at a nearby restaurant. Waiting for their order, Joy again discussed the physical and medical implications of her father's condition, as if slipping into nurse mode would tamp down her anxiety. Dorothy was stoically attentive while Rick, preoccupied with private thoughts and feelings, remained largely absent from the conversation. *I need Doc Grey's words of wisdom—words I can't express. Won't express.*

The following afternoon, during Rick's Creative Writing class, a strange, ghastly world descended from out of nowhere, overwhelming him with a sense of being trapped in a place that wasn't quite real—a place where students' heads seemed to merge in front of him; where walls receded in the distance. He felt as if two hearts were pounding in his chest, bathing his body in sweat. Engulfed in panic, he wanted to leave the room but his legs felt like rubber. *I'm going crazy!* Rick thought, then told himself, *breathing is the gift that keeps me alive…right here, now. Slow, deep breath in…slow, complete exhale. Dear muscles, you know how to get me through this.* He lowered his head and waited for what seemed like an eternity until his hyperventilating and fear subsided enough to lean into Gabe, who had sensed something unusual was happening to his friend.

"That's it for me," Rick said, his voice little more than a whisper. "Explain later."

Gabe affectionately patted Rick's arm. "Should I come with you?"

"I'll be okay, but thanks." Walking unsteadily to his car, Rick repeatedly wiped his brow and tried to make sense of his bizarre experience. He stopped and looked up at the swirling dark snow clouds. *Maybe a signal from Dad. Have you left us? Are you trying to say goodbye? No. Ridiculous.*

Rick phoned Joy as he waited for the light film of frost to evaporate from his windshield.

"Hey, Sis, where are you?"

"Hospital. Hold on while I step into the hall."

"Is Mom there too? How's Dad."

"Mom's still wrapped up in that book, and Dad's the same—comatose. Every so often he gives a deep sigh like he's trying to come back…or something. Where are you? We need you here. Dad needs you here."

"I'm on my way. Need to tell Dad something. Just in case…just in case."

Joy waited patiently as Dorothy sat beside her husband where she'd been for most of the afternoon. Every few minutes, she'd read Joy another segment from *My Stroke of Insight*, then stare at Dick as if seeking confirmation that he'd heard what she'd read aloud.

Rick staggered into the room, hugged his mom and sister, then searched for signs of life in a man who look mercilessly and completely ravaged by the stroke. Himself ravaged by cascading emotions, Rick pressed the palm of his hand to his father's forehead and released that which was foremost in his thoughts—thoughts that, until now, were imprisoned in a small corner of his mind.

"Dad, it's me, Ricky. I need to tell you something—something I should've said long before this. Please hear me, Dad...I love you." Rick put his lips closer to his father's ear and slowly enunciated, "I love you, Dad." He tried to swallow but his throat felt full of sand. Wondering if his dad was forming sentences he couldn't speak, and drenched in desperation, Rick reached for his father's hand and again belaboured each word. "I...love...you...Dad."

Despite Dick's apparent lack of consciousness, at some level of awareness he must have sensed that time was pressing down on him since what happened next could only be described as a small miracle. His eyes opened barely enough to look entreatingly at Rick. With every ounce of dwindling energy, Dick forced his mouth partially open and lifted his tongue to his top teeth where he held it for a couple seconds, as if struggling to say something.

Rick, frozen in disbelief, watched as his father's eyelids fluttered and closed, his mouth drooped, and his breathing became jagged and heavy.

Dorothy and Joy looked on in stunned silence.

"Mom! Joy! Did you see what I saw? Dad tried to tell me he loved me. He listened...he heard me. He would've said the whole word and more if he could've. I know it! He would've!" Rick felt light-headed, not fully registering what had just happened.

"I think so too, Ricky," Joy said in a calm, comforting voice. "Let's all assume that's what he tried to do. Makes sense to me." She reached for her father's other hand and listened to his irregular, noisy breathing—a sound she knew too well.

With a protective, maternal look, Dorothy said, "Yes, Ricky, I believe that's what your father tried to say."

Rick put his ear to his father's chest and listened for a heartbeat. Only then did he tap into the raw reality of the moment. "Dad's barely of this world," he said, then sat up and folded his arms tightly across his chest as if to stop from plummeting into that tidal wave of panic he'd fought to control earlier.

A nurse briskly entered the room and checked the ECG, and as she approached Dick's bedside, Dorothy anxiously said, "My husband's breathing doesn't sound normal. It sounds…oh no, is that the death rattle?"

In a comforting, quiet voice, the nurse said, "I'm afraid so, Mrs. Wright. The death rattle is a common term for fluid accumulation and muscle weakness that makes swallowing difficult. Sadly, I'm afraid it won't be long now."

"Nothing can be done?" Rick asked.

The nurse slowly shook her head. "Your father signed papers that requested no heroic interventions should he reach this state, which is why the medical team has now limited his treatment to comfort care. He isn't in pain, but he could go on like this for an hour or more."

Not one to keep people waiting, Dick soon gave a long, slow gasp and surrendered to that ultimate summons. No more second chances.

The nurse made an emergency call and within seconds a physician rushed in to check Dick's vital signs. She looked caringly at Dorothy. "No pulse, Mrs. Wright, and dilated pupils. Your husband is unresponsive."

Dorothy covered her face with both hands and quietly asked, "Has he left us?"

The physician looked at each family member. "I'm sorry. There was nothing more we could've done for him." She extended heartfelt condolences and exchanged a few words with the family before leaving the final closure in the nurse's hands.

Looking mainly at Rick, the nurse said, "One tremulous breath and he was gone…without a fight. Almost as if he were ready."

Dorothy steadied her voice. "Does the hospital have a priest on call to administer Last Rites, or should I contact our own?"

"Father Kinkaid administers Last Rites to families who request his services. We'll call him, if you like."

"Please," Dorothy said.

"He'll be here soon. Is there anything I can get you while you wait? A beverage—tea, coffee, hot chocolate?"

"Thanks, but we'll just wait here with my husband until the priest arrives," Dorothy said. "We're so grateful for all you've done."

Rick tried to hold back tears as Dorothy walked over, patted his arm, and said, "Let the tears fall, Ricky. This is goodbye. How comforting that in the end, love flourished." She leaned over and gently kissed her husband's forehead as a sudden shaft of sunlight streamed through the window.

"Dad's now at peace…soaring with the eagles," Dorothy said as Rick began his signature pacing.

Disconsolate, Joy stared straight ahead without so much as a blink, as if she'd drifted into a human variant of hibernation.

Rick wiped his cheeks with the back of his hand. "A mind so unstoppable…." After a long pause, he added, "In the end, death was Dad's salvation."

Joy covered her mouth and died her own little death, then stumbled to the other side of Dick's bed and buried her face in his neck. "I fully imagined this, Dad," she said, her voice thin. "Witnessed it with families who watched their dying loved ones, but it feels like this hasn't really happened…to you. To us." She lifted her face and scanned the walls and ceiling. In a stronger voice, she said, "Your spirit's filling the room. You're still here, Dad, comforting us."

"Yes, honey, it feels like Dad's still with us. Even though he knew he was dying, he was thoroughly at peace in his final hours, comforted by a strong belief that heaven awaited him. For the last couple of days, your father and I experienced a state of grace. This might sound weird," Dorothy said, "but I don't feel sad."

Looks serene, Rick thought, then asked, "If not sad, Mom, what do you feel?"

Dorothy walked over to the chair she'd spent so many hours in, nudged it closer to Dick's body, and sat down. "If I try to explain it, I'm afraid it'll disappear. I need to stay in the moment…it's soothing."

In their own way, Dorothy, Rick, and Joy allowed each other time to privately grieve. Rick resumed his restless pacing while struggling to accept that death had cheated him of the fatherly relationship he'd longed for since childhood. He glanced around the sterile room that embodied his father's indomitable spirit. *Richard Wagner Wright has taken his place among the billions before him, and our family, with all its turbulent history, has shrunk to a tight bond of three. In a couple generations and without so much as a lingering anecdote, he'll be reduced to obscurity. A mere relic of time and history.*

Chapter 14

Uncle Harry and Aunt Rose, sorry to say we've got a bad situation here. Dad left us a few minutes ago. Priest arriving soon. Home later.

"Have you let Al know?" Rick asked Joy, who shook her head and pulled out her phone.

Al quickly replied: *On a rescue. Will call soon. Love you.* Joy put her phone in her pocket and looked up at Father Kinkaid, who'd entered the room.

The priest introduced himself, offered consolation to each family member, and stepped close to Dick's body. After making the sign of the cross, he administered Last Rites, then stepped back and talked with Dorothy about funeral protocol.

"Tomorrow I'll call Father McFarland," Dorothy said, "and talk to the rest of the family about final details. My husband was quite adamant about being cremated…even more adamant about a Catholic service."

After blessings and the priest's departure, Rick kissed his father's forehead and whispered, "We made it, Dad…you and me. We truly made it."

Looking utterly forsaken, Rick and Joy lingered over Dick's lifeless body until Dorothy pulled them close, put her arms around each, and led the way for their final, weepy departure.

At home with Dorothy and Joy, Rick texted Liv: *Dad's gone. Rough day.*

Liv replied immediately: *So sorry, Rick. Wish I could comfort you.*

Rick tapped: *Is that an invitation?*

Liv answered: *Yes, come over if you like. Anytime. I'll keep the bed warm.*

Rick replied: *Thanks. Need that. Mom's nuking leftovers for our little family of three. See you in about an hour. XO*

Rick had no sooner hit send when another text arrived: *Sorry we couldn't have been there with you. Rose and I insist you all come for dinner tomorrow, 5 o'clock. Chinese take-out. She'll call your mom later. Much love.*

Rick read Harry's text to Dorothy and Joy, then said, "Liv also texted that she'd like to comfort me tonight. I'd like to let her do that…after we have supper. Right now, I need time around the table with my mom and sis…our shrunken little family."

"Shrunken but solid," Dorothy said. "I'm so glad you have Liv's loving support at a time like this." She then reminded Rick that he'd agreed to help her write a short obit for the local newspapers.

"We'll do that tomorrow, Mom. Promise. I'll be home before noon."

Joy looked at Rick. "You're lucky to have Liv, and I'm lucky to have Al. He'll come to my place after his shift." Looking suddenly startled, she grasped her mother's arm. "But there'll be no one here for you, Mom," she said, tears flooding her eyes.

"Please, don't worry about me, honey," Dorothy said, running her fingers through Joy's bowed head of hair like she'd so often done when her daughter was a child. "I'll be okay. Phone me when you wake up tomorrow and come for breakfast. Al too if he can."

Joy lifted her head and sighed. "Will do. But know this, Mom. In our heart of hearts, we're all with you. You're never really alone."

With Liv's warm body nestled against his, and vivid memories of his father's astounding farewell, Rick felt wrapped in the arms of love. *Just where I need to be*, he thought. *Never knew love could be this good. Never imagined it could be this good.*

At home the next morning, after emailing his profs a request to defer his midterm exams, Rick and Dorothy drafted Dick's obituary while Joy and Al searched for a photo to accompany the submission to local papers and the church bulletin.

Later that afternoon, en route to Harry and Rose's, Dorothy passed Rick her Visa and asked him to stop at the liquor store for a bottle of white wine and a small brandy. "If ever we needed an elixir, it's today."

"Agreed, but the best elixir is family," Rick said. "I've never been so grateful to have one."

Over refreshments and appetizers at the kitchen bar, Dorothy described Dick's final moments to Harry and Rose.

"Mom!" Joy said. "You left out Dad's desperate attempt to tell Rick something before he died." She opened the palm of her hand toward Rick.

Dorothy quickly replied. "Purposely did so. That marvellous ending is yours to tell, Ricky."

Rick welcomed the gesture and relayed, in great detail, how convinced he was that his father struggled to say he loved him. "Just before coming here, I read a poem by Theodore Roethke, who wrote that in a dark time, the eye begins to see." Rick looked directly at his uncle. "That was Dad. That was me."

"So sorry I missed something memorable," said Harry.

Dorothy looked at Harry and said plaintively, "Yes, in his dying moments, Dad and Ricky gave each other the redemptive power of love—such precious gifts. I'll never forget their goodbyes."

Bleary eyed, Harry folded and refolded the paper napkin in front of him. "Should that memory go in the eulogy, Rick, and have you thought about giving it?"

Rick turned and faced his uncle. "How about you doing the honours?"

"Rather not. You're the writer in this family, but if you insist…and if you write it. Then again—"

"Let's work on it together," Rick said. "I'll write it if you'll edit it. We'll decide later who delivers it."

Harry agreed and suggested someone from the choir sing a solo tribute to Dick.

Dorothy's eyes lit up. "Great idea, Harry. I'll request 'Ave Maria,' his favourite hymn."

Rick said, "And Mom, ask if the church choir will sing 'How Great Thou Art.' The congregation could join in and I'll belt it out—loud enough for Dad to hear." Rick raised his hands to the ceiling. "I can see it all now, him smiling down on us...even though I'll be off key."

Appreciative laughter eased family tensions, but it wasn't long before Rick felt a chill sweep over him, as if the kitchen had become a dark, dank morgue.

Harry must have sensed his nephew's sombre struggle. "You could add some humour to the eulogy by telling the story of how your dad, when he reached adolescence, decided he wanted to be called Richard, but in our little town, everyone knew him as Dick, so he toughed it out. Johnny Cash's 'A Boy Named Sue' was his favourite song."

Rick chuckled, then sat back and thought about the story behind his own name and how, after years of calling him Ricky, his uncle was now comfortable honouring his nephew's request that everyone call him Rick. *Hope others notice.*

Rick suddenly realized that, unlike a week ago, when tension hovered over Harry and Rose's dinner table, he felt a comforting togetherness as the family moved to the dining room and relished a broad selection of Chinese food.

Deep in thought, Joy studied the beautiful floral arrangement on the buffet. "Have any of you noticed how summer flowers change to a deep, vibrant hue at sundown...like a beautiful prayer to end the day? Dad's final moments were like those flowers."

"Jesus, Joy," Rick exclaimed, immediately regretting his blasphemy. "Apologies for swearing, but what a metaphor! *You* should write the eulogy."

Joy forced a laugh and shook her head at such an idea. "It came out of nowhere, just like your brilliant idea that I write the eulogy. Not a chance."

"Here's another thought," Harry said. "Unless Dick told you where he'd like his ashes spread, how about scattering them at the

Bird Sanctuary? Songbirds will serenade us when we visit him, and Rose, you can name all the wildflowers fertilized by Dick Wright."

"Great idea, Uncle Harry!" Rick said, chuckling. "Dad's grave new world."

Rose giggled. "Dick will fertilize the trees that house the birds...and feed the flowers that bloom in spring."

"In vibrant colours at twilight," Joy added, laughing as if to give permission for levity. Everyone joined in wholeheartedly, except Dorothy, who looked serenely bemused.

After a shot of brandy and sweets from the dessert tray, Joy reached over and squeezed Dorothy's hand. "You can hardly keep your eyes open, Mom."

"Yes, but I'm loving your comic relief." Dorothy rubbed her eyes and tried to stifle a yawn. "I like the idea of spreading Dick's ashes at the Bird Sanctuary."

"Since the eulogy is now on me, I'll start writing it tonight," Rick said, hoping his comment would hasten the end of a necessary but pleasantly exhausting evening.

Which it did.

Dorothy pushed her chair back from the table. "Please, let me cook dinner for a change...day after tomorrow. Nothing fancy, just a simple meal that will occupy my mind until the funeral."

Rose winked at Joy, then turned to Dorothy. "I'll bring a Greek salad—if not for dinner, for your lunch next day."

Joy said. "And I'll bring Dad's favourite brandied sweet potatoes with roasted pecans."

Warm thanks and hugs soon followed, and when Dorothy, Rick, Joy, and Al stepped into the brisk evening air, Rick looked up at a faint canopy of twinkling stars. "Tonight is unusually quiet. Someone must've grabbed the remote and put the city on mute."

"Good one," Al said, looking back at Rick, who was checking an incoming text.

Rick nudged Dorothy. "Hey, Mom! A message from Liv." Rick scanned it again, then stepped into the car and read it aloud.

Thinking of you always! Team went all out today. Can I help you wish anything? XO!

Dorothy raised her eyebrows and looked over at Rick. "Wish anything? A typo?"

"Unlikely. The letters *s* and *t* aren't close enough for a typo. Freudian slip, me thinks."

Rick quickly replied: *Thanks Liv! There's lots you can help me 'wish.' Wish for many nights of bliss together. Will phone tomorrow.*

At 10:30 p.m. with heavy heart, Rick began his eulogy. To his disbelief, and great relief, words effortlessly energized him well into the night.

Thank you for coming to say goodbye to my father, Dick Wright, a man who was dedicated to his family and the company he and his brother, Harry, started some thirty years ago. Dad considered his employees family, and I'm sure he'd want me to thank those of you who are here today, not only for paying your respects, but for helping Wright Brothers become a successful business venture.

I'd like to tell a brief, largely untold story of Dick Wright's life. Unfortunately, when Dad was twelve years old, his mother, Molly Wright, died from a prolonged illness. Shortly after, Dad and Uncle Harry joined a small group of teens for Bible Study…and thanked the Lord for the hearty lunches that followed. No doubt Dad also thanked the Lord for his athletic prowess at the hockey rink and on the football field, where he excelled throughout adolescence.

Sadly, it wasn't long after their mother died that Uncle Harry and Dad were hit with another tragedy—they lost their father. Grandpa Wright was killed instantly in a head-on collision with a semi-trailer truck, leaving Dad and Uncle Harry orphaned at eighteen and sixteen.

After high-school graduation, Dad landed a job with an established home construction firm. A hardworking employee who never shirked extra duties, he was soon promoted to an assistant managerial position that gave him broad experience in the construction industry. The following year, after Uncle Harry graduated, Dad was instrumental in getting him a job with a new company that specialized in building condos.

Grandpa Wright's friend Ben gave Dad and Uncle Harry financial guidance such that after saving two years of their salaries and investing money from their inheritance and the sale of the family home, they had enough to finance a move to Calgary—the little city on the Bow with a view of the Rockies, as Dad once described it. With excellent references, he was soon hired by a large construction corporation that offered good opportunities for advancement. Meanwhile, Uncle Harry earned a Business Administration diploma, and with Ben as their venture capitalist, Dad and Uncle Harry started their own construction firm and hired qualified, loyal personnel—loyal because their employment packages outperform those of competing firms.

Rick visualized coworkers nodding in agreement as he faced the side room and swept an open arm toward his mother.

One such loyal employee was my mother, Dorothy Wright, who Dad hired for her proficiency in word processing and spread sheets. But Dad saw much more than that in Mom. A year later he proposed, and fourteen months after their wedding, Mom replaced Excel spread sheets with crib-sized bed sheets and developed unique word processing skills to process baby babble—mine. Twenty months later, my sister, Little Miss Joyful, came into the world—so named, Dad said, because as a tiny infant, she smiled profusely and adorably at the sight of any human face.

Rick pictured Joy, crestfallen in a torrent of tears. His own were close to the surface.

Thanks to you, Dad, despite extreme childhood adversity, your optimism and dedication to hard work helped make Wright Brothers a respected, well-established business. I hope to emulate your courage in the face of hardship, your dedication to family, and the unwavering self-confidence that helped you succeed at whatever you put your mind to.

Thank you for working so hard to give so much to all of us. We will remember you.

We love you.

Rick walked to the window and looked deep into the darkness until the power of an intimate, courageous ending enveloped him.

I love you, Dad.

After validating the final draft with tears, Rick stood in front of his full-length bedroom mirror and recited what he'd written until he got the inflection right. He flopped on his bed and deeply regretted that he hadn't known earlier and thought deeper about the wreckage in his father's family. Such knowledge, Rick hoped, would help him read the eulogy without choking on his words. *Dad's poor, wounded heart…and my cursed, unpredictable emotions.*

When Rick awoke late the next morning, he pulled the duvet over his head as if to hide from looming, crushing obligations. Over the next two days, he needed to polish his eulogy and read it to the family, brace himself for the funeral and reception, deliver the eulogy with composure and compassion, then drive to Liv's campaign headquarters and anxiously await election results. *If I can make it through all that with dignity and diplomacy, I can make it through anything.*

That afternoon, Liv arrived with a large bouquet of yellow roses that Dorothy graciously accepted and nestled among the other floral arrangements, most of which were from Dick's employees. She briefly chatted with Liv before opening the door to downstairs and shouting, "Ricky, Liv's here."

"Be right up!" Rick hollered, then quickly brushed his teeth and combed his thick, wavy hair that Liv once described as "a bumper crop you always cut too short."

Dorothy made tea and as Rick laced his fingers between Liv's, the three of them talked about the flowers, the funeral arrangements, and the closing days of Liv's election campaign.

Rick watched Liv take her last sip of tea, then looked at his mom. "Sorry to interrupt our nice visit, Mom, but would you please excuse us."

The moment they stepped inside his suite Rick reached under Liv's sweater and ran his fingers over her cool, satiny skin. "You're so thoughtful, Liv. With E-day closing in, you must be juggling chainsaws, yet you've found time to bring us flowers."

Together on the love seat, Rick put his arm around Liv as she leaned into him and said, "I hope you and I can celebrate...or commiserate after all the votes are tallied. Mom, Dad, and Zeke are arriving soon to help tidy the office and prepare for the election party—win or lose. Zeke has to work the next day, so they'll leave for Edmonton as soon as there's a projected winner. Do you think you'll feel like joining us at some point after the funeral?"

Rick said, "On election day, I'll vote for you, and in the evening, I vote we celebrate each other...and your win."

"Wonderful! I want us to be together then," Liv said, nestling deeper into Rick. "How did it end for your father? Were you able to say goodbye?"

"After Dad's heart attack, a heavy, moral responsibility weighed on my conscience. The time had come to tell him that I regretted all the times I've vehemently argued with him; all the times I've pushed him away. Then I said those two important words: I'm sorry."

"You must've touched him deeply."

"Dad's eyes never rested so comfortably in their sockets. He looked at me and thanked me for apologizing. Sincerely thanked me!" Rick talked about his father's apology and gratitude for a second chance to be a better husband and father. "I was shocked, but thankful for the possibility that a respectful relationship might be within reach."

Liv smiled tenderly as she looked up at Rick. "I wish I could've met him, but then came the stroke."

Rick nodded and told Liv about his father's dying moments. "I watched Dad's life drain away in that godforsaken hospital bed and thought about all the years I've been chasing a dream. Didn't have the guts to tell him what was buried deep within until finally, on the day that proved his last, I put my face next to his ear." Rick paused, tongue-tied. "That's when I told Dad I loved him. To my utter amazement, he tried to tell me the same."

The two quietly cuddled until a satisfying thought crossed Rick's mind. "If I hadn't told Dad I loved him, he never would've been dead and buried. We'd both be roaming through my dreams, waiting endlessly for apologies. Instead, as Dad's life ended, something beautiful began—respect and love for each other. Redemption."

Liv sighed. "Ah, redemption. Now that you've both said what went unsaid for so many years, are you at peace?"

"A strange kind of peace. Even though Dad's gone, he's with me more than ever. Did it take dying for me to see all of him? To love him? Does death exaggerate one's virtues? Sanitize the memories? Does that even make sense?"

"Does it matter? You're both free now."

"Yeah, but death robbed us of the chance to prove our love. I'll never know how things might've been."

Liv looked as if she were seeing Rick anew. "The ending...so special. I forget who famously said that those who think deeply can love deeply."

Rick thought deeply. "Last night, after a family dinner, Uncle Harry and Mom reminisced about Dad...shattered my hardened view of him. All my life I've wanted him to not be him, and he wanted me to not be me. Therapy has proven the futility of such childish demanding. Helped execute the old me—the one I've put to rest with Dad."

Liv's fingers rode in and out, up and down between Rick's. "In two months, I've learned so much about you. I don't have the words, but I love how close I feel to you at this moment."

Rick's smile was almost too big for his face and it occurred to him that neither he nor Liv was ready to say those three powerful words.

Liv stood and stretched. "I hate to end this beautiful time together, but please know that now, *especially* now, you're always in my thoughts. When things slow down, I hope we can grab our skis and head for the slopes."

"Yes, my dear. Can't wait."

Upstairs, Liv hugged Dorothy and Marg, who had dropped in for tea. "You've made a real contribution to my campaign, both of you," Liv said. "If I win, it'll be because of efforts like yours. Thanks so very much."

Dorothy said, "I'll check the election results and leap to my feet when I hear you've won."

Liv beamed. "It's nice to know we'll all be thinking of each other on such an important day. I plan to attend Mr. Wright's service, but I hope you'll understand if I sneak away as soon as it's over."

Rick walked Liv to the front door, kissed her, and held her close. "Mmm," she murmured, evocatively. "Good luck with the eulogy."

"And good luck with the erection," Rick said, then fiercely shook his head and laughed uninhibited. Relieved by the unintended humour, Liv laughed along with him and said, "I'll vote for that tomorrow night."

As he passed through the living room, Rick noticed the edge of a note tucked into a large bouquet of fresh flowers. Curious, he read the message.

Dorothy dearest, I'm thinking of you morning, noon, and night.
Abiding love,
Efner

Rick felt his stomach tighten. *Glad for Mom, sad for Dad.* He walked into the kitchen where Dorothy and Marg sat talking about tomorrow's dinner menu. "Later," he said, patting his mother's arm and marching to the downstairs door.

At his desk, Rick reread the final draft of his eulogy before grappling with another heavy obligation.

Dear Dr. Grey,
Please accept my sincere apologies for not terminating therapy in person. Emails are a cowardly way to end relationships, but I'm not up to struggling through another goodbye.
Dad had a fatal stroke and I'm delivering the eulogy tomorrow. Before he died, I told him I loved him, and in his final moments he tried valiantly to tell me the same. You enabled our loving reconciliation and for that, I'm sincerely grateful. Recently, I've spent more time trying to

understand Dad and less time judging him. I'm also more aware of my demanding, unreasonable beliefs that trigger inappropriate emotions and behaviours. I believe that without your helpful guidance, Dad and I wouldn't have reconciled, and Liv and I would be lost to each other. Today, our love blossoms.

Without knowing it at the time, The Incident was a threatening opportunity for therapy and self-discovery. You've shown me how I disguise my fears—fears that damaged past relationships, especially Dad's and mine. With you, I also felt deeply heard. Hopefully, I've learned to be a better listener. I remember your apology for being too teachy, something I never felt. Loved, in fact.

Dr. Knowles, my psychology professor, has been teaching me about dogmatism and I now see that Dad and I were racing to the finish line of the dogmatism derby—he, driven by a search for respect and dignity, me, driven by a need to prove that I'm smarter than everyone else. If I were so smart, there'd be no need to arrogantly prove it. I'm confident I won't go back to that which I now have a name for. That which still tempts me.

What I do in life counts, but who I am counts more.

You've made me think.

With gratitude,

Rick Wright

Dorothy and Marg spent the better part of the next day making dinner for Harry, Rose, Joy, Al, and Rick—beef tenderloin with mounds of sautéed onions and mushrooms braised in beer, bay leaves and garlic, homemade dinner rolls, and Dick's favourite dessert, flapper pie.

In the dining room that night, Dorothy took her usual place at the end of the table, then stumbled through a tearful grace that acknowledged Dick's absence in the empty chair across from her. Rick gave a toast of thanks to his mother, and people enjoyed a quiet meal as if they'd said all they needed over the last two weeks. During dessert, Rick put his fork down, swallowed hard and said, "So I've been thinking, maybe we get wiser and more courageous near the end. Pity it takes so long."

"Rick, you're exceptionally wise at twenty-eight," Harry said, with a hard wink.

Rick smiled and reached for a folder on the side table. "Uncle Harry, I've decided to give the eulogy during the reception. Writing it was less daunting than I thought. I'd like to read it now and have all of you suggest changes."

Everyone agreed and listened closely as Rick read the opening paragraph, after which, for the first time in front of others, Dorothy wept openly. The family gave heartfelt support, then waited solemnly until Rick resumed reading his tribute. When he ended with, "I love you, Dad," Harry's eyes glistened.

"Perfect eulogy, Rick. Your way with words…you've clearly chosen a mighty good career path," Harry said.

Dorothy gave a proud smile of approval and glanced across the table at Joy, mopping her face with the sleeve of her sweater.

"It's great, Ricky. Keep every word," Joy said, blinking rapidly.

The family discussed arrangements for a small gathering of mourners at the house after the funeral. When voices became strained, Joy seized and eased the moment. "I'm so glad we've spent precious time together to talk about Dad and plan our final goodbye. Thanks for Dad's honorary dinner, Mom, and thanks to you too, Uncle Harry and Aunt Rose, for taking such good care of us through everything. Let me help clear the table, then we…" With pleading puppy-dog eyes, she looked over at Rick and said, "On second thought, will you please help tidy up? I'm as dragged out as our dear mother."

With that, everyone looked content to call it a day. As Rick scrubbed the roaster, Dorothy dealt with the few leftovers and lamented, "I truly regret what I told you about Efner and me. Should've had the decency not to burden you with it, especially that unforgiveable alley scene."

"Sorry you feel that way, Mom. I'm thinking Efner's love is especially helpful now." *Dad's death has accomplished what divorce might otherwise have*, Rick thought, wiping clean the countertop.

Dorothy lowered her head. "This is a time to remember Dad. After thirty years, I owe it to him to do just that." She looked deep into her son's eyes. "But you're right. My family's love, along with Efner's, is immensely comforting."

"Love will comfort us tonight," Rick said, helping load the dishwasher.

Dorothy looked near collapse as she propped herself against the kitchen counter. "Love and exhaustion, my best friends right now."

Rick felt his phone's alert as he descended the stairs.

Hello Rick,

Thank you for your thoughtful message and the informative chart on dogmatism. It's given me much to think about.

Clients seldom know the impact they have on therapists. Of the many people I've worked with over the years, none will be more memorable than you—you who had the courage to look at who you are and who you are not, then do the hard work of becoming who you'd rather be.

Best wishes for your relationship with Liv and all future endeavours, including that bestseller you'll write. I look forward to reading it!

Marion Grey

As people arrived to give their last goodbyes to Dick Wright, directionally confused snowflakes wafted about in the cold, dreary stillness of another wintry day. Funeral hymns played in the background, and lightly scented candles welcomed mourners as they signed the guest book and thoughtfully paused in front of an attractive photo of Dick, taken in his late forties.

The Wright family was seated behind a heavily curtained side room reserved for relatives of the deceased. Rick peeked out and saw a long-term employee of Wright Brothers urging people to sit near the front instead of scattering themselves throughout a room too large for the number of guests, about thirty in all. Some were current or former employees of Wright Brothers or corporate suppliers; others were members of the church congregation or hospice volunteers, including Efner. Five campaign workers had arrived to support Rick: Liv, John, Gabe, Brittany, and Edna.

"We've gathered today to remember Richard Wagner Wright," Father McFarland said, "a man faithfully devoted to God, church and family." He acknowledged Dick's immediate relatives, including the deceased, then read from scripture.

Rick nudged Joy, who was drowning in a puddle of tears, and whispered, "Imagine Dad smiling down on his Little Miss Joyful," a comment that offered little consolation.

One of Dorothy's church acquaintances sang an operatic rendition of *Ave Maria*, followed by prayers and traditional hymns. With newfound strength, Joy leaned against Rick and said, "I'm sure Dad heard it all, looking down from the firmament."

With a glint in his eyes, Rick said unabashedly, "Wait 'til he hears my eulogy."

Dorothy had remained resolute throughout the service and as she and the family joined guests for the church's customary refreshments, Rick took his place at the small podium. He winked at Gabe and Brittany, and to his utter delight, caught sight of Liv standing along the back wall. With a wink and broad smile, she turned his uneasy voice to silk.

When Rick gulped down the last four words of his eulogy, Harry strolled up to the podium, blurry eyed and open armed. "Your dad would've hung on every word. We're all so proud of you."

Rick glanced at Liv, who threw him a kiss and mouthed 'later', then slipped out the door.

"I hope you'll excuse me," Rick said, after visiting briefly with a small gathering of family, Marg, two hospice workers, and long-time employees who'd come to the house following the reception. "Election results will soon be rolling in and I'd like to join Liv Janson at campaign headquarters. He winked at his mother and added, "As some of you may know, she's my girlfriend…and future premier of the province."

Dorothy said, "We understand, Ricky. You need to be with her."

"And Joy," Rick said. "We need lunch or coffee soon—in a couple of days." He hugged her and quietly asked, "Are you alright?"

Joy lowered her head. "Like everyone who loses a parent, I'll have my tearful times, but I'll carry on. Dad would want that."

As he backed onto the street, Rick saw Efner walking toward the house. He lowered the car window and shouted, "Nice to see you, Efner. I'm off to watch Liv's election results."

Efner punched the air and shouted, "Here's to a Janson victory!"

At campaign headquarters, excited optimism filled the air when the first poll results flashed across a rented, 60-inch TV screen. Conservative Ron Mallore had a slight lead.

Liv caught sight of Rick and went straight to him. "Gather me in. This is a close one. Might need a little sheltering tonight," she said, with the seriousness of a supreme court judge.

"I'm here for you, no matter what. To me, you'll always be a winner." Rick felt strong. Needed. He wanted to hold her forever.

Momentarily, new poll results flashed across the screen as people burst into triumphant shouts and applause. With several outstanding polls to report, the count marginally favoured Liv over the other two candidates. "Mallore's now trailing Janson by two percent," the TV reporter announced.

All smiles and glossy-eyed, Liv hurried back to her family's side as Rick caught sight of Noah standing near the back door.

"Hey, Noah," Rick shouted, sprinting toward him. "Looks like this one's too close to call. Can I get you a drink?"

Noah dug his hands deep into his pant pockets. "I'm good, thanks. Thought I'd swing by on my way to a friend's election party. Liv's got this one in the bag."

Rick looked over at John. "Wonder how we did last election on the remaining polls."

Noah's strained smile signalled the end of chit chat. "Don't know, Rick. I'll wish Liv the best and be on my way."

Rick felt good about acknowledging Noah as he watched John crane his neck at the numbers on his computer. "What's your best guess on the outstanding polls?"

John gave a long, slow sigh. "Most of them had strong Conservative support last time around. I'm worried. Things could change rapidly."

As poll results dribbled in, people chatted excitedly about various scenarios until a string of final results from all but three constituencies covered the screen. A news reporter started summarizing the total votes, then stopped. "Breaking news," he said. "The CBC has just declared Ron Mallore the projected winner for Mount Vista. Not a resounding victory, but one that likely won't warrant a recount."

Oxygen left the room.

Barring a serious irregularity, family, friends, and volunteers knew Liv couldn't possibly gain enough votes to tie, much less win. *She looks like a turtle that's just lost its shell.* Rick edged his way to the front of the room.

Liv stepped up to a makeshift platform and scanned her supporters' dejected faces. "My friends," she stammered. Everyone broke into applause as if sensing she needed time to regain her composure. Liv looked at Rick's adoring eyes and continued. "Your support has meant more than words can convey. We gave it our all, but it wasn't quite enough...*this* time."

"We'll be ready," shouted John from a side wall. Fists pumped the air, and overlapping shouts of "Janson in four" gave Liv all she needed to keep going.

"Each of you, in your own way, donated far beyond what I dreamed possible. I won't single out anyone for special thanks, except my family, here from Edmonton. To my Mom, Lavonne Janson, my Dad, Gunnar Janson, and my brother, Zeke, your loving support has never faltered. I love you so." Liv stepped back and beckoned the family to join her.

Gunnar, seeing tears in his daughter's eyes, took the microphone. "It's been a pleasure meeting and working with each one of you. We'll be back for the next election. By then, given Mallore's age, he likely won't be the incumbent, but there *will* be a return candidate with renewed energy, commitment, and campaign experience." Gunnar put his arm around Liv. "You, Liv Janson, are the grit in integrity.

Amid raucous applause, Rick trembled as a torrent of loss plunged him into a threatening vertigo. Dreading a repeat panic attack, he slipped out the back door while his legs could still carry him and sprinted to his car where he curled up in the back seat and buried his face in his arms. Shielded by the comforting darkness and the ghost of a loving father, Rick mourned three deaths—his dad's, a potentially loving father-son relationship, and Liv's election loss.

Inside campaign headquarters, Liv frantically gasped as she leaned into Zeke. "Where's Rick?"

Still crumpled up in the back seat, Rick was asking a different question: *Where's Dad? Where are you, Dad?* Heartsick and emotionally drained, he remained there until he pulled himself together enough to drive home and trample a few more fibers in his living room carpet. *Accept life as it is,* he told himself—*beautiful despite the finality, the banality, the brutality.*

He texted Liv: *Sorry Liv, was overwhelmed with grief. Please come over when you can. Take sidewalk to back door. It's unlocked. XO*

Rick occupied himself with haphazard tidying as he listened to the discouraging TV coverage of final election results. When a reporter interviewed Liv, he marvelled at her diplomatic composure, then let his mind raggedly wander. *Dad would want me to be strong. Philosophers claim free will's a delusion. Fuck it. Have Joy and Al left? Where's Mom?* He went upstairs, tapped on the kitchen door, and opened it. Lights that were on when he drove into the driveway were now off, and Rick assumed that his mom had gone to bed—with or without Efner. Likely without.

At campaign headquarters, Liv and volunteers divvied up what food and drink remained. "I'll throw a thank-you party to celebrate our great team," Liv said. "A clean-up crew is coming tomorrow, and so, to all of you…we're done!" A few colleagues invited her to debrief at a nearby bar, but she graciously declined, saying that she'd planned to be with Rick, "who's having a tough time with the loss of his father." Volunteers readily understood since, by the last week of the campaign, it was no secret that Rick and Liv had strong feelings for each other.

Brittany and Gabe were the last volunteers to leave. Liv watched with fascination as they stepped out onto the sidewalk and Gabe reached for Brittany's hand.

Liv reached for her phone. *Okay Rick, let's get on with that real celebration. On my way.*

Rick took Liv's coat, picked her up, and kissed her long and hard, then let her body erotically slide down his. She took his face in her hands and peered into his very soul.

"The strength of your support when you said, 'I'm here for you' was…" Liv stalled. Blinking away tears, she continued. "Without that echo, I would've been a mess in front of everyone."

Rick squeezed her hand. "Can I get you something to drink—tea, coffee, a beer?"

"Just you," Liv said. "You're all I want. Naked under the covers."

Classical romantic music softly filled the room as Rick lifted Liv and carried her to his bed. Together, they caressed their vanquished bodies and spirit.

"Liv, my dear one, courage, honesty, and hard work…you ran a superb campaign against a tough competitor."

"But Rick, I've let everyone down, everyone who worked so hard for me. That hurts. *Really* hurts. Loss…." Liv buried her face in the warm crook of Rick's neck and sobbed.

"Mm-hmm," Rick softly murmured, then let the presence of love cushion his sorrow. *How many people in this world feel what I'm feeling now?* His heart swelled as he stroked Liv's shoulder. In a voice clear and mellow, he said, "No loss will eclipse my love for you, Liv. A lifetime together wouldn't be enough."

Liv's sobs dwindled to sniffles. Looking fondly into Rick's eyes, she replied, "I feel your love…a safe place for sorrow. I haven't lost anything, Rick." She held his penetrating gaze and tweaked his nose with hers. "I love you, too…and this story isn't over."

Rick broke into an enormous, radiant smile. "How's this for a title to our never-ending story? *Everything's on Schedule.*

About the Author

 Judy J. Johnson, Ph.D., is Professor Emerita in the Psychology Department of Mount Royal University, Calgary, Alberta. She is the author of *What's So Wrong with Being Absolutely Right: The dangerous nature of dogmatic belief.* Amherst, NY: Prometheus Books, 2009. A practiced clinician, Johnson has also taught university psychology courses to students in Calgary and Israel.

Her website is at: https://www.dogmatism.ca.